SOUL HEELER

BOOK III
OF
THE DUDLEY FILES

SOUL HEELER

BOOK III
OF
THE DUDLEY FILES

by
Cary Robinson

Golden Hound Press

info@goldenhoundpress.com

www.dudleyfiles.com

ISBN: 978-0-98906006-6

Cover design: Cary Robinson, Kari Carlson, and Robyn Flatch

Editor: Catherine Jones Payne

Printed in the United States of America

Library of Congress Control Number: 2016932452

*"If man only had the character of the canine,
lack of character would cease to exist."*
—Careless

CHAPTER 1

What is that horrible smell? Speaking of smells, this was the first time I'd ever smelled one. I didn't like it much. In fact, I wondered how it even occurred. It seemed to be coming from the front of my face, but that's all I knew. I was excited to have a face, but I couldn't see anything. Everything seemed dark. But I felt nice, warm, and cozy. I liked it. Then, I heard sounds—high-pitched squeals surrounding me and coming from all directions. But everything remained dark.

Later, that smell lingered, but it wasn't as bad. It smelled somewhat like me and yet a little different. Soon, I found myself drinking a warm, nourishing liquid. Whatever it was, it tasted yummy. When I finished drinking, I got sleepy. I also felt soft, furry, warm things snuggle up to me. At first, I wasn't sure how I felt about it, but it seemed right, so it didn't bother me. In fact, I think I enjoyed it. Yes, I definitely did.

Sometime later, I found that not only could I smell, taste, and hear, but I was able to see. It started off a little blurry. At first, I could only make out shapes moving about, but then my eyes adjusted. Those little furry, smelly things that kept me warm looked similar to me. But they were all a little different.

It was feeding time again. Something that looked like me—but much larger—licked me and the rest of the furry things. It felt good. The other things liked it, too. Then, we all began drinking the warm, good-tasting stuff coming from her. It filled my belly and left me happy and content.

Somehow, I knew this thing was my mother. She was beautiful. She had short, coarse golden hair like mine. When we finished drinking, we all walked around and sniffed one another. We explored—but not too far, since a wall encircled us. I was getting sleepy again, so I lay down next to my mother, and the six other things joined me.

When I woke up, they were walking around and squealing. Mother seemed excited as well. She made some new sounds I'd never heard before.

A strange voice said, "Good morning, Juna."

I'd never heard anything like this. My mother wagged her tail in circles. If she was happy, so was I. My tail spun around in circles. I couldn't control it. All the other things wagged their little tails, too, but theirs went from side to side. My mother's name was Juna. I liked that name and everything about her.

Juna stepped over the wall surrounding us and strode over to a creature even larger than she. She nuzzled up against it, and a hand stroked her. As she craned her neck upwards, the hand rubbed her up and down and back and forth. Her whole body relaxed. If Juna liked this thing, so would I. The hand rubbed her long, floppy ears, and she made a low, rumbling sound. I wanted to be just like Juna, even though my ears weren't as long and floppy as hers.

I imitated the sound. Juna cocked her head and looked at me. Then, the strangest thing happened. Two hands reached down and grabbed me. They smelled different but good. When they lifted me into the air, I wasn't afraid— I was curious! I came face-to-face with the creature. It had whitish-tan skin and golden hair on the top of its head that was much different than Juna's. It didn't smell like Juna or the other things. Juna kept a mother's watchful eye on me.

"What a big puppy! What are we going to call you?"

I must be a puppy. All of the things like me are puppies. Of course, I am the best puppy. The other puppies must be my brothers and sisters. I was beginning to warm up to them, but still I knew I was the best. "You know, you are the pick of the litter," she said to me.

I didn't understand, but I knew she was happy with me.

She held me close to her chest while stroking my coat with her hand. I could hear her heart beat. *Thump thump, thump thump.* Then she brought me close to her face. Not only did she smell good, but I was fascinated with her long hair. I couldn't quit looking at it. I didn't know what to do, so I did what came naturally—I licked her face. It tasted salty. She liked to be licked, just like I liked to be licked by Juna.

"I think we'll call you King," she said. "Yes, King it is."

Now I know my name. It is King. I am King.

Another creature walked over and said, "Good morning, Heidi."

Heidi said, "Morning Cabby." Cabby looked and smelled different than Heidi.

"Big pup there. Given him a name yet?" Cabby asked.

"Juna and I just named him King," she said. After I licked Heidi's face a few more times, she handed me to Cabby. He raised me up and down and turned me over and back again. His hands were strong, dark, and wrinkled. He wore something on his head, and I felt the strangest urge to chew on it.

He called me "Mutton Chop" and handed me back to Heidi. I didn't know what that meant, but I bet it was something good. She stroked my hair a few more times and put me down with the other puppies. I didn't really want to be with them.

I wanted Heidi to hold me, but instead she picked up each puppy and said, "You are Bella. Cinco. Greta. Stella. Rex. And you are . . . Rookie." When she finished naming each of us, she set us back down with Juna again.

I have the best name. I am King.

CHAPTER 2

A few weeks later, my brothers, sisters, and I were growing and getting much larger and stronger. Bella was my favorite. She was nice, calm, and always by my side.

Rex and Rookie mostly stayed to themselves and always wrestled. Rex grabbed Rookie's neck while Rookie turned Rex over on his backside until they either fell asleep or needed to eat. The others mostly watched from a safe distance. None of the puppies challenged me. Bella and I walked, sniffed, and watched things. Each time I slept, Bella circled around me several times and lay right next to me with her head resting on my neck.

Heidi came to see us two or three times a day. Her voice soothed me. I wanted to say something back to her, but I didn't know how. At first, I could only make a small sound, but then something strange happened. I said something. I'm not sure what I said, but I think Heidi understood me.

She said, "You're going to be a talker." She was happy, so I talked again.

Later on, Juna no longer wanted to feed us. We tried to drink from her, but she would just turn while pushing us away with her snout. I didn't know why, but all the running around and playing really made me hungry. Then, something strange and new happened. Heidi brought bowls of something and set them down in front of us. It sure smelled good. I stuck my face in the bowl and ate the warm, good-tasting stuff.

"Eat your food, little puppies," Heidi said. Juna also ate from a bowl but not with us. Heidi fed her separately. She liked her food in a bowl. So did I.

We kept to a strict schedule—wake up, play, walk around, do our business, eat, and go back to sleep. Then one day, Heidi walked up with two humans. I didn't like them. I didn't recognize their smell. The woman said something, but I didn't like her voice. I'd never really felt this way before. She reached down and tried to pick me up.

I said something again. That made Heidi happy.

"That one's already spoken for," Heidi said.

The woman put me down and picked up Rex. Rex squirmed in her arms and licked her face. She smiled. The male human next to her stroked Rex's back. Rex liked these humans. I did not.

The woman said, "We'll take him!"

The man pulled some papers from his pocket and asked Heidi, "How much will that be again?"

The papers smelled like many people. Intrigued, I moved forward to peer up at them.

Heidi said, "That'll be sixteen hundred dollars. He's a fine puppy. He looks just like his brother, King." Heidi pointed at me. I acknowledged this by saying something. She reached down and picked me up, clutching me in her arms. I licked her hands, and she laughed. "This little guy is a birthday present for my daddy. Black Mouth Curs are some of the finest hunting dogs there are. King will love it at Daddy's ranch. But they also make great pets."

The man gave the papers to Heidi.

Heidi shook hands with him and said, "Let me get you Rex's papers." She set me back down with the other puppies, but Rex stayed with the two new humans. When Heidi came back, she handed the man some papers that smelled different than the other ones.

Both humans said, "Goodbye," and walked away with Rex. Rex looked back at us, confused. I was not happy, and I let the people who were taking my brother away know it.

Heidi looked at me and said, "Don't worry, King. They're nice people. Rex will be fine."

I never saw Rex again, and it was the first time I felt angry and sad.

CHAPTER 3

When we slept that night, we knew Rex was missing. It was strange at first, but after a few days we got used to it. It didn't seem to bother Juna. She still checked on us and licked us, but she kept more and more to herself. She and Heidi were inseparable.

I remained with the other puppies in a fenced-in area where we ran, wrestled, ate, and slept. I was getting bigger and stronger every day. One day, a human showed up with Heidi. I smelled him before I saw him. He didn't smell like other humans—he had animal smells on him. He wore a big, black hat that I really wanted to chew on.

He and Heidi stopped walking when they reached the fence, Juna at their side. All my brothers and sisters rushed over to the fence and started barking. Heidi and the human laughed.

"Go ahead and pick the one you want," Heidi said.

He looked at my brother and sisters. Then he reached down and picked me up. I wanted to be with Heidi, but at least I was out of the fence.

"I like this guy," he said, holding me up.

I said something.

"Oh, I'm sorry," Heidi said, "he's not for sale. He's a birthday present for my daddy. King's gonna help out at the ranch, aren't you boy?"

I didn't know what *for sale* meant. Maybe that was what happened to Rex. Maybe that's why he never came back. I didn't want to be for sale. I wanted to stay with Heidi.

"Too bad, I really had my eye on him," he said.

He put me down in the fenced-in area. I didn't want to be back there, so I said something again. They both chuckled. He looked at us as Heidi and Juna kept a watchful eye on him. I did the same. He was looking at all of the puppies, but I saw him staring at me.

I am NOT for sale!

A few minutes later, he looked at Bella. I didn't like this. I hoped she was not for sale. Bella was my favorite. He bent over and reached for her. He was about to pick up Bella, but I stood in front of her and said something. He looked at me for a moment and then picked up Cinco. She didn't mind, and neither did I. As long as it wasn't Bella.

Cinco licked his face. She liked this human. If she was for sale, at least she had a new friend.

"I'll take this one. What's her name?" he asked.

"Oh, that's Cinco," Heidi said. "She's a good little girl and will make a fine ranch dog. You know, these dogs can track anything."

I didn't know what tracking meant. I decided to watch Juna to see if she tracked. I knew Cinco was about to leave and never come back. I didn't like this. I said something.

Heidi said, "That will be sixteen hundred dollars, please."

The human pulled some papers from his pocket. These papers also smelled like many people, which confused me because I didn't see any other humans.

"I'll get her papers," Heidi said, walking away. When she came back, she gave him some papers. He put Cinco down, and she ran back to the outside of the fence. She wanted to be with us. She whined, and he tried to pick her up.

I wasn't happy, and I'd become stronger and bigger than the rest of the puppies. I looked at him and said something. Then I jumped over the fence. I hadn't even known I could jump the fence.

I stood between him and Cinco, and the hair on my back bristled. Juna stared at me while Heidi put her hands on her hips.

"King," she yelled, "I saw you jump over that fence. Bad boy!" She bent over, reached down, picked me up, and put me with the other puppies. Then she smiled at me. Bella ran up to me and nuzzled me with her head.

The human picked up Cinco. I still felt the urge to chew on his hat, but if I jumped over the fence again, I'd be a bad boy.

I didn't want to be a bad boy.

Grabbing the front of his hat with his hand, he tilted it down and then back up. He walked off with Cinco as she gazed back at us. That was the last time I saw her. Heidi didn't seem to mind. I hoped no more of my sisters or my brother were for sale.

CHAPTER 4

Several days later, Heidi walked up with two humans who were holding hands. I'd never seen this before. Sometimes I held Bella's paw but usually in my mouth. That was only when we roughhoused. Heidi said, "Here they are, Marc and Tyann. You said you want two females?"

I smelled Cabby walking toward us. Sometimes I can smell things before I see them.

Heidi turned and said, "Hey, Cabby." He walked up and patted Juna on her head.

"Morning, Heidi," he said.

"Cabby, this is Marc and Tyann."

Cabby shook Marc's hand. He did the same with Tyann. "Pleased to meet you. These are some of the finest puppies Heidi has offered."

"Cabby's my neighbor," Heidi said. "He comes over and helps me with the puppies."

"I just popped by to see how they're doing." Cabby peered down at us. "It looks like some of them are already gone. I'm sure they'll be happy in their new homes."

Heidi smiled. "I'm sure they will."

Reaching down, Tyann picked up Greta. Greta liked that and seemed to like Tyann. Marc looked at Bella and reached for her. I was having none of that, and of course said something.

Marc laughed and hefted Stella up into his arms. While I didn't want Stella to be for sale, at least he didn't try to take Bella. *Bella is not for sale.*

Tyann and Marc looked at Heidi and said, "We'll take them."

Cabby said, "You've made a great choice. Those are two of the best females in the litter."

Marc handed Stella to Tyann. She cradled Greta and Stella in her arms. Marc pulled out some papers from his pocket and handed them to Heidi. She walked away and when she returned, she gave him some different papers.

"These really are some fine dogs you've picked out," Cabby said. "Heidi raises the best Black Mouth Curs I've ever seen. They'll bring you many years of enjoyment."

As Tyann and Marc walked off together, Greta and Stella stared back at us, and I knew I would never see them again. At least I had Bella. If my brothers and sisters had to leave, at least I had her.

"Well, just three left," Cabby said.

"Two. King is staying with us until I go see Daddy. He is going to be Daddy's best birthday present ever."

"Right, I keep forgetting that."

"Daddy is going to love King, and you're going to love Daddy, aren't you, King?" she asked.

I said something. *I am happy. I'll stay right here with Bella, Juna, and Heidi.*

Cabby looked at Heidi and said, "I hope your father appreciates King. Those are sure some fine dogs."

I saw an expression on her face I hadn't seen before. "Cabby, would you like one of the puppies?"

"Oh, they're well out of my price range. I could never afford a dog of that caliber."

"How long have we been neighbors?" she asked.

"Over twenty years."

"You always help me when I need it and never ask for anything in return. I insist you take either Rookie or Bella," she said.

Water sprang from his eyes. "That's the kindest thing anyone's ever done for me," he said.

He looked at Heidi and then at Rookie. I was glad he had his eye on Rookie. He picked up Rookie and held him in his arms. Cabby had dark, wrinkly hands, and it looked like Rookie was having fun chewing on them. Cabby smiled. Water still trickled down his cheeks.

"You have no idea how much this means to me," he said.

"It's my pleasure, Cabby. I know you'll take great care of him."

"You can bet on it," he said. He hugged Rookie, and Rookie reached up and licked the water flowing from Cabby's eyes. They both seemed to like that. Then Cabby walked away with him.

"Looks like it's just you and Bella, King," Heidi said.

CHAPTER 5

The next day, Bella and I did all the usual things—woke up, snuggled, stretched, walked around, sniffed each other, did our business, played, and waited for Heidi to feed us. When she came, she brought two bowls of food. We ate every bit.

Heidi picked up the bowls, looked at Bella, and said, "Today's your big day, girl. You'll be meeting your new owners. You'll love them." She turned to me. "No worries, King. You're not going anywhere yet. You'll stay with Juna and me until Daddy's birthday. He'll be so excited!"

The day went great until a golden-haired human walked up with Heidi and Juna. She smelled like flowers and was younger than Heidi. Bella and I ran over to the fence to see what was going on.

Heidi reached down and picked up Bella. Now it was clear to me. Bella was for sale. Bella was for sale, and I was not happy. Heidi hugged Bella and then handed her to the human. I knew what was about to happen. This time, I was determined to do something about it. Once Heidi took the papers from the human, Bella would leave forever. And I would never see her again.

With a running leap, I hurtled over the fence. Heidi's eyes widened as I dashed up to the woman holding Bella and jumped up on her. I tried to grab Bella but wasn't able to reach her. The woman shrieked. I might have hurt her. I didn't want to hurt her, but I didn't want her to take Bella away. I wasn't going to lose Bella.

The woman gripped Bella tightly.

Heidi looked at me, and for the first time, anger shone in her eyes.

"Bad boy!" she yelled. For a reason I can't explain, for the first time, I felt shame. I'd never seen Heidi angry before.

Heidi picked me up and sternly said, "Bad boy," again. I didn't want to be a bad boy, and I felt bad, but I guess I was a bad boy.

Heidi said to the human, "King's a little rambunctious."

I said something. And I said it with some authority. Even Juna took notice.

"He's quite attached to Bella," Heidi said. "He's going to be a present for my father on his ranch in Kerrville." Heidi held me in her arms. I licked her face, and her anger melted. She smiled and said, "You know I love you, King. You may not have any manners yet, but I'll always love you." She kissed me on my head.

The woman said, "I really like this one. How much is she?"

"Sixteen hundred dollars."

I knew what was happening, but I wasn't sure Bella did. I squirmed in Heidi's arms, but she just held me even tighter. There was nothing I could do. I was going to lose Bella.

The human held Bella with one arm and reached into her pocket with the other. She didn't give Heidi papers. She pulled out a paper from a blue thing. "Do you mind if I write you a check?"

"Go right ahead. I'll need your driver's license number on it, if you don't mind," Heidi said.

"No problem. Would you mind holding Bella while I write the check? And who should I make it out to?"

"Golden Hound Kennels."

"Thank you," she said, handing Bella to Heidi. She started doing something with the paper, and I knew this would be my last chance to make sure Bella didn't go with her.

I said something, and Bella understood because she started licking my face like she had never done before. I think Juna understood me as well. She also looked at Bella. I was happy because Bella was going to stay with us.

I was wrong. The human finished writing the check and gave it to Heidi. Heidi handed Bella to her. I squirmed, but Heidi clutched me tightly. Bella wriggled in the human's arms and whined.

Heidi turned and walked away with me in her arms. "Come, Juna. We might as well introduce King to the house since he'll be staying with us for a while." I looked back at Bella. We both knew we wouldn't see each other again, and for the first time, I felt deep sadness. Bella howled as Heidi carried me away.

"Now, now, King, everything's going to be alright. Bella will be just fine," Heidi said.

I said something as Juna, Heidi, and I went into the house. It was different. It had lots of smells. Heidi closed the door we'd just come through and set me down on the floor with Juna. I walked up to her and sat. I didn't know what to do. Heidi picked up some papers off a big wooden thing and walked toward the door.

"Now, King, you stay here with Juna. I'm just going to give that nice young lady Bella's papers," she said.

I didn't say anything. I had a plan. I waited until Heidi opened the door, and I burst into a full run toward it. Darting under Heidi's legs, I raced back out to the yard toward Bella.

She was still there. She said something. Heidi almost stumbled when I ran past her. The human saw me coming and knew what I wanted. She placed Bella on the ground, and I ran full blast until I reached her. Maybe this human wasn't so bad.

Heidi ran up and said, "I'm so sorry." I guess I was a bad boy again, but I didn't care. I was with Bella.

The human smiled at Heidi and said, "It's okay. King just loves his sister. I think it's sweet. Let them have a moment together."

Bella and I nuzzled one another for the last time. When Heidi picked me up, the woman picked up Bella, and they walked away. I raised my head to the sky and howled. Bella did, too. When she walked out of sight, I knew she was still close. I could smell her. As Heidi meandered back to the house, I eventually lost track of Bella's scent. I'll remember it. If I ever meet her again, I'll remember it.

Juna waited for us in the house. She was amused at what had just happened. Heidi closed the door behind her and put me down. I walked right up to Juna and sat by her side. I had no one else to sit by. I was the only puppy left. Heidi pointed her finger at me. "You were a bad boy! Bad boy!"

I am a bad boy again. I don't want to be a bad boy.

Heidi smiled and said, "But you're my bad boy." I was confused. She patted me on the head, and then I went exploring. The whole house smelled like Heidi and Juna.

Juna walked over to something on the floor and curled up to sleep on it. I tried to snuggle up next to her, but only half of my body fit—the rest of me spilled out onto the floor. She looked at me, sighed, and went to sleep. I heard Heidi laughing.

"Don't worry, King. I'll get you your own bed to sleep on."

I liked the bed. It was soft and smelled like Juna. Even though I was still a little mad about Bella, I was tired, so I fell asleep with my head resting on Juna. We slept until I heard Heidi's voice and felt her picking me up.

"Come on, King. You have to go do your business outside. I know you can't hold it like Juna, and you're not going to have an accident in my house."

I groaned as I stretched after my nap. I followed Juna and Heidi outside. Juna squatted down and did her business. I watched her and ran over to a fence, lifted my leg, and did my business. It felt good, and Heidi was happy. "Good boy, King! That's a good boy."

I am a good boy. Doing my business had never made me this happy before. I wanted to do my business for a long time on that fence just to hear Heidi tell me I was a good boy.

The next day, Heidi gave me my own bed, right next to Juna's. It was perfect. Whenever I was tired I walked to my bed and slept on it. Sometimes when Juna wasn't around, I slept on her bed because I liked the way it smelled.

Many months passed, and I grew very strong and very fast. One day when I was eating, Heidi said, "King, now eat all of your food. Don't leave those vitamins on the floor." I wanted to make Heidi happy, but I didn't like the vitamins. I could tell from her voice and the look on her face she was not happy. After that day, she brought the vitamins out but covered them with something that smelled great. She thought she was tricking me, but I knew they were vitamins.

"King, you want some crunchy peanut butter?"

It smelled good so I ate it. It made Heidi happy, and I just happened to like peanut butter.

CHAPTER 6

Heidi said, "I can't believe it, King. You are already twelve weeks old." My legs were getting longer, and my feet were bigger than Juna's. I especially liked to jump. I jumped on a lot of things—on doors, on the cabinets when Heidi got out food, and sometimes even on Heidi. When I did, she smiled but then got angry and said, "No!"

I really tried to stop myself from jumping on things because I liked to make her happy. But I felt confused when she was happy and angry at the same time. Sometimes, I just had to jump.

We had the same routine every day, which made it easy for me to remember what to do. I am a dog, and a dog needs a routine. Heidi rarely picked me up anymore. I walked by myself and did my business outside. Every night when Juna went to sleep, I circled around and lay down next to her with my head resting on her back or her side.

Every morning, I woke up and saw her next to me. I always woke before she did and stared at her while she slept. As soon as she opened her eyes, I stood up and licked her face. I couldn't stop myself.

The weather changed, growing colder. Heidi said, "Well, it looks like fall is here. It's cooling down." I jumped up and down in circles around Juna. Heidi clapped her hands and said, "Dance, King, dance."

I heard Heidi say something the next morning. She was holding something next to her head. I was curious, but I was waiting for Juna to wake up.

Heidi's voice soothed me. "Yes, Daddy, I can't wait to see you. I have a big surprise for you. No, I'm not going to tell you what it is. It's a surprise, silly. I'll give you a hint. It's something you need and something that will be useful at the ranch. You'll just have to wait and see. You're going to love it. No, I'm not going to tell you. I'm going to pack up the car and leave soon. I'll see you in about four hours."

Heidi stopped talking and set down the thing she was holding as she turned to look at me. I still hadn't moved because Juna wasn't awake yet. "I know you're awake, King."

I heard my name so I said something.

"Rise and shine, sleepyhead. Time to wake up, Juna," Heidi said. When Juna heard her name, both her eyes opened. That was my sign to begin our morning ritual. I jumped up and licked her face. She smelled like home.

"Oh King, you're so silly. Whatever will we do when you're not here? I almost wish you could stay with us," Heidi said.

I looked at her and said something. Then I groomed Juna some more, but she'd had enough and lifted herself off the bed. We both stretched at the same time, and that made Heidi happy. She walked over to us and began rubbing our ears.

"Okay, go outside and do your business. Then I'll feed you breakfast," she said. I knew the command *do your business*, so I went outside with Juna. When we came back in, Heidi had our food ready, and Juna and I ate every bit of it. She finished well before I did.

"Come on, King, we don't have time to fool around today. We're going to Daddy's, and it's a long drive." I took the food from the bowl and dropped it on the ground. I nosed a few pieces here and there and ate them. Once I finished, I looked at Heidi and she said, "Good boy."

She picked up my bowl and my bed. I didn't know why. *What am I supposed to sleep on? What am I supposed to eat from? Does she want me to sleep on the floor? If she wants me to, I will. Is she not happy because I played with my food before eating it? Does she want me to eat out of Juna's bowl?* Heidi walked outside with my bowl and bed. I was confused.

Am I . . . for sale?

I didn't want to be for sale. I liked it just fine with Heidi and Juna. If I was for sale, I wondered if I would see Bella again.

Heidi came back into the house and put some of her clothes in a bag. She spotted me looking at her and said, "Don't worry, King. I'm putting your things in the car to go see Daddy."

I said something.

She lifted up the bag and swung it in the car. I looked at Juna, and she was as confused as I was. I said something, but she ignored me and focused on what Heidi was doing. Heidi made several more trips from our house to the car while Juna and I followed behind. When she came back into the house with us on her heels, she closed the door behind her.

She looked at Juna and me and said, "Okay, Juna, it's time to say goodbye to King. He's going to be leaving us. I don't want you to worry. He's going to have a great life at Daddy's ranch. Cabby will come by and take care of you while I'm away."

Juna was uneasy. I could feel it. This made me uneasy, and I said something.

Heidi said, "I know, King! You are such a good boy. Juna and I will really miss you, but we'll come visit." Now I knew I was for sale. I didn't want to leave our house. I didn't want to leave Juna. I didn't want to leave Heidi.

Juna sat down, and I ran to her. I said something, and for the first time, she gave a mournful response. I leaned my body into her and placed my head on her neck. She licked my head as if she knew what was about to happen. She probably did know, and there was nothing she or I could do about it.

"Now, now you two, you'll see each other at holidays. I know it's a little sad, but at least you'll be with Daddy. You'll have a great time at the ranch and forget all about us," Heidi said.

But I wouldn't forget. A dog never forgets. We may give unconditional love, but we never forget.

Juna was still licking my head, but then Heidi walked over and put her arms around me. Normally I liked this, but this time it was different. Heidi pulled at me so she could lift me up. The harder she pulled, the harder I pushed my body up against Juna. I didn't want to leave Juna, and I wanted to make sure she knew it. Maybe if I just made her understand, she'd let me stay.

"King, don't make this harder than it has to be. Daddy's already expecting you, and you're coming with me. I'm sorry, Juna, but it will be okay. I promise."

Our tug-of-war went on for several minutes, and I think Heidi might have been impressed with my resolve, but she eventually won out and separated me from Juna, who remained seated with her eyes fixated on me. She didn't even blink. Neither did I.

I knew this would be the last time I would see her. I said something. Juna responded in kind. As Heidi walked toward the door, she looked back at Juna and said, "Don't worry, Juna, Cabby will be here soon. He'll take good care of you." She closed the door and carried me to the car. For the first time I could remember, I was unhappy with Heidi.

She held me with one arm and opened the car door. Once she shoved me inside, she closed the door behind me. There was no way I could get out. She walked around the car and joined me. I was in the back but decided to hop in the front to be closer to her.

Heidi put her hand on my head. "Everything will be alright. Maybe you just need a little air." She pressed a button on the side of the car, and the window opened. As the car moved forward, I stuck my head outside. There were many smells, some of which I didn't recognize.

I didn't think there was enough room to squeeze my body out of it, but that wasn't going to stop me from trying. I enjoy riding in the car with Heidi, but I'd much rather be in our house with Juna. I gathered up all of my courage and squeezed my head and shoulders through the open window. Before Heidi knew what was happening, I managed to fit my entire body through the small space. I was as surprised as she was that I made it through. Even though the car was moving, I landed on my feet. Our house wasn't far away. I could see it and smell it, and I ran as fast as my legs would move.

Heidi said something, and the car stopped moving. She was angry, but I didn't care. I made it to the door and heard Juna just on the other side of it. I said something to her, and she said something back. I think it was goodbye.

CHAPTER 7

Heidi walked up behind me, picked me up, and looked into my eyes. "King, you are a *bad boy*. A very bad boy. You could have really hurt yourself."

I didn't care. I just wanted to be with Juna, back in our house. Heidi lugged me back into the car. She pushed me over to one side as she got in behind me. The first thing I checked was to see if the window was open so I could jump out and make my way back to our house again. It was closed.

There was no way out of the car. Heidi was watching me. She wasn't mad anymore. She smiled and petted me. "You're a smart, brave dog. I hope that combination doesn't get you in trouble."

The car moved away from our house. I watched behind us through a window until it disappeared. Once I could no longer see it, I lay down with my head on Heidi's leg. She looked at me, took one hand off the round thing she was holding, and placed it on my head.

"I know, King. It'll turn out fine. You'll see," she said.

She put her hand back on the round thing and looked straight ahead. I closed my eyes. Riding in the car made me tired. For the first time in a long time, I went to sleep without Juna. I slept for a while.

"Come on, King, we're at Buc-ees. We're going to get out of the car in a minute, and you need to do your business."

She placed her hand on my back and gently shook me. I must have been more tired than I'd thought because I hadn't moved since we left Juna at home. Heidi shook me a few more times, and I stood up and stretched. The car was no longer moving. I looked through the back window to see if our house was behind us. It wasn't. I licked Heidi's face. I felt disappointed, but I put it behind me.

Heidi was happy but tried to push me away. I guess she'd had enough licking, but I wasn't finished yet, so the harder she pushed me away, the more I leaned into her.

Laughing, she said, "King, you are just too much. I almost want to turn the car around right now and take you home and keep you forever."

I heard the word *home*. My tail spun around in circles, and I said something. I wanted Heidi to know that I wanted to go home. I wanted to stay with her and Juna forever. She had to know. If only she knew, I wouldn't be for sale.

I carefully watched her. I saw in her eyes that she wanted me to stay with her. I knew she wanted to take me home to Juna. She sat deep in thought. After a few minutes, her facial expression changed, and she said, "No, King, as much as I really want to keep you, you must go to the ranch with Daddy. You need to watch over him and help him. He'll love you like I love you. You'll see. Soon enough you'll be having so much fun, you'll forget about Juna and me."

But I wouldn't forget. Dogs don't forget. We move on with our lives because we have a purpose. We don't forget. I didn't say anything, even though I knew what she was thinking. I just had nothing to say about it.

Heidi opened the car door and got out. I clambered behind her. I didn't know where we were, but it was definitely not home. She walked to a grassy area, and I ambled by her side.

I knew there had been other animals and dogs here. I could smell them, but the scents were old. "Go do your business, King," Heidi said.

I walked around for a few minutes and sniffed here and there. None of the smells were familiar to me. But Heidi wanted me to do my business, so I did. I wandered around a little more, and then Heidi walked back to the car, and I followed.

When she opened the door, I jumped in, and went back to my seat. She looked at me and said, "King, I'm going to fill up with gas and get some coffee. You stay here, and I'll be right back. Okay?" She closed the door.

I knew she was talking to me, so I said something.

She picked something up and put it in the side of the car. It smelled awful. As I watched her through the window, the smell overpowered my nose. I couldn't smell anything else.

"It's okay, King. I'm finished now. We've got a full tank. We won't need to stop again," she said. "I'll be right back. I'm just going to grab a cup of coffee."

Pressing my nose up against the window, I watched her walk away. *She may need me for something, so I want to make sure I can track her if I have to.* I looked around for a way out of the car. All I wanted was to be by her side, but the doors and windows were closed. There was no escape for me this time. My breath fogged up the window. I'd never seen that before. I was curious. When I moved my head, my nose made a squeaky sound against the window.

Meanwhile, I watched Heidi disappear through some doors and into a building with lots of humans in it. I could see her through the windows. She walked around, picked up a few things, and handed some papers to a man behind a counter. My eyes were fixed on her. When she walked back toward the car, my tail spun around in circles. I couldn't help it. I was just so happy she'd come back.

She opened the door and climbed back in. Something smelled good. As she sat down, I lunged at her and licked her face nonstop. "Okay, King, I missed you, too. Sit down. I've got a surprise for you," she said.

But I didn't want to sit down, and it didn't matter how long she'd been gone. I was so happy she was back. She tried pushing me back to my seat, but the harder she pushed, the harder I pressed my body into her.

She smiled and said, "Okay, I guess you don't want your surprise." She pulled something that smelled amazing out of a bag. I stopped licking her and sat down, staring at the good-smelling thing. "This is a hamburger. You shouldn't be eating this, but they didn't really have anything else. Besides, we're on vacation. We can do whatever we want when we're on vacation. Am I right?"

I didn't know about vacation, but I knew I wanted the hamburger, so I said something at it.

She smiled. "Good boy, King."

I remained seated and she handed me the hamburger. I snatched up the whole thing in my mouth, chewed it up, and swallowed it. *I like hamburgers.* Hamburgers taste better than the usual food Heidi gave me. She laughed and rubbed my head. *Hamburgers make me happy.*

She put her drink down. "Did you fog up the window? I can see your nose print on it. You big goofball."

She took a small, white piece of paper from a box on the floor and wiped the window. I followed her hand movements with my head. Then I licked her drink. It smelled and tasted good. "Leave it! That's *my* coffee. I'll get you a drink when we get to Daddy's. Besides, that's not decaf, and you already have more than enough energy."

I stopped licking her drink and said something. I like hamburgers and coffee. I sat back in my chair, and the car moved forward. I fell asleep.

CHAPTER 8

"King! King! Wake up. We're here. We've made it to Daddy's!"

When I opened my eyes, Heidi stood outside of the car. She opened my door and called me. Behind her was a house I'd never seen before. It was much bigger than our house. The scents were different, too, and the air felt cooler and a little dryer. I smelled different kinds of trees and several animals. I wasn't sure what kinds of animals they were, so I decided to investigate.

I jumped out of the car and trotted in the animals' direction. Heidi called me, but I didn't listen. Something drove me toward the smell. "King! King! Come back here. You are a bad boy," she said.

I didn't want to be a bad boy, but that smell . . .

I decided I didn't want to be a bad boy so I stopped, sat down, and waited for her to catch up. It didn't take long.

"King, what has gotten into you? I knew you shouldn't have had that caffeinated coffee," she said.

She put her hand on my head. I looked up at her. That's when I knew I was a good boy. The smell of an animal was right in front of me, so I looked around. A fence stood between me and it.

"Oh, look at that beautiful mare. Isn't she gorgeous?" Heidi said.

The mare's big head was hanging over the fence, looking right at me. I didn't know what to do, but I knew she liked me. I just felt it. I said something and started licking the mare's face. Her breath was hot and strong. She nudged my head with her nose, and then she said something. I'd never heard anything like this before. It was a strange sound, but I liked it.

"So, I see you've met Big Red," a voice from behind us said. It was a human's voice, kind of like Cabby's. He smelled different than Heidi and Cabby—more like sweat and the outside air. I knew he was there, but I couldn't take my eyes off of Big Red.

"Your dog better be careful around Big Red. She doesn't take too kindly to strangers," the human said.

"Daddy!" Heidi screamed out.

This alarmed me. I turned away from Big Red and saw Heidi run to the human and throw both her arms around him. She seemed thrilled to see him, and she pressed her face to his. She often did this to me, so I knew she liked him. I wasn't sure about him yet. Something about him bothered me. It was just a feeling.

"Actually, King's not my dog, Daddy—he's yours," Heidi said as she separated herself from him. "King is the pick of Juna's last litter, and I'm giving him to you to help you around the ranch. Here are his pedigree papers showing he's a purebred, championship stock Black Mouth Cur."

She pulled some papers from her pocket and gave them to him. "He's very friendly and smart. Look, he's already made friends with Big Red."

"Thank you, Heidi. He's a good-looking pup," Daddy said.

"King, come over and meet Daddy. He's going to be your new best friend," Heidi said.

She said my name, so I licked Big Red one last time and turned and trotted over to Heidi. I sat by her side.

"How you doin', boy?" Daddy asked. He reached down and patted me on the head. I could tell he didn't mean it. "Come on, Heidi, let's go to the house and catch up."

I looked back at Big Red and said something. She made a strange sound and snorted air through her nose. I liked Big Red.

We all walked to the big house. Daddy opened a door, and Heidi passed him as she went in. I started to walk in, but Daddy slammed the door shut in my face.

Inside the house, Heidi said, "Daddy, where's King? Did you let him in?"

"No animals allowed in the house. That's the rule."

"King's used to sleeping indoors. He'd be much happier inside with us."

"No, honey, he can't come in the house. He'll be fine. He can sleep on the covered porch or in the barn with his friend, Big Red. I'll put some water and food out for him," he said.

"Alright, Daddy, but I sure wish you'd reconsider. Won't you please just think about letting him live inside with you?"

"Heidi, he can't live in the house. If you can't follow the rules, you're just going to have to take him home with you."

"Okay, just promise me you'll take good care of him. He's a very special dog," she said.

"Don't worry, he'll be fine," Daddy said.

I said something, and I know Heidi heard me, but the door never opened. I didn't like Daddy.

I went to sleep outside, and early the next morning, the door opened and Daddy walked out. I thought he was going to feed me. I was really hungry.

He looked down at me and said, "I don't need a damn dog."

He was not happy. I followed Daddy anyway because I'm a dog and that's what we do. We follow our humans. But I didn't like him. He went to the barn, and Big Red trotted over. She lowered her head over the fence, and I licked her. Big Red liked me.

Daddy was watching and said, "Damn dog!"

He threw some dry grass over the fence, and Big Red walked over and ate it. Then Daddy walked over to a small house and opened a door. A lot of animals ran out. I wanted to chase them down and kill them, but he yelled, "You better not touch my chickens! Leave 'em alone! Damn dog!"

It was all I could do to keep myself from running them down and shredding them, but Daddy looked like he meant business and he already didn't like me, so I didn't.

He fed a couple more animals as we walked along. Daddy was good at feeding animals. I hoped he was good at feeding me because I was hungry. I really wanted to eat those chickens, but Daddy said, "No. Damn dog."

I didn't like the sound of that, and I told him so. I could tell he was not happy when I made noise. His face showed it. When he finished feeding the animals, he walked back toward the house, and I followed him. "No animals in the house. No exceptions! I don't care how much Heidi cries about it."

When we reached the house, Daddy opened the door and went in. Heidi came out later and set some food and water out for me.

"Here you go, King. I know you're hungry. Don't worry, Daddy will get used to you. He'll warm up to you soon." I grabbed a mouthful of food and dropped it on the porch. I nosed it around a couple of times until I had it just the way I wanted. Then I started eating it a few morsels at a time. As I finished the food, I heard Heidi and Daddy talking inside the house.

"That dog's making a big mess. Why does he eat that way?" he asked.

"I don't know. That's the way he's always done it. He just has a big personality. Kind of like you," she said.

"I guess so," Daddy said. He didn't mean it. A dog can tell when a human doesn't mean it.

The air was cool when I finished my food and water, and I felt like going exploring. I walked over to Big Red, and she came over to the fence to greet me. She lowered her head, and I licked her on the nose. She liked that. Then I went to see the chickens. I barked at them but didn't eat them. Daddy wouldn't be happy about that. I barked at the other animals as well, and they took notice.

I am King. I am the boss.

When I got bored, I returned to the porch to lie down. *This must be where I'll be sleeping from now on.* I didn't like it and much preferred to be home with Juna. Slowly, I dozed off. A little while later, I heard Heidi walk out of the house and sit beside me. She didn't know I was awake. I still had my eyes closed. She stroked my back.

"King, I know you want to come home with me, but you're going to stay with Daddy. You already made a new friend. I think you and Big Red will have fun together. I have to go now. I'm going to miss you," she said.

I stopped pretending to be asleep and said something. I knew what she'd said. I was for sale, and she was leaving me with Daddy. There was nothing I could do about it.

Heidi hugged me. I turned around and pushed my body into hers. Water trickled from her eyes. She was not happy, and this made me uneasy. The way she held me reminded me of the very first time she'd held me. A dog remembers these things.

"I love you so much. Juna and I will come visit you. We'll be here before you know it," she said. She tried to push me away, but the harder she pushed, the harder I pushed back. I wasn't going to let her leave.

I thought she couldn't escape while I was pressing against her, but Daddy came out and leashed me. He tied me to a post, and Heidi stood up and strode away. I tried to follow her, but the leash around my neck held me fast.

I said something.

Heidi turned and hurried back to me. I knew she couldn't leave me. She ran to my side and hugged me. I licked the water off her face. "Goodbye, King," she said.

I was for sale.

"Honey, you best be getting along before it gets too late. Don't worry about King. I've got big plans for him. He'll be fine," he said.

He was not a good human. A dog knows these things. I watched Heidi walk to her car, get in, and drive off, leaving me behind.

CHAPTER 9

Once Heidi drove out of sight, Daddy untied me. "King, I'm going to take you for a ride. You like to ride in the truck, don't you?"

I didn't say anything. I didn't like Daddy. He kept the leash on me and led me to his truck. He opened the back of the truck and patted his hand on the floor. I jumped up into the truck. He closed the door behind me, but it was wide open in the back, with no windows or walls. He climbed inside of the truck and closed the door.

He started driving, and he was right—I did like it. As he drove, I stuck my face in the wind and took in all the smells. Maybe Daddy wasn't so bad after all. My tail spun around in circles. There were so many smells coming from so many directions.

I didn't know how long the drive lasted, but we went up and down several hills and past many trees. Daddy stopped the truck and got out. "Okay, little fella," he said. "I'm setting you free. You can live on your own now."

I stayed in the back of the truck. I wasn't sure what he wanted me to do. "King, get down. I don't have time for this. Come, King, come!"

He patted his leg. Now I knew what he wanted. I jumped down, walked over to him, and sat by his side.

But something didn't seem right. He was uneasy, and that made me uneasy. He looked at me, pointed his finger in my direction, and said, "Stay!"

I stayed while I watched him walk quickly to his truck. He never looked back. I waited for him to call me. I wanted to ride in the truck again. I liked riding in the truck with all the smells and the wind blowing in my face. But he never called me. Instead, he drove off in the truck while I was still sitting there.

I couldn't wait any longer, so I jumped up and ran hard after Daddy.

I am King. My legs are strong, and I am fast.

I thought I was going to catch up to Daddy, but he looked back at me, and the truck went even faster. I gave it my all, but the truck proved too fast and I lost sight of it in a cloud of dust. I was confused.

Why did he leave me? Why is he mad at me? Did I do something wrong? Will I ever see him or Big Red again? I didn't know what to do, but I decided to track him. I lifted my nose in the air and followed his scent. It was still strong.

Soon I felt hungry and thirsty, but I lumbered ahead tracking Daddy. I looked for water and food as I walked. *Maybe Daddy will come back and feed me. Maybe he will remember he forgot me and come back.*

I continued on for a long time. The weather was cool, and I had a lot of energy. *What's that smell?* I made a quick detour into the woods. My nose drew me to something hopping along the ground just ahead. It was small and brown with a white tail. I had never seen anything like this before, and my body started doing things on its own. The more it hopped, the more I wanted to kill it.

I crouched low to the ground and extended my neck. My pace slowed, and my eyes fixed on my prey.

Maybe I will eat this thing.

Gone were the thoughts of Daddy, Big Red, Heidi, and Juna. The only thing I could see, hear, smell, or think about was my prey. It didn't even know I was tracking it. I was going to shred it and eat it. I wasn't sure how I knew what to do. I just did.

I stayed low to the ground, creeping closer to it. Just as I was about to pounce, I smelled and heard something else. It was rustling through the nearby leaves. I wrinkled my nose. I'd never smelled anything like this. My body stopped in its tracks. I really wanted my prey, but I stopped and waited.

All at once, a long, thick animal jumped out of the grass and struck my prey. Then I smelled something bad. I didn't want any part of that smell, so I slowly backed away. As I watched, my prey stopped hopping and began to twitch. It was hard for me not to pounce on it, but that bad-smelling animal was waiting nearby.

My prey fell to the ground and stopped moving. The long, thick animal moved in and opened its mouth wide. It began swallowing my prey whole. I had never seen anything like this before. I couldn't take it anymore, and I ran forward, jumped up in the air, and landed on the long, thick animal. It was busy eating my prey and never saw me coming. Before it could make a move, I bit its head off. It didn't take much effort.

I am King. I am strong and fast. Faster than that bad-smelling animal. For the first time in my life, I had the taste of blood in my mouth. It felt natural.

I didn't eat my prey or the animal I'd just killed because they both smelled bad. I was still hungry. I left them both and started tracking Daddy again. His smell wasn't as strong, but I could still follow him. I stretched my neck out, extended my nose, and moved forward. I was going back to Daddy's. *I'm sure he just forgot me.*

As I trodded along, I grew tired. When the sun went down, I found a nice spot on which to lay down and go to sleep. I made sure it was a grassy area with no rocks. Rocks are too hard to sleep on. As I lay there getting ready to close my eyes, I thought of home. Home, with Juna and Heidi. Home, where I had my own bed. Home, with food and water. I went to sleep thinking about home.

CHAPTER 10

The next morning, a cold rain poured from the sky, soaking me. It was time to move on. I lifted myself up and started tracking Daddy. I could just barely make out his scent. The rain made it really hard to follow him, and I felt a little weak because I hadn't eaten anything. I sipped some water from a puddle.

As I walked ahead, the rain finally stopped. I was only thinking about getting back to Daddy's and eating some food. The sun peeked out from the clouds and lit up the sky. Soon, my coat dried, and I warmed up.

I smelled something up ahead—food. I moved a little quicker. In a clearing, I saw a large animal lying on the ground. This was definitely where the smell was coming from. I also smelled something else, something I'd never smelled before. For some reason, the hair on my back stood straight up—all the way from my shoulders down to my tail. This had never happened to me before, and it made me anxious.

My nostrils and eyes were wide open. I pinpointed where the smells emanated from and cautiously moved into the clearing. The animal was much bigger than I was, and it lay next to a large tree with its back toward me. Just past the tree, I heard running water. I couldn't smell the water because the animal in front of me was overpowering my nose, but I knew it wasn't far away.

The hair on my back still pointed straight up as I crept up to the animal. I expected it to get up and do something. If I could smell it, surely it could smell me. When I walked right up to it, it still didn't move. It was brown and white and had pointy, hard things on the top of its head. Its feet were hard and black. Something made me nervous. I almost turned and ran, but I wanted to see whether the animal would move or not.

I raised my front paw up and pushed it. I jumped back, waiting for it to run away. It moved forward a little bit and then fell back into place. I walked around the other side of the animal, and I saw it had been injured. There was blood on it and on the ground. Something had killed it.

I was starving, so I took a bite out of the animal where it had been wounded. It wasn't as good as the food Heidi fed me, but it was good enough. I ripped and chewed it into small pieces and then swallowed it. It was salty from the blood. I was hungry and took several more bites. I had blood on my face. My energy started to return.

As I gorged myself, my ears perked up. The hair on my back still stood straight up. I knew instinctively that something was sneaking up on me. I detected the same smell I'd noticed earlier, but now it was strong and coming from right behind me. I stopped eating and swallowed what I'd bitten off. As the footsteps drew closer, I jumped up and over the dead animal, turning around as soon as I landed.

Facing me was an animal golden in color. It was smaller than the dead animal on the ground but bigger than me. It looked right at me with the eyes of a predator. I knew I was in trouble, and I growled. My jowls curled up, exposing my teeth. Water dripped from my mouth. I was angry, and so was the animal facing me. It stopped walking and stared at me like it was getting ready to pounce. I waited.

The animal made a loud hissing sound. When it did, I heard more sounds coming from the tree behind me. There were three smaller animals in the tree that looked just like the one I was facing. I realized at that moment the animals in the tree were its babies. It didn't take its eyes off of me. It was protecting its young and the prey it had killed. But I needed the prey. I stood my ground.

The large animal stalked toward me. Instinctively, I stepped backwards. I knew I shouldn't be here. *Why did Daddy leave me here?*

Behind me, I heard the river. As I backed away, the sound of the water grew louder.

The animal kept moving toward me, its eyes fixed on me. Letting out a loud growl, it lunged at me and swiped at me with its paw. I felt the force of it but thought nothing of it. I didn't hurt at first.

Then I smelled the blood coming from my leg. And it did hurt. The animal was trying to kill me, but I didn't want to end up dead on the ground like the prey animal. I had to get back to Daddy. He needed me. My leg was hurt, but I could still use it. The animal lunged again but stopped just short of pouncing on me. I jumped backwards and stumbled down a hill toward the sound of the water.

I rolled down the hill with no way to stop myself, and the animal didn't follow. I bumped up against rocks and pointy things that stung when my body touched them. At the bottom of the hill, I rolled into the river, plunging underwater. When I made it back up to the top, I started swimming. I had to get back to Daddy. The river carried me away. I saw the animal up on the hill. It was watching me but not moving. It stayed with its babies.

When I reached the shore, I fell to the ground, exhausted. I stayed there for a while and licked my wounds. It still hurt, but the bleeding had stopped. Putting my head down, I went to sleep. When I woke up, it was dark outside. I didn't smell or hear the animal that had hurt me, so I stood up, drank from the river, and began walking. My leg still hurt, so I couldn't put all of my weight on it, but I trudged on. I was going home to Daddy's ranch. I walked for a long time. I couldn't smell Daddy any longer so I wasn't sure which way to go. I just moved forward, away from the animal that had hurt me.

When I started feeling tired again, I came to a clearing and found a grassy field lit up by the moon. I threw my body down in the soft grass and licked my wounds. I had to rest. At least when I went to sleep, I could think about being back home with Juna and Heidi. I was so happy there. When I sleep, I am happy. When I sleep, I dream. Oh yes, we dogs do dream.

CHAPTER 11

I woke up the next morning and watched the sun come up. My body was covered in the morning dew. The warmth felt good. For a moment, I forgot about being hungry, thirsty, and hurt.

I made myself stand up and start walking again. My leg was feeling better—still injured, of course, just not as painful. I walked all the way across the grassy field. None of the smells around me were familiar except for one—Big Red. Now I knew I was close to Daddy's ranch. I raised my head and began tracking Big Red.

In the distance, I saw Daddy's ranch. He would be so happy to see me. He would probably call me a good boy for coming back after he forgot me. I quickened my pace. I couldn't move that fast because my leg was still hurting, but I did pretty well.

I was closing in on the ranch, and now I could see Big Red. I heard her whinny and stomp her hoof on the ground. I trotted straight over to her and sat down. She lowered her head and smelled me, nudging me with her nose. I started licking her like I'd never licked anyone before. I was so glad to see her.

While I was licking her, I heard Daddy say, "Well, I'll be damned!"

I was so tired and so busy licking Big Red, I didn't even hear him come up behind me. I stood up and walked toward him. My tail spun in circles. I was glad to be home.

Daddy took a look at me and said, "What kind of trouble did you get into, boy? And how on earth did you find your way home? I've never seen a dog track like that! I guess Heidi was right about you. Come on, let's get you fixed up."

I licked Big Red one last time and walked toward the house with Daddy. He went inside and shut the door behind him. I was sure he was getting me food and water, but when he returned, he was holding a leash. He slid it around my neck and said, "Come!"

I followed him because I am a dog, and that's what we do. Daddy and I walked to his truck, and he opened the back of it. "Okay, King, up you go," he said as he patted the truck. I didn't like this. I remembered the last time I went in Daddy's truck and he forgot me. And I couldn't jump into the truck because my leg was hurt.

"Okay, King, if you won't jump, I'll lift you up."

His two arms circled underneath me, and he lifted me up and into the back of the truck. After he climbed inside, he drove for a while, and the smells all seemed familiar because I'd just traveled that way back to the ranch. Pretty soon the woods gave way to buildings. Now I was sure he was taking me back to Heidi and Juna. I would miss Big Red, but Daddy and I never bonded. I never felt like I was his and he was mine. A dog needs that.

We drove for a little longer, and most of the smells from the ranch and the woods dissipated. Cars and trucks drove next to us. I saw lots of humans in their cars smile at me. A few smaller humans in the backseats of their cars waved. I thought I would like small humans. They seemed nice. Daddy drove the truck up to a building and stopped.

I could smell other dogs in the building. Lots of dogs. I wasn't sure what this place was, but it couldn't be bad if it had dogs in it. Daddy got out of the truck, and I was sure he was taking me to visit the other dogs. Maybe even my brothers and sisters who had been taken away because they were for sale. I hoped Bella was here.

Daddy walked over to me and lowered the back of the truck. "Okay, King, let's go. Don't make this any harder than it has to be," he said.

I didn't like the tone of his voice or the feeling I was getting from him. I did jump out of the truck but only because I wanted to see Bella. Daddy grabbed my leash, and we walked toward the building. The smell of dogs got stronger. I didn't smell Bella.

We went inside, and a human said, "May I help you, sir?"

I said something. I wanted to see Bella.

The lady looked at me and smiled. Daddy didn't look at me.

"I just want him to go to a good home. I can't keep him," he said.

"Sir, he's an older, larger puppy who's all banged up. His chances of being adopted are not as good as the young puppies we have. And we have quite a few puppies right now, so it's likely he'll be put down."

"I'm sure somebody will come pick him up. He's a good boy, aren't you, King?" Daddy said while looking at me. "Look, I even have his papers. Somebody will want a dog with papers. I'm sure of that."

"Sir, that's definitely a plus, but he's hurt and in need of medical attention. He's got some big cuts on his front leg and a lot of cactus needles stuck in him that need to be removed. We can't spend the money fixing him up if he's not going to get adopted. We just don't have the funds for that."

I didn't know what she'd said, but I saw Daddy was angry. Dogs can tell when people are angry.

"I drove all this way to turn him in. Are you going to take him or not?"

"We take all dogs. Especially when they are not appreciated," the lady said. Now *she* was angry. Everyone was angry except for me. I just wanted to see Bella again. "I just need you to fill out this paperwork for me, and while not mandatory, we do ask that a donation be made to help defray the cost of caring for him and adopting him out."

Daddy handed the leash to her and gave her some papers he was holding. He took some different papers from her. Pulling a pen out of his pocket, he scribbled on the papers and handed them back to her. "I don't see why I need to make a donation since you're probably going to put him down anyway." He turned and stormed out of the building.

I must be for sale again.

CHAPTER 12

This human reminded me of Heidi. She stroked my coat. "Don't you worry, King. We're going to try really hard to get you a good home. That mean man will never bother you again."

I said something, and she smiled. She hugged me just like Heidi used to do. My tail spun around in circles. A dog knows when he's wanted. She picked something up and said, "Jen, I have one for you at intake."

A young lady appeared from another room. Her hair was the same color as mine. "Jen, would you mind taking King to the back and doctoring him up? He's got some cuts on his leg that need to be cleaned and a whole heck of a lot of cactus needles to remove. Let's see if we can gussy him up and get him adopted by a nice family."

Jen smiled, patted me on the head, and took the leash. "Come on boy, let's get you taken care of," she said.

She opened a door, and I walked with her into a room containing a lot of dogs in kennels. She lifted me up, put me on a table, and took my leash off.

"Okay King, this is going to hurt a little bit. I'm sorry," she said.

She started pulling out the cactus needles. It did hurt. Every time she pulled one out, I winced. They were in deep. After all the needles were pulled out, Jen washed my leg with water and put something on it. "Looks like you had a run-in with a mountain lion. These claw marks are pretty deep. You're lucky to be alive. I'm going to put medicine on it. It's already starting to heal up."

When Jen finished, she lifted me off the table and put me back on the ground. "Come on, let's go outside for a few minutes," she said. I followed her into a fenced-in grassy area. I did my business just as Heidi had taught me.

"Good boy," said Jen.

I was happy to be a good boy.

After a few minutes of walking around, sniffing, and doing my business, Jen said, "Come on, King." I followed her back into the building, and she led me to a small, gated area. "Okay, King, you have to stay in here for now. I bet someone will come pick you up and take you home soon. You're so handsome and very sweet."

She opened the gate, and when I tried to follow her, she blocked me with her body. There were other dogs on both sides of me. None of them were Bella.

When Jen came back, she brought a bowl of food and some water. She set them down and watched me. I lapped up all the water and turned my attention to the food. I grabbed a mouthful and spit it on the ground. After I nosed it around a little bit, I gobbled it all up.

Jen laughed. She put her hand over her mouth, but I knew she was smiling. "You are so silly, King. How could anyone ever drop you off at an animal shelter? That person should have his head examined." I finished my food and said something. She laughed as she walked away. I couldn't see her, but she stayed close. I could smell her.

She returned again with a blanket and toys. When she joined me in the dog run, my tail spun around in circles. She placed the blanket on the floor and put the toys on top of it. Taking my head with both of her hands, she rubbed my ears. "Who's a good boy? Who's a good boy?"

She put a few good-smelling things down on the blanket and said, "Treats!"

They smelled good, so I ate them.

"Okay, King, I have to go take care of more dogs. I'll come back soon. Don't worry." She walked out of the dog run. I saw her petting other dogs and taking them outside. She lifted some of them up on the table and helped them. I watched her, hoping she'd come back to me.

Some of the dogs took notice of me as they walked by with Jen. Some just smelled me. Most of them were nice, and a few of them stopped to see and sniff me. I knew they wanted to play, but Jen always shooed them along. A few of them were not so nice. I knew who they were right away. She kept them on a tight leash. Sometimes the hair on their backs would rise up. If they were mean, I would only see them once or twice. After that, they never came back. I didn't know where they went, but I was glad I didn't see them anymore. They made me anxious. Maybe they were for sale and went somewhere else. I was glad they were for sale.

I was in the dog run for a long time. I didn't understand why I was here, and it confused me. Jen took me outside a lot and fed me, but I didn't like being held in the dog run. I would have been more useful at Daddy's ranch. Even though I didn't like him, I would have found things to do. I would have spent time with my friend, Big Red.

I stayed there so long that one day, I couldn't take it anymore. I was bored. When dogs get bored, we tend to do bad things. I was about to do something bad. I loved being with Jen and wanted to be a good boy, but I couldn't help myself. My leg had healed, and I was strong again. I walked to the back of the dog run and sprinted toward the gate as fast as my legs could carry me. Just before I reached it, I leaped into the air. I hooked my front legs over the top of the gate and walked up with my back legs. When I reached the top, I pulled my body over the edge and fell to the floor. I landed on my feet.

I looked for Jen, but she wasn't there. I walked around to see the other dogs. Most of them were nice and happy to see me. They were bored, too. After I met all of the other dogs, I walked around looking for things to do. My nose led me to some treats on a table. Jen gave me these pretty often. I couldn't help myself, so I jumped up and grabbed the box with my mouth. I shredded it and ate all of the treats. When my belly was full, I got sleepy. I saw a sofa up against a wall, jumped up on it, and took a nap.

Later, Jen entered the room. There wasn't anybody with her, but she was holding something up to her head. I opened one eye and followed her movements. She was busy talking and didn't notice me. She sat down on the sofa right next to me and kept talking.

"I know, I know, there are a lot of dogs here that are running out of time. There are some really good ones, but we're just out of room. Not enough people are adopting right now. I have one here I really like. He's terrific, but he's not a little puppy so people are passing him up. His name? His name's King. Will you please come down here, take pictures, and post them on the internet? If we don't do something soon, a lot of dogs will be put down. Okay, thanks. I'll see you soon."

She still hadn't seen me, but I heard my name so I said something, stood up, and tried to lick her. Just as I did, she turned her head, and my tongue went into her ear. She screamed and jumped up. I couldn't tell if she liked it or not. When she calmed down, she looked at me and smiled. I guess she liked it.

"King! What the heck? How'd you get out? I see you found the treats, you naughty boy," she said.

I guessed I was no longer a good boy. But I wanted to be a good boy.

"Come on, let's see how you managed to escape," she said. She walked over to where I'd been held and checked the gate. "It's still locked." She looked at me. "Come on, King, I don't know how you did it, but back you go."

She strode into the dog run, and I followed. She closed the gate behind us. "Now, you stay here, King. I bet someone let you out, or I didn't lock the gate properly. Stay here and be a good boy," she commanded.

I was a good boy again. But not for long.

Jen left me in the dog run and cleaned up the shredded treat box, turning her back toward me. I no longer wanted to be confined to a dog run, so I repeated what I'd learned earlier. I am a dog. Dogs remember.

I walked to the back of the dog run, ran as fast as I could toward the gate and jumped. I looped my legs over the top of the gate and walked up it with my back legs. It was pretty easy. Jen heard the commotion, but by the time she turned around to see what had happened, I was standing right behind her and began licking her face. She laughed.

"Oh, no you don't. I don't know how you did that, but we're going to do a little test. Come!" Jen led me back to the dog run and locked me inside. But I didn't want to stay there. I waited until she turned her back and escaped again. This time, she saw what I did.

She smiled and patted me on the head. "You are a clever one, aren't you, King?"

I heard my name so I said something.

She looked at me and rubbed my ears. "Okay, you can stay out of your dog run and do my chores with me. As long as you behave. Good boy," she said. She patted me on my head.

I would behave, because I was a good boy.

"This may be your last day with us. If you don't get adopted soon, it could be trouble. The shelter is filling up, and you've been here longer than most of the other dogs. I'm afraid your name is on the list," she said.

Now she was sad, and water trickled from her eyes. She hugged me. I liked it when she hugged me. I hoped I hadn't done anything wrong. I wanted to be a good boy for her.

CHAPTER 13

I walked around with her that whole day. She cleaned the dog runs for the others who didn't seem to know how to do their business outside. She also filled the water and food bowls. I walked outside with her and the other dogs. She put fresh blankets and toys in each dog run. I didn't need the blanket and toys because I wouldn't stay in my dog run any longer. Now that I knew how to let myself out, why should I?

Jen and I walked a lot of the dogs outside. This gave me something to do, and I liked playing with them. She had them on leashes while walking. I didn't wear a leash because I walked by her side. She knew I didn't need a leash.

When Jen finished walking and feeding the other dogs, she turned to me and got down on her knees. I stared into her eyes. No human had ever done this to me before. She grabbed my head and touched her head to mine.

"Oh, King, I'm so sorry. I wish I could take you home, but I already have two dogs, and my landlord doesn't even want me to have them. If I brought another dog home, he would kick me out. Then we'd both be homeless. You wouldn't want that, would you, King?"

I heard my name, so I said something.

She laughed and said, "That's what I thought. I'm going to give you a special meal tonight. What would you like? Anything you want! Do you like hamburgers? There's a Jack in the Box right across the street. You stay here. I'm going to get you a hamburger. I'll be right back."

I do like hamburgers. Heidi gave me a hamburger once, and it tasted good.

Jen walked through a doorway. I tried to follow her, but she told me to stay. I stayed, sitting on the sofa and waiting for her to return.

When she came back, she held something that smelled good. Water dripped from my mouth. "For your dining pleasure tonight, we have the Ultimate Cheeseburger from Jack in the Box. I'm not sure what's on it, but after seeing a picture of it, I renamed it the King Burger. Because Burger King was already taken." She laughed. "I think you're really going to like it."

I already liked it even though I hadn't tasted it yet. The smell drove me crazy. All the other dogs smelled it, too. They were jealous.

Jen took the hamburger out of some paper and set it on the ground, right in front of me. I looked at her, and she said, "Go on boy, eat it!"

I normally play with my food first, but this smelled so good, I shoved the whole thing in my mouth, chewed it up, and swallowed it. It tasted as good as it smelled.

"I'm so sorry, King. I checked the schedule when I went out, and you're slated to be put to sleep at nine o'clock tomorrow morning."

This time I didn't say anything. I was still licking my chops. Water came from her eyes again, and she kissed me right on the top of my head. "I'll come in early tomorrow morning, King. I'll stay with you until the end if necessary. You won't be alone," she said.

I licked her face. Now, she smelled like a hamburger. I didn't understand what she'd said, but she wasn't happy. I hoped I wasn't a bad boy.

She walked me back to my dog run, and we went in together. She closed the gate behind us and bent down and hugged me again. "Get some sleep. Stay in your dog run. Stay! Tomorrow's going to be a big day. I'm going to call everyone I know about you and put your face all over the internet. I'm going to save you. My friend was supposed to come take your picture but I'll just do it myself."

She pulled something out of her pocket and pointed it at me. "Smile, King," she said.

I knew she was talking to me, so I said something. When I did, I saw a bright light. I didn't know what it was, but I wasn't afraid. I trusted Jen.

She left my dog run and closed the gate behind her. "I'll see you in the morning, King. You be a good boy."

I was a good boy. I stayed in my dog run the whole night because she told me to stay.

The next morning, I got bored and left my dog run. I waited for the other dogs to join me outside of their dog runs, but they never did. I heard and smelled Jen behind the door. My tail spun around in circles. The door opened, and she walked in. She didn't look surprised that I was waiting for her outside my dog run. She pretended to be happy, but I could tell she wasn't. Something was wrong. I felt it.

"Let me get you some breakfast. I'm really sorry, boy. I've done everything

I can," she said. She put some food in a bowl and set it on the ground in front of me. But something wasn't right. It took me a long time to eat my food. Longer than normal.

A human opened the door while I was eating and said, "Jen, it's 9:05. We really need to stick to the schedule. I'm sorry. I know you're attached to him."

"It's just not fair, Sean. I know you're right, but he's just such a good boy. He deserves better."

"He does Jen, he really does. But, we have a job to do. Let's try to get through this and concentrate on saving more lives after he's gone."

"We'll be along in a minute."

He left. I said something and finished my food. I walked up to her and pressed my body into her leg. She stroked my back.

CHAPTER 14

Jen petted me for a few more minutes. "You're a good boy, King."

I am a good boy. But why isn't she happy?

She put a leash on me and commanded me to come with her. I did. I would do anything for her. We walked down a hallway toward another door. "I'm so sorry, King."

I was uneasy because Jen was uneasy. I couldn't help it. She opened the door, and we walked in. I stopped. Sean was in the room, and he wasn't dressed like anyone I'd ever seen before. He was holding something with both hands. My hair went up. I sensed danger. There was a strange smell in this room, and I didn't like it. It reminded me of the smell when that long, fat animal killed my prey in the woods.

But Jen would protect me. She wouldn't let me get hurt.

I became even more uneasy when Sean walked toward me with the thing in his hand. The smell was strong on him. My jowls curled up, and for the first time, I snarled in anger at a human. He stopped in his tracks.

"Are you going to be able to control him, or do I need to call someone to help us?" Sean asked. "We really need to get this done. I have a very tight schedule."

"Can you just give me a minute alone with him? I want to say goodbye, and I think it'll calm him if you leave the room," she said.

Sean looked at her and then at me.

"Please, Sean? Just one minute?"

"Okay. I'm sorry. I don't like this any more than you do. I'll wait outside, but please make it brief." He put the thing down and walked past me. I snarled at him as he passed by. I wasn't going to bite him. I just didn't want that smell next to me.

Jen bent down. I was hoping she would tell me I was a good boy. Just before she said something, the door flew open, and Sean rushed in. I didn't like this. I didn't like it at all. But this time, things felt different.

Jen stood up and yelled, "I just asked you to give us a minute!"

He walked past us and put the smelly thing in a cabinet. Jen looked at Sean and seemed confused.

"What on earth are you doing?" she asked.

He grinned. "Take all the minutes you want. Someone's here to adopt him. They're in the waiting room and want to meet him right now!"

Jen hugged me, and water streamed from her eyes. This time she was happy. "I knew it, King! I just knew it!" She stood up and hugged Sean. Sean was surprised but hugged her back.

"I'm just glad we were running late," he said. "Timing is everything, isn't it?"

"It sure is, Sean. It sure is," she said.

"Come on, let's take King to meet his new family."

"Hell yeah. But I thought you were too busy?"

He smiled. "You know, sometimes we just have to take a moment and enjoy the good things that come our way."

They walked me out of that smelly room, down another hallway, and into a room with a sofa in it. Three humans—two of them small—sat on the sofa.

Jen extended her hand. "Hi, I'm Jen, and this is Sean. And this is King. He's *very* happy you're here to adopt him!"

She looked at me. I heard my name, so I said something.

She grinned and said, "Yeah, he's a talker."

The small humans on the sofa giggled. I liked them.

"Hi, I'm Lacy, and these are my daughters, Olivia and Caroline. We're here to take King home with us," the woman on the couch said.

I walked over to them and lay down. Then I rolled over on my back. Olivia and Caroline started rubbing my belly. Jen smiled, and water came from her eyes again. I had never seen a human with so much water coming from her eyes.

"I'll be right back with the adoption papers," Jen said, sniffing. "You guys get to know King. He's a very special dog. You'll love him."

When Jen came back, she brought some papers with her. She gave some of them to Lacy and said, "King is actually a purebred Black Mouth Cur. He came with papers and everything. He'll make a fine pet. Won't you, boy?"

Olivia and Caroline rubbed my face and kissed my nose. Jen smiled. I'd never seen her this happy. Lacy took some papers from her pocket and handed them to Jen. Jen bent down and gave me a big hug. My tail spun around in circles, and the Olivia and Caroline laughed. I said something as I licked Jen's face.

"I love you, King," she said. "Have a long, happy life." Lacy, Olivia, and Caroline walked me out of the room and out of that building. I knew I would never see Jen again.

CHAPTER 15

I followed them to a truck like Daddy's. I wondered what had happened to Daddy. He was probably really upset that I wasn't with him. I didn't know if I'd ever see him or Big Red again. I was sure he missed me.

But now I was with Lacy and the small humans. Lacy opened the door, and I jumped in. Everybody else got in, and I sat between Lacy and Olivia. We drove for a while. I'd had a lot of excitement, so I lay down and rested my head on Olivia's leg. She placed her hand on my head and said, "Don't worry, I'm going to take great care of you, King."

I wasn't worried. I went to sleep.

I woke up when the truck came to a stop. "Come on, it's time to wake up," Olivia said. She gently shook me, and I opened one eye to see the three of them outside of the truck. I leaned forward and stretched. As I did, I gave a little yawn, and that made them happy.

A lot of scents hit me. Not only did I smell the three humans in front of me, I smelled all kinds of animals, in all different directions.

Go time.

I jumped out of the truck and over the heads of the small humans. First, I found some animals with white feathers and orange feet and noses. They saw me coming, but I am King and I was too fast for them. They waddled away from me, but I was closing in on them. I was going to shred and eat them.

"*King, no! Bad boy!*" Lacy yelled. I didn't want to be a bad boy, so I stopped chasing the animals. I didn't know why I'd chased them. Something made me do it.

I trotted back over to the humans, and Lacy said, "Good boy, King. That's a good boy. Don't eat our ducks."

I was a good boy. *I bet ducks are delicious.* I didn't eat them, but I thought about it. Two dogs came running up to me. I wasn't sure what to do, so I stood my ground.

"King, meet Peggy Sue and Cricket."

Peggy Sue was small and the same color as I am. Cricket was a little bigger than Peggy Sue, but she was many different colors. The three of us sniffed one another. They seemed friendly enough.

After we all checked each other out, they ran off together. I followed them. We went to a house. Food and water lay in bowls next to the house, so I drank some water. The small humans walked over to us and giggled.

Olivia said, "Look how King bobs his head up and down while he drinks." They pointed at me and giggled. I was curious why they were so happy. I turned my head and said something. Water dripped from my jowls. They didn't mind.

Later, Cricket, Peggy Sue, and I walked around. I saw and smelled all kinds of animals. Caroline walked with us and said, "King, you can't kill the pigs, rabbits, goats, or cows. Don't chase them either. You leave them alone. Okay, King?" I was told not to chase them, so I didn't. But I really wanted to. *Sometimes being a good boy is hard, but I am King. I am a good boy.* I said something to acknowledge her command.

I really liked the pigs. They were nice like Big Red. They lived in a fenced area, and when I walked up to them, they stuck their heads through the fence, smelling me and snorting.

That night, the two other dogs and I went to the house to eat. Lacy put some food out, and while the other two dogs ate it quickly, I played with my food first. Everyone chuckled while watching me eat. Afterward, another truck drove up, and the small humans ran out and jumped on a human getting out of it.

"Daddy!" they yelled. I looked around to see where Daddy was, but I didn't see or smell him anywhere. I was confused. I thought for sure he'd come to get me because he missed me. But Daddy was nowhere to be found. The human holding Olivia and Caroline kissed them on the head. He saw me and cocked his head.

He put them down. "Did you feed Cricket too much because he's grown a lot bigger since this morning." He pointed at me.

Since he was talking to me, I said something.

They laughed. "No, silly, that's King. He's our new dog. We got him today while you were at work."

"Oh! That explains a lot." They ran over to me and the other two dogs and started petting us.

"King, say hi to Daddy."

I heard my name, so I said something. They called the human 'Daddy.' He must have the same name as Daddy. Daddy, Olivia, and Caroline laughed and clapped their hands. They liked it when I said something.

The small humans and Daddy went into the house and closed the door behind them. They didn't want me in the house. I would sleep outside with the other dogs. They were nice, and I didn't mind. I heard Daddy talk to Lacy inside. I peered in the window. He was sitting in a chair next to a table. Lacy brought him food, just like she'd brought us food. His food smelled better.

"Honey," he said, "do we really need another mouth to feed right now? We already have two dogs. He's a fine-looking animal. I bet he'd make a great hog dog or hunting dog. Looks like he has a good nose on him."

"Oh no, King isn't ours. Our weekend neighbors from Katy called me this morning and asked me if I'd go pick him up from the shelter in Kerrville. Someone from Kerrville posted pictures of King on the internet—he was scheduled to be euthanized early this morning. He reminded them of a dog they just lost to cancer. I gathered the girls up and drove to the shelter to get him. He's a great puppy and as sweet as can be. They'll be here tomorrow to pick him up."

"That was really nice of you and the girls to drive all that way to save him. You all should really be proud of yourselves," he said.

When he finished eating, he moved into another part of the house and turned out the lights. I could still hear and smell all of them. The other two dogs went to sleep, but I wanted to sleep inside the house. I like being inside with my humans. When it got quiet and I didn't hear any more noises, I said something. The other two dogs just looked at me without moving. I said something several more times, but no one ever came to let me in.

I jumped on the door. It didn't open, so I jumped a few more times. After several attempts, my paw caught on something and pushed it down. The door swung open. The other two dogs must have been impressed because they stood up and walked in the house behind me.

They went back to sleep in the room where the humans had been eating. I tracked the small humans, swiftly and silently following their scent to another room. They were sleeping in beds next to one another, just like Juna and I used to. I was certain there was more than enough room for me. And I felt sure they wouldn't mind sharing.

I crawled in bed with Olivia, and she woke up. She smiled and said, "King, you're going to get in big trouble."

I circled around a few times in her bed. It was much nicer than any bed I'd ever slept in. I came to rest with my head on her chest. She looked at me, and I peered into her eyes. That's what dogs do. We can tell a lot about a human just by looking into their eyes. She put her hand on my head, closed her eyes, and went to sleep.

CHAPTER 16

The next morning, I heard animals making loud noises. They sounded like birds. I wanted to get up and eat them, but I remained still with my eyes open, staring at Olivia. I waited for her to wake up. While lying there, I heard Lacy walk in. She made her way toward the bed.

"King! What are you doing in the house?" she asked. Olivia opened her eyes, and I licked her face. She was happy. Lacy was not. "Olivia, did you let King in the house?"

"No, Mama. He just showed up. I was sleeping when he came in."

"I bet your father did it. Come on, King. Let's get you fed and outside. Your new owners are coming to pick you up today!"

I heard my name, so I said something.

Lacy looked at me and said, "You know, it's almost like he knows what I'm saying."

The small humans were happy, and Carolyn said, "He does, Mama."

I jumped off the bed and followed Lacy.

After she fed Cricket, Peggy Sue, and me, Lacy said, "Hurry up, King, we have chores to do." I finished eating my food, and the two girls dashed outside. Daddy's truck was gone. I didn't see, smell, or hear him. We all walked around together.

When we stopped, Lacy said, "Okay girls, it's time to milk the cow."

They pulled on something underneath the cow, and something squirted out of it into a bucket. It wasn't water. It smelled and looked different. She put food out for the cow, and we continued on to a little house. She opened a door, and some birds strolled out. I froze. I pointed my nose at them ready to pounce. I was going to kill and eat them.

Lacy was watching me and yelled, "*No, King!* Leave the chickens alone!" I did leave them alone, but it took all my might. Something inside made me want to tear the chickens apart. Lacy told me 'no,' so I didn't. But I wanted to.

The small humans walked ahead and gave food to some horses that reminded me of Big Red, but they weren't as nice. I missed Big Red. Lacy fed the ducks and the pigs and then picked things growing on some plants.

When they finished their chores, we made our way back to the house. The small humans went inside and closed the door behind them. Lacy looked at me and said, "King, stay out here with Cricket and Peggy Sue. Do you hear me?"

I heard her, and I said something.

She smiled and said, "Okay then." She went in the house and closed the door. The other two dogs curled up and fell asleep on the porch. I wasn't ready to sleep. I still had a lot of energy. I chased the chickens and ducks for a little bit. I didn't run too fast, or I would have caught them. Lacy wouldn't like that.

It was fun, but I soon got bored because I couldn't finish the job. I meandered over to see the horses, but they ignored me. I didn't bother trying to become friends with them. Why should I? They made no effort.

Now, the pigs were different. When I went to visit them, they trotted right up to me and made strange noises with their noses. I jumped over their fence, and they chased me around. I, in turn, chased them. I jumped up on them, and they jumped up on me. We had fun. They got tired and lumbered over to a big mud hole. I watched as they rolled around in it. They seemed to be having fun, so I joined them.

The pigs went to sleep, so I jumped back over their fence and continued to walk around. I was getting a little tired and decided to join Cricket and Peggy Sue on the porch. They were still sleeping, so I went to sleep as well. I'd been sleeping for a while when I heard Daddy's truck drive up. I opened one eye and watched as he stopped the truck and got out. He walked over to the porch and looked right at me. He had a strange look on his face. "Lacy, can you come out here?" he asked. The door opened, and Olivia and Caroline ran out.

They screamed, "Daddy!"

A moment later, Lacy walked through the door. She looked at me. "King, what have you done now?" she asked.

The small humans turned around and looked at me. They were happy. I make people happy.

Now I had both eyes open, and I stood up. "King, how did you get mud all over yourself? You're just filthy, and your new owners are coming today. Girls, take King down to the river and wash him off. We can't let him go home looking like that," Lacy said.

"Mama," Carolyn said, "King was rolling around in the mud with the pigs. That's how he got so dirty."

I heard my name and the word *pigs*, so I said something.

When I did, Carolyn said, "See? I told you that's what he did."

"I think you're right, honey," said Daddy. "I think that's exactly what King did. Maybe he thinks he's a pig. Are you a pig, King?" All of them were laughing, so I knew I was a good boy.

Olivia and Caroline walked to some water behind their house. It reminded me of the river I fell in when that animal attacked me in the woods. I ran to the water and jumped in, drinking it in. It was cold but good. Caroline splashed water on me with her hand. I tried to catch it in my mouth. They smiled. I ran around in the water, and when it grew deep, I swam.

I am King. I am a good swimmer.

Olivia said, "Okay, King, the mud is all washed off. Let's go back to the house."

They walked away, and I followed them. When we got to the house, they went inside and closed the door. I joined the other two dogs lying in the sun on the porch. This warmed me up and dried my hair.

CHAPTER 17

A car pulled up the dirt road toward the house. I heard it before I saw it. When the other two dogs finally heard it, they jumped up, started barking, and ran toward the car. They barked at it until it stopped next to Daddy's truck.

I stayed on the porch to protect the house. The other two dogs continued to bark until Lacy and the small humans came out. I remained silent and, for once, didn't say something. Two humans climbed out of the car and walked toward us. I was motionless. I wasn't sure what was going on.

I hoped I wasn't for sale. I didn't want to be for sale.

Lacy said, "Hi, come on over," as she gave some papers to one of the humans. He put them in his pocket and gave her some papers. They all looked at me, and then Lacy called my name.

I meandered toward her. I didn't want to go to her, but I am a dog and when my name is called, I must come.

"King, I want you to meet your new owners, Scott and Gayle. They are going to take you home with them," Lacy said.

"Come here, boy," Scott called out. I liked his voice and his scent. I looked him over and decided he was a good human. He was standing with open arms, and I ran to him. As I got closer to him, I jumped and landed in his outstretched arms.

Maybe it was because I could tell how much he really wanted me. Dogs can feel when we are truly wanted. While in his arms, he held me like I hadn't been held since I'd been with Heidi. Of course, I was much bigger now. Gayle came closer and rubbed my head. I'd finally found my own humans.

The small humans walked over to me and petted me. "Goodbye, King. We'll miss you." I knew I'd be leaving with Scott and Gayle because I was for sale. I would miss the small humans, but I liked Scott and Gayle. Scott carried me to his car and put me in the back. I could smell another dog had been back there, but the scent was not very strong. Scott closed the door, and he and Gayle got in. As we drove away, I saw Lacy and the small humans waving. I stuck my face up against the window and pressed my nose to the glass.

"Look at that, he's fogging up the window with his nose, just like Coco used to do," Gayle said. She looked at me and smiled. When we passed by the pigs, they were rolling in the mud again.

We weren't in the car for long. We stopped at a small house just down the road.

I can go visit Lacy and the small humans whenever I want.

Scott let me out of the car, and I went exploring. There were all kinds of scents for me to follow. I started tracking my prey, but Gayle called me, so I ran to her.

"Come on, King. Let's go in the house. I'll rustle you up some dinner," she said.

I followed her inside. Just like in the car, I could smell another dog had been there. The scent was faint. The dog hadn't been there for a while. I searched anyway. If there was another dog, I would find it. I walked around the home, sniffing at everything.

"Look, honey, he smells Coco. I wonder if King can sense that Coco's in heaven," Gayle said.

I heard my name, so I said something. Gayle put her hand over her mouth, and water streamed from her eyes. I sensed the other dog had gone where I could no longer track him. A dog can always tell.

Gayle put some food and water down for me. I drank the water right away. They both laughed as they watched me drink.

"Look how he bobs his head up and down while he drinks. Isn't that the cutest thing? King's going to be a great dog," Gayle said.

Once I quenched my thirst and finished my food, the three of us walked outside. There were lots of smells to keep me busy. Scott and Gayle watched me from the porch, but I was busy watching something else.

I smelled my prey. Something was moving in the brush. My nose went forward, and I stood still. I wanted to kill and eat it. I wasn't even hungry, but my instincts took over. I took off. Leaping from the porch, I hit the ground at full stride. My prey sensed me and bolted. I followed close behind. As I overtook it, I moved in behind and grabbed it with my teeth, just below the head. I sharply turned my head to the side and snapped its neck. When I heard the cracking sound, I knew it was over. I didn't know if this would make Scott and

Gayle happy, but I brought my prey to them and dropped it at their feet, the taste of blood still in my mouth.

I waited to see if I was a good boy. I waited for a while. They were watching me but didn't say anything. So I said something.

"Good boy, King," Scott said. Gayle looked at him, and he said, "I think that's what he's supposed to do, Gayle. A dog can't go against his nature any more than we can. It's obvious he's some type of hunting dog. Maybe he's a hog dog or a varmint dog or something like that. He sure got that rabbit in a hurry!"

"We can't have him going around killing things willy nilly. We'll have to work on that."

Scott smiled and said, "Good boy, King!"

He picked up my prey and took it into the home. I walked by his side. He didn't let me eat it, but he tore it apart just as I would have, except he used something sharp to do it with. Later, he put my prey in something hot, and I could smell it. Water came from my jowls. Gayle came in and walked over to me. She stopped and looked up. So I looked up as well.

"Honey," she said, "I think we might have a leak in the roof."

"No, I don't see a leak in the roof, but I do see the leak, and he's standing right next to you." Scott chuckled.

She looked down at me and saw the water dripping from my jowls. I couldn't help it. The smell of my prey was strong. I was ready to eat what I'd killed.

Gayle smiled. "Okay, King, let's get you wiped up." She dried my mouth with a white cloth and then cleaned the floor. When the rabbit came out, they gave me a section of it. It was good and hot. Water came from my jowls again. Gayle dried me up again and put the rabbit away somewhere else.

It had been a long day for me, and I was tired. I found a bed like the one Juna and I slept on at Heidi's house. The smell of the other dog was strong on the bed, but I didn't mind. It was a good smell. Scott and Gayle watched as I circled around several times.

I heard Gayle say, "You're looking for your sweet spot, aren't you, King?" I heard my name, so just before I lay down and closed my eyes to go to sleep, I said something. They looked at one another and then at me and laughed.

"It's a good thing we saved him, but he sure is a goofus," Scott said.

I went to bed that night knowing I was a good boy and in a good home where I'd be cared for. And possibly a *goofus*, whatever that was. I was certain it was something good. Finally, I could rest easy, and that's just what I did.

CHAPTER 18

The next morning, I heard a strange sound and movement coming from outside. I opened my eyes and didn't see anyone, so I got up and moved toward the noise.

The door was open, but there was another door behind it. I could see through it and feel the breeze from outside carrying a multitude of scents. I spotted Scott with something that was making the sound. I really wanted to join him. My curiosity got the better of me, and I nudged the door with my nose. It didn't budge. I am King, and I don't take no for an answer, so I tried several more times.

Gayle walked up behind me. I didn't need to turn and see her to know she was there. I smelled her even before I heard her footsteps.

I was too occupied trying to get out of the house to acknowledge her presence. I nudged the door a few more times, and it almost opened. But then I lost patience and rammed the door with my head. This time it paid off. It made a loud ripping noise as the bottom of the door came loose, and my body passed through it. It rubbed against my back, but it was soft and didn't hurt.

Once I was outside, Gayle yelled, "King!" I continued to walk but looked over my shoulder. The door was still closed. I saw her standing behind it with her arms folded. She was not happy. I walked up to Scott. He did something, and the noise stopped.

Gayle came out and said, "King, you're a bad boy."

Scott said, "What happened?"

"He just busted through the screen door."

I don't like the screen door.

Gayle said, "You're going to have to fix that door."

"How long have we wanted a doggie door? You've been asking me for years to build one. Now, we have one. You're welcome!" He pointed to the screen door and smiled. He rubbed my head and said, "Good boy."

I was confused because I wanted to be a good boy, but Gayle told me I was a bad boy.

I said something.

They both laughed for a long time, and I started dancing around because they were so happy. I said something again. It was a good day. I learned how to walk in and out of the house without opening the door. I just walked through the doggie door.

They walked inside, and I followed. Gayle said, "It's time for breakfast." She put some food in a dish for me, and like I usually did, I played with it before I ate it. She made some food for herself and Scott. When I finished, I went over to the table where they were eating. It smelled good. Water dripped from my jowls.

Scott said, "I'm sorry boy, you will not be fed at the table." I lay underneath it just in case someone accidentally dropped food or secretly handed me a morsel here or there. Scott and Gayle ate three times a day. I only ate two times a day. Three times a day would be better, but I never went hungry. Sometimes Scott handed me food under the table. Gayle always called him a *bad boy* when he did this. I'm sure he wanted to be a good boy, but I liked it better when he was a bad boy.

After breakfast, Scott and I walked outside, and he climbed into the thing that had caught my attention earlier. He sat down, and I followed him in and sat next to him. He turned something, and it made the same noise I'd heard before. I turned my head sideways. He looked at me and laughed. He did that a lot. He adjusted a couple of things, and we moved forward. I liked this because all the scents came to me instead of my having to search them out. I knew where everything was without even seeing. I knew which direction animals were traveling. The wind blew through my hair.

While we were moving, he said, "King, you would have loved Coco. He was such a good boy. He rode with me in this utility vehicle all around the property. Just like you're doing. You even look a little like him. We lost him to cancer, you know. Gayle cried for weeks. When I saw your picture online, I knew she needed you. She does need you. She's even smiling and laughing again. Thank you, King. You're such a good boy."

I heard my name, and I was a good boy, so I said something. He was happy. I lay down on the seat and rested my head on his leg. I sighed. He placed his hand on my head. "That's exactly what Coco used to do."

When we got back to the house, we jumped out of the utility vehicle. I walked through the doggie door, Scott following behind me. Gayle was sitting on the sofa, talking into something she held next to her head. She was looking at a paper.

"Well, we picked him up at the shelter in Kerrville. And we were just in time because he was scheduled to be put down right before we got there. Yes, yes, I'm sure. I got your name off the papers he came with. Yes, his name is King. He's a little banged up, but nothing we can't fix."

I heard my name and Heidi's voice, so I said something. Then I heard Juna say something. My tail spun around in a circle. I couldn't help it. She heard me. I lifted my head, opened my mouth, and howled. Juna howled back. I couldn't smell her, but I heard her. Gayle was confused. So was I.

"Well, do you want him back?" Gayle said. "Of course we'd love to keep him. Absolutely, we'll give him a great home. Thank you! Thank you very much!" Heidi stopped talking, and I no longer heard Juna. Gayle looked at me and said, "Well, King, I guess you're stuck with us. That was Heidi on the telephone. She said we can keep you."

I heard my name, so I said something. I was glad to be with Scott and Gayle. Scott walked over to the sofa and sat next to Gayle. Since everyone was sitting on the sofa and looked so comfortable, I joined them. I lay down next to Scott and placed my head in his lap. Gayle looked at him, and Scott said, "What? He's part of the family now."

Scott smiled, and Gayle said, "He's not allowed on the furniture. You know that."

"So, who were you on the phone with?" Scott asked.

"Well, I called the telephone number on King's papers and had an interesting conversation with his breeder. Her name's Heidi, and she's very nice," Gayle said. My ears perked up when I heard Heidi's name.

"Heidi's a little upset. She told me King was the pick of the litter and that people come from all over the country to buy her Black Mouth Curs because they come from some of the finest bloodlines. She sold all of the puppies for sixteen hundred dollars each except for King. Can you believe that?"

I looked up at Scott, and his mouth was wide open. Maybe he was hot. That's what I do when I'm hot. He must be hot.

"That's amazing. Who would pay that for a dog when you can get one at the shelter for almost nothing?" Scott said.

"I totally agree, honey, but it turns out that our King is a special breed of dog. According to Heidi, Black Mouth Curs are bred for speed, intelligence, loyalty, and agility. They're even great at tracking and hunting. Now we know why he was able to kill that rabbit so quickly. She told me a lot of people use them for hog dogs," Gayle said.

"Why was she upset?" Scott asked.

"Turns out that King was the pick of the litter, and Heidi never sold him because he was supposed to be a gift for her father, who's a rancher. When she last spoke to her father, he told her King had wandered off the ranch and never returned. Now she's caught her dad in a lie, and she's furious. She knows he dropped King off at the shelter because we have King's papers that she gave him. She's really angry because she would have taken King back had she known her father didn't want him. He could have died at the shelter. I felt bad when I told her he almost did. Anyway, she asked me if we would give him a good home, and I told her of course we would. She said King had been through enough, and if he was happy here, she wanted him to stay."

"You hear that, boy? Looks like you're stuck with us," Scott said.

I could tell from his voice that he was happy. That made me happy, so I said something. Scott placed his hand on my head, and I went to sleep.

CHAPTER 19

Two days later, Scott and Gayle walked me down to the river. I saw some ducks swimming around and making noises. I needed to kill and shred them. I jumped in the water. I was becoming a good swimmer.

Scott said, "He must have webbed feet to be able to swim like that."

I swam to the middle of the river to clamp down on a duck, but just before I could, it flew into the air and landed further down the river. That made me even more determined, but every time I got close to a duck, it flew away. I knew I might not be able to catch a duck, but that didn't stop me from trying. Something drove me to get those ducks.

Eventually, Gayle called, "King, come here! Leave the ducks alone." I am a dog, so that's what I did. I swam back to shore, and when I left the river, I shook my coat dry.

I sprayed Scott and Gayle with cold river water, and they both said, "King!" They were happy, so I knew I was still a good boy.

That evening when it got dark, a new animal wandered into my line of vision. I couldn't help myself—I sprang into action. Scott and Gayle hadn't yet seen my prey, but I knew exactly where it was. I followed my nose. I jumped off of the porch and hit the ground running. Soon, I overtook it. I'd never seen anything like it before.

It was gray and covered by a hard shell. I was about to sink my teeth into it when it stopped and rolled up into a hard ball. I was confused. It didn't try to escape like most prey. The head, tail, and legs just disappeared. Only a hard ball remained.

Where did it go? It still smelled like my prey, but it wasn't moving. Sniffing it, I nosed it, and it rolled like a ball. I nosed it again, and it rolled away. If my prey was gone, at least I could have fun rolling the ball around.

I rolled it again, and Gayle called me back to the house. "Come on, King. Come home." I went back and sat next to Gayle and Scott on the porch.

"Now, King, you must leave Dilly alone. He lives out here in a little hole underneath a tree stump. He's our resident armadillo, and I don't want you doing to him what you did to that rabbit," Gayle said. I was glued to her eyes and listening to her every word.

I said something so she would know I was listening. I wanted to be a good boy. While Gayle was talking to me, I heard Dilly, the armadillo, unroll and scramble around in the brush. I dared not turn my head away from Gayle and take off after Dilly while she was talking to me. That would make me a bad boy. When Gayle finished talking, Dilly had already made it safely back to his hole. Just like the ducks, Dilly had gotten away from me. I could still smell him, so I decided to revisit him tomorrow.

I followed Scott and Gayle into the house. This time I didn't have to use the doggie door because Scott opened the door for me. They gave me food and water. When I finished eating, I sat under the table while they ate their food. Scott gave me some while Gayle wasn't looking. I liked eating with them.

"King, we need to go to bed early tonight because we've got some chores to do in the morning. Tomorrow's our last day out here before we head back to Katy," said Gayle.

I went to my bed and curled up to sleep. It had been a fun day. When I slept, I dreamed about Dilly.

Scott and Gayle turned the lights out and went to sleep in their bed. I got up and watched them for a little while. Then I looked out the window, checking for any movement. I couldn't help it. But I only saw some animals flying around next to a light that was high up in the air. They were swooping down from up high and eating bugs right out of the air. I watched them for a few minutes and then decided to go to sleep.

I am King. I watch over my humans.

In my dream, the chase was on. I found myself back in the river, swimming after the ducks. This time, when a duck flew out of the water, I caught it just in time. I swam back to shore with it in my mouth. Once I walked out of the water, I shredded it. Feathers flew everywhere, and I ate it.

When I finished eating the duck, I walked back over to Dilly's hole in the ground and waited. I crouched downwind from the hole so he wouldn't smell me. I didn't have long to wait. Dilly crept out of his hole and walked forward. My whole body twitched, but I remained silent and still. At just the right moment, when I knew he couldn't possibly make it back to his hole, I sprang into action and grabbed him with my mouth. I shook him until his neck broke, and then I shredded him. I couldn't help myself. Dilly didn't taste good, so I didn't eat him.

CHAPTER 20

I felt someone pushing me. Then I heard a voice. Dilly was gone, and I was no longer outside. "King, if you're going to sneak into bed, you're going to have to be still. Stop running in your sleep and making noises. Are you having a dream? Your name fits—if you're going to sleep with us, we're going to need a king-size bed," Gayle said.

Scott laughed. It wasn't loud, but I heard it. I licked her face, stood up, circled around, and came to rest with my head on Gayle's chest. She put her hand on my head and went back to sleep.

The next morning, Scott and Gayle woke up early. The sun was not in the sky yet. Gayle pushed me away from her. I didn't want to move away, so I leaned into her. She laughed but managed to slip out of bed. Unmoving, I watched her.

"Scott, get out of bed," she said, yawning. "It's time to get to work."

Gayle fed me and watched me eat as she made food for herself and Scott. She made happy noises a few times, and when she did, I looked up at her. *When she's happy, I must be a good boy.* When they finished eating, Scott walked outside, and I trotted behind him. He put a few things in the utility vehicle, and we drove for a while and stopped. I remember when Daddy drove me to an area and stopped. That was the day he forgot me, and I went hungry. I hoped Scott wouldn't forget me.

"Come on, King, let's take care of business. We need to chop these dead cedar trees down and bring back some firewood. It'll be cold soon. You stay here and watch. I don't want you to get hurt by the chainsaw."

I said something.

Scott said, "Stay," so I did. He lugged the chainsaw out of the utility vehicle and pulled at it. It made a loud sound, and smoke came out of it. He pushed it up against the cedar trees, and they fell to the ground. I'd never seen anything like this before. He toppled five trees, and then he used the chainsaw to cut them into small pieces.

"Okay, King, here's the hard part. We have to take some of this wood back and stack up the rest of it," he said.

He picked up the small pieces of wood and loaded them into the utility vehicle. I wanted to be useful, so I bit into a piece of wood and dragged it over to Scott. He was happy and said, "Thank you, boy—you're a big help!"

I was a good boy, and not long after that, he finished loading the utility vehicle with wood and stacked up the rest. We jumped in the vehicle, and he started driving. "It sure is hot outside today, King. It's usually not this hot late in the year."

I said something.

"You know what I'm talking about, don't you, boy? We may have to go back down to the river and cool off. I bet you'd like that, wouldn't you?" he asked.

I said something. I liked the river.

When we got back to the house, Scott carried the wood to a spot next to the house and stacked it up. I dragged some with my mouth to him. Gayle came out and watched us. She was happy—I was a good boy and helped with the wood.

"Scott, Paulito called for you. He wants you to call him back," she said.

"Let me finish unloading and stacking the wood, and I'll call him," Scott said.

Dragging the wood made me hot. I went through the doggie door and drank a whole bowl of water. After Scott came in and drank his own water, he picked up the telephone, pushed it with his fingers, held it up to his face, and started talking. "Paulito? What's up? Sure. Sure, that'd be great. Come on over," he said. He put the telephone down.

"What did he say?" Gayle asked.

"It's hotter than hell outside. He wanted to know if he could come swim in the river," Scott said.

"It is pretty hot for this time of year. Today would be a good day to take a dip in the river."

I lay down in my bed and waited for our next activity. A truck pulled up, and, on guard, I went outside to see who it was. Scott walked up behind me and said, "It's okay, King, it's Paulito. He's nice. You'll like him."

A human got out of the truck, and Scott walked over to him. I walked at Scott's side. Paulito smelled liked something I'd never smelled before. It wasn't bad, just different. Scott and Paulito walked to the porch, and I trailed them.

Paulito said, "Man, I'm ready to go sit in the river. And I brought two cigars for us." He held up two long, brown things. Now I knew what he smelled like. He smelled like cigars.

"Terrific," Scott said. "I'll go change to my swimsuit, and we'll go down to the river."

I heard the word *river*, and after a moment, I wandered away and walked down to it. When I got there, an older human was sitting with a puppy next to the water. The puppy was small and reminded me of when I was a puppy and lived with Heidi, Juna, and my brothers and sisters. Especially Bella. She was my favorite.

I was curious, so I walked up to the puppy and sniffed it. It was a young male like I used to be, but it had longer hair. He sniffed me back, also curious.

The human yelled, "No! Get away!" He was not happy. I wasn't being a bad boy. I was doing what dogs do. We sniff one another. We learn a lot about each other after a sniff or two. Scott and Paulito came running up behind me. I heard and smelled them long before they reached me.

"We heard all the shouting. What's wrong?" Scott asked.

The other human said, "I walked up the river to swim here, and I have a six-week-old German Shepherd puppy. Your dog's right next to him. Does he bite?"

Scott said, "I don't think so, but I just got him, so I'm not sure."

I sniffed the puppy a few more times and sat next to it. The human seemed happy, and he, Paulito, and Scott walked into the river and started swimming. I wanted to join them, but I was curious about the puppy and stayed with it. The puppy liked me.

He missed his human, who was swimming far out into the river. He walked toward the water and tried to enter it. I didn't like this. I walked in front of him and nosed him back. He tried several times, and I kept nosing him back.

When I got distracted by a sound, he ran past me, right into the river, and swam out to be with his human. Struggling against the current, he started to whine.

He needs help.

His human was too far away to get to him. I jumped forward and lunged into the water after the puppy. I swam to him and turned around. He climbed on my back and up on my shoulders, and I swam him back to shore. He held on tight.

The three humans swam back, and Paulito said, "Did you see that? King saved that little puppy. We were so far away—there was no way we could get to him quick enough. I wish we would have caught that on video!"

The human looked at me and said, "Thank you, King! Thank you for saving my puppy!"

I was a good boy, and everyone was happy. I licked the puppy's face, and the human picked him up and walked down the river with him. The puppy looked back at me until they disappeared around a bend.

Paulito and Scott patted me on the head, and both said, "Good boy!"

I was tired after all the swimming. Scott and Paulito sat down on the river bank. Paulito had two cigars in his hand. He gave one to Scott, and they made the ends of the cigars red. Smoke came from them, and they placed the cigars in their mouths. I was curious.

Paulito said, "That was amazing when King rescued the puppy from drowning! I'll never forget that."

Scott said, "Neither will I." After their cigars got smaller, they walked back to the house, me by their side.

Paulito said, "Goodbye," and patted me on the head. He got in his truck and drove away.

"Well, King," said Gayle, "let's start closing up the house. We'll head back to Katy this evening. It's going to be a long drive, so we should get started soon. It won't be that bad, and you'll love our house in Katy. We have a big back yard and a swimming pool."

I said something back to her. Scott and Gayle packed up all their stuff and put it in their car. I did my business outside and walked inside to sleep on my bed. When I woke up, everyone was outside. I joined them.

Even though I was tired, I smelled animals moving around. I was about to give chase when Scott said, "Let's go, King."

He patted the seat with his hand. He wanted me to jump in the car, so I did. "It's time to go home."

I was confused because I thought we were home, but I jumped in the car anyway. As we drove, I saw and smelled a lot of animals. I put my nose right up to the front of the car where the air came in. I smelled everything. When the road got bigger, the smells of animals were not as strong. I lay down and put my head on Scott's thigh. He set his hand on my head, and I went to sleep.

CHAPTER 21

I'd been sleeping for a while when I felt the car come to a stop. I opened my eyes. We were at another house. Scott drove the car into a big room with another car in it. We all got out of the car and went into the house. I found a bed that smelled like another dog, the one from the first house.

"Come on, King, I'll show you around," Gayle said.

I followed her from room to room in the home. "This is the kitchen," she said as we walked into a room. It smelled like food. This was my favorite room so far. Then Gayle and I walked outside behind the house.

A river!

"This is the swimming pool." It looked pretty inviting.

I did my business on the ground next to the swimming pool. "Oh, King, did you have to go on the pool deck?" she asked.

I did, and I said something. I am a good boy. I do my business outside.

She walked over to the house, got a bag, and picked up my business with it.

When we walked back inside, Gayle fed me. After I finished my food, I went to the doggie bed and sniffed it. I definitely smelled the other dog's scent. I circled around several times, lay down, and went to sleep.

Later that night, I heard Gayle and Scott talking, so I got up to go find them. They were both in their bed, and I jumped up on it to join them. Gayle laughed and raised the covers up. I walked underneath the blankets, circled several times, and lay down right next to her with my head on something soft.

Scott said, "Is he sleeping with his head on the pillow?"

Gayle just laughed.

The next morning, I woke up before everyone else. My head was on Gayle's pillow. Staring at her, I waited for her to wake up. When she opened her eyes, she smiled, put her arm around me, and started singing. I rolled over on my back and stretched all four legs straight up in the air, and she rubbed my belly. "It's rolly polly time, it's rolly polly time, rolly polly time time time, rolly polly time time time," she sang.

"What are you singing, and what is he doing?" Scott asked with a chuckle.

Gayle stopped singing and said, "Don't get jealous just because I have a new man in my life." I rolled over and pushed my body against Gayle so she would know how much I loved her.

"Looks like you've got a spooner there, honey," he said. They both laughed.

"Okay, boy, let's get out of bed and have some breakfast," Gayle said. She tried to push me away, but I leaned into her. I didn't want her to get up. She laughed and crawled out of bed. "Come on, let's go eat and start our day. Scott and I have to go to work," she said.

When I walked back inside after eating breakfast and doing my business outside next to the pool, Gayle and Scott were wearing different clothes.

Gayle said, "Okay, King, we have to go to work now. You wait for me in the backyard. I'll come home during lunch and check on you."

"Is that really a good idea?" Scott asked. "What if he gets out? We don't even have a collar or tags on him yet."

"He'll be fine. The gate is locked, and the fence is six feet tall. Besides, I'll come home and check on him soon."

I didn't know what she'd said, but I followed her outside. I walked around for a while, but when I was ready to come back in, I found the door was closed. I couldn't get back in the house. I barked to let them know I was ready to come inside, but no one opened the door. I jumped up on the door to see if it would open, but it didn't. I jumped again, but nothing happened. *Where are Scott and Gayle? Why did they leave me? I hope they didn't forget about me like Daddy did.*

I walked around for a while looking for something to do. Nobody was there to play with me. I jumped in the water and swam, but with no purpose, I got bored. I patrolled the perimeter of the yard but found no way out. With a sigh, I sat down and waited for someone to come get me. While I was waiting, I smelled an animal. Then I saw it—small and fast with a long, bushy tail—dart across the top of the fence.

I sprang into action and gave chase. It saw me coming and scurried away even faster. Just as I got close, it jumped over the other side of the fence. I wasn't going to let him get away. I leaped up on the fence and hooked my front legs over it, using my back legs to walk up it. Once over the fence, I dropped and landed on all fours. I looked around, and the animal had vanished. Its scent was faint, but I could still track it, and I did. I walked for a long time looking for the animal, and it finally led me to a big tree. The scent went straight up, but I didn't see it. My prey had eluded me—this time.

I was ready to go back to the house, but when I looked around, it was nowhere to be found. I'd traveled far in search of my prey. It would be no problem for me to backtrack. I'd just follow my own scent. As I turned to go back, I noticed a black dog ahead of me. It was by itself, and it hadn't seen me yet.

My curiosity got the better of me, and I ran over to introduce myself. She was friendly enough, and we played and ran around for a while. When she walked away, I followed her. We walked for a long time, crossing many roads. Some of the cars and trucks made noises at us. One almost ran into us. We came to a big field with stacks of large, long, round things on the ground. She walked inside a large round thing and lay down. I joined her. She reminded me of my sister, Bella. I was tired, and we both went to sleep.

When I woke up, the black dog was standing up. It was dark outside, and I knew I needed to get back to Scott and Gayle. I didn't want to be a bad boy. I sniffed the black dog and walked out of the round thing. Looking around, I raised my nose in the air. I would let my scent guide me home.

I moved my head from side to side to determine which direction I should go in. I didn't smell anything that would lead me home. The black dog walked over and sniffed me. When she walked away, I followed her. I didn't know where else to go. She seemed to know her way around. I was thirsty and hungry. She walked over to some water on the ground and started drinking it. I did the same. It wasn't as good as the water Scott and Gayle gave me, but I needed it.

She walked further ahead and up to something big. It had a lot of bags in it, and some of them had fallen out because it was so full. The black dog tore into some of the bags on the ground and started eating. I followed her and started eating as well. The food tasted bad and smelled even worse.

I wondered if Scott and Gayle missed me. I missed them. After we ate, we met up with two other dogs—a black male and a mixed-color female. They sniffed us both, and we sniffed them. We all got along fine. We drank more water from the ground and walked into another big, round thing. It was almost as if I were with my brothers and sisters again. We lay down together and went to sleep.

CHAPTER 22

The next morning, I heard a lot of strange noises. I walked out of the round thing and saw something big moving around, black smoke billowing from it. It picked up other round things and moved them around. I watched for a little while. The other dogs joined me. Some humans wearing orange things on their heads saw us and starting shouting. My tail spun around in circles because I liked humans. But these humans picked up rocks and threw them at us. A rock hit me in my ribs, and it hurt. I didn't yelp.

I am King—I don't yelp.

I'd never met a bad human before, but we ran away and stayed away from them.

When night fell, we came back and drank water from the ground and ate more bad-smelling food. I wasn't feeling as strong as I usually did. That night was one I'll never forget. An angry, large, gray dog wandered into our territory. He had a big head and a strong, muscular body covered in bite marks. He approached us, and the hair on his back stood up. The other dogs were afraid, but I am King, and I don't scare easily.

He walked up to me and snarled. I waited. He lunged at me and bit my leg, but I turned and grabbed the back of his neck. As I twisted my head back and forth, I heard his neck snap, and he fell limp to the ground.

I am King, and I am the top dog.

The other dogs watched, and the black female walked over to me and licked my wounds. I limped back to a round thing with the other dogs and went to sleep with them. *I am the leader.*

The next morning, I heard the big things moving stuff around again. We all watched. I saw some different humans this time, and they called out to me.

"Here boy," they said, trying to get me to come to them.

The humans wearing the orange things on their heads stood right behind them, so I knew not to go. I didn't want rocks thrown at me again. They continued to call, but I limped off with the other dogs. Every day and every night, we repeated the same pattern. A few other dogs joined us, but they were friendly, so I didn't have to put them in their places. We roamed around during the day, and at night we drank, ate, and slept in the round things.

One day, a truck like Daddy's pulled up, and two humans got out. I'd seen one of them before. He called me several times, but I didn't trust him. He was always with the humans wearing orange things on their heads. The other human I hadn't seen before. I kept my distance.

"Careless, over here's the forty-eight inch pipe you wanted to look at. It's in pretty good shape. If you want to buy it, I'll have it loaded on our trucks with the John Deere," he said, pointing at the big thing picking up the round things.

"Pipe looks good, David. Go ahead and ship it over to our pipe yard. When do you think it'll be delivered?" Careless said.

"I can ship it tomorrow. That okay?" David asked.

"Sure, that'd be great. Thanks," Careless said. I looked at him, and he noticed me. "Hey, are those your dogs over there?" He pointed at me. He looked kind, not like the other humans with the orange things on their heads I'd encountered there.

"No, just a bunch of junkyard dogs. I've tried to feed and catch them, but they'll never come to me. They always run away when I walk toward them. I want to take them to a shelter," David said.

"Well, that golden-colored one looks like some sort of hunting dog," Careless said. "Here, boy! Come here!"

He patted his thigh with his hand. I wanted to go to him. I wanted to have a human again, but the humans with the orange things on their heads walked over, and I was on guard. Careless walked toward me, and for a moment, I stayed. But then David and the other humans followed him, so I limped away with the other dogs. I heard them get back in their truck and drive off.

I wouldn't get another human.

Many days passed, and we continued our routine. I wasn't feeling well, and some of the other dogs that had joined us had lain down and not gotten back up. Even the black female wasn't moving around as much as she used to. One day, I felt so weak I could barely stand up. I tried to walk around, but I just couldn't. My leg hurt, and I couldn't stand anymore. I lay down in the grass. The black female nudged me with her nose a couple of times, but I just didn't have the strength to stand up.

Then something happened. David drove up in a truck and stopped. The black female ran away. David walked over and looked at me. All I could do was look up at him.

"You poor thing. Let me help you," he said.

He placed both his arms underneath me and lifted me up. I was limp in his arms. He put me in his truck and drove off. He placed his hand on my head and said something.

He didn't say my name, but hearing a human's voice and feeling a human's touch again did soothe me. I wanted to say something, but I was too weak. He stroked my head as he drove.

We came to a stop. He lifted me out of the truck and carried me into a building. All I could do was watch. "Good afternoon, sir, welcome to the shelter. How may I help you?" a woman asked.

"Hi, my name's David Gilmore, and I found this poor animal in my pipe yard. He didn't look like he was going to make it through the day. Will you guys fix him up and make sure he's adopted to a good home? I'll be glad to make a donation to sponsor him," David said.

"Yes, sir, we can do that. Just fill out these forms, and I'll call someone to take him to the back and get him on the road to recovery. Do you happen to know his name?" she asked.

"No, I found him in the pipe yard. He didn't have a collar on," David said.

"Okay, how about we name him Dudley? Does that sound good to you?"

"Sure, that sounds as good as any name. Dudley it is," he said.

CHAPTER 23

The human picked up a telephone. "A dog needs immediate medical attention. Please send a vet tech to intake."

Another human showed up almost immediately and said, "Okay, sir, I'll take him now." Even though I wasn't feeling well, I could tell David didn't want to let me go. He hesitated.

The other human said, "Mr. Gilmore, I can assure you Dudley is in capable hands. The sooner we get him into care, the better off he'll be. He's in pretty bad shape, and his leg wound is definitely infected."

David said, "Okay, Dudley, you're going to be alright, boy. Don't worry."

When a human saves a dog, an instant, unbreakable bond forms. It doesn't matter if they just met. It's as if they've known one another their entire lives. I knew David felt this. He gently handed me to the human.

As the human carried me away, I looked back at David. He's a good human. But I was for sale. He reached into his pocket and gave the human some papers.

He looked at me and said, "Goodbye, Dudley."

My name is King.

I didn't know why he called me Dudley.

I was brought back to a room that smelled bad. It reminded me of that room Jen had brought me to after Daddy left me at the other shelter. It smelled like death. The human carrying me placed me on a table under bright lights. An older human approached and said, "Well, what do we have here?"

"Somebody brought this stray in, Doctor Washington. Pretty bad shape. He's probably starving and looks like he's dehydrated. He also has what appears to be an infected bite wound on his leg."

"That looks pretty bad. I don't know if we'll be able to save the leg. Let's take a blood sample and clean that wound up. It's definitely going to take some stitches. Start an I.V. and give this poor boy a sedative," Doctor Washington said. I felt a small pain in my front leg and got sleepy.

I was running with Juna at Heidi's house. My leg was completely healed.

I was so happy to see her. I stopped running and nuzzled up against her. I'd never forget her smell. We ran like crazy, right up to Heidi's house, and she opened the door. She gave us both big hugs and rubbed our heads and ears. I said something, and she smiled. Juna licked my face. Heidi gave us some treats, and Juna and I went to our beds to take a nap. I pressed my body up against her as hard as I could. I'm even bigger than she is now. I was so happy to be with them.

When I opened my eyes, I was lying on a soft blanket in a small, metal cage. I'd only dreamed of being home. I could barely move, and there was no opening for me to climb out of. I tried to move, but my leg was in so much pain, I couldn't. There was also something attached to my other front leg. It smelled bad, but I was too tired and in too much pain to do anything about it.

A human walked by. "Well, hi, Dudley. How are you doing, big boy? You hungry? I've got some delicious food for you. I have to put your medicine in it first. Doctor Washington saved your leg. She said you'll be as good as new in no time," she said.

She's a good human. She reminded me of Jen. I said something, and she smiled and opened the cage. "I knew you were going to be a smart one. You answered me back," she said while rubbing my ears.

I liked this human. She let me walk out of my cage and took the thing off my leg. I was still in pain, so I limped over to her. "Don't worry, Dudley, that leg will heal up in no time. You'll be walking and running on it soon enough," she said, smiling. She called me Dudley just like everyone else did.

My name is King.

She put a bowl of food down. I was hungry, and I ate most of it very quickly. It had a strange taste, but I didn't care. It was better than the bad food I'd eaten with the other dogs. When I got to the last few bites, I picked them up and dumped them on the floor. I nosed them around and played with them before finishing. There was something that smelled bad in it, so I left that on the floor. I just ate the food.

"You are a smart one, aren't you? You need to take your medicine," the human said. She picked up the funny-smelling thing and walked away. When she came back, she gave me a treat. I could smell the thing in the treat, but I ate it anyway because it tasted good, and the human wanted me to.

"Come on, Dudley, let's go outside so you can relieve yourself," she said as she patted her leg for me to come. I limped over to her and followed her.

I guess I'm Dudley.

We walked out of the building. Even though it was a little cold, it felt good to be outside. I did my business, and the human said, "Good boy."

I like being a good boy.

When I finished, we walked together back into the building. She gave me a bowl of water. I was so thirsty, I drank the whole thing. She laughed so loud, I stopped what I was doing and looked at her. Doctor Washington walked in and also laughed.

I said something.

Doctor Washington said, "I don't believe I've ever seen a dog bob its head up and down like that while drinking."

The other human walked over to me with a white paper and said, "Here, let me wipe your mouth up. You're dripping water all over the place."

Doctor Washington came up to me as well and said, "Let's give him the once-over, Katelynn."

She lifted me onto a table. She felt all over my body with her hands, but I didn't mind. She said, "The leg appears to be healing up well. He does have heartworms, but he's low positive. I think he's strong enough to be treated. Let's get him started on the heartworm injection and up for adoption."

When she finished, Katelynn put me back in the cage. I was still pretty weak, so I went to sleep on my blanket.

I'm now Dudley. That's a good name. I like it. Dudley!

CHAPTER 24

One day, they brought me back to see Doctor Washington. She felt my body with her hands and said, "Go ahead and hold him down while I give him the heartworm injection."

I didn't know what that meant, but a human held me tightly, and I felt a sharp pain in my backside. It hurt so bad that I yelped. I tried to pull away, but I couldn't. It stung and smelled terrible. I'd never felt pain like this before. I didn't know why they were hurting me. I thought they were good humans.

One of them said, "It's okay, boy. It'll be over soon. You're a good boy." Even though my leg still ached, my back hurt more. When they finished hurting me, they put me back in a cage.

For the next few days, we returned to my usual routine. My leg was feeling much better, and my backside didn't hurt as bad. Since I was now eating good food and drinking plenty of water, my strength was coming back. Now, when I went outside to do my business, I walked around and checked everything out.

This is a good place. Except for when they hurt me, these humans are nice. I didn't like living in a cage, but at least they let me out and gave me food and water.

I did my business and saw a fence that looked like it needed to be climbed. I liked it here, but I didn't want to live in a cage. And they *did* hurt me. I leaped up, hooked my front legs over the top of the fence, and walked up it with my back legs. I was almost to the top when a human yelled, "Dudley! You get back down here right now!"

She ran over to me, and I let go of the fence. She bent down and hugged me, saying, "Good boy! You can't escape like that, Dudley. You'll get hurt again out there. Just wait, when we get you all fixed up and heartworm free, we'll put you up for adoption. A handsome guy like you? I bet you'll get adopted in no time."

When we went back inside, Doctor Washington was waiting with something in her hand. I knew what it was. I smelled it. Last time, it had made my backside hurt. I backed away.

"Katelynn, please hold him down while I give him his last heartworm injection." She picked me up and put me on the table. I tried to get away, but she held me tightly.

"You're such a smart boy, Dudley. I know it will hurt, but without it you'll have heartworms and probably die. Be a good boy. This is the last shot," she said.

I knew what was about to happen. A dog remembers. But a dog also has to do what a human tells him. I said something and licked her face. She held me while Doctor Washington made my backside hurt even worse than it had before.

I yelped again. I couldn't help it. When they finished, they put me back in my cage. It hurt so bad I couldn't move. I don't know why the humans did this to me.

CHAPTER 25

Days went by, and my backside and leg hurt less. I grew stronger and stronger. One day, a human came to get me and she said, "Today's your lucky day, Dudley. Doctor Washington said you're well. We're moving you to the adoption ward."

A man walked by and asked, "Do you need any help with him, Katelynn?"

"No, I got this big ol' boy." She put a leash around my neck and said, "Come on, let's go." I walked by her side.

Another human, named Elaina, who had also been caring for me, bent down and hugged me. "I knew you would make it, Dudley! Have a great life. I'll miss you!" She kissed me on my head.

We walked out of the room and continued on through the building. That's when I heard it and smelled it. There were many dogs nearby. I couldn't see them, but I knew they were close. We strolled through some doors, and then I saw them. There were a lot of dogs, all in kennels like the one I had just come from.

I was led past them. Some of the dogs sat quietly. They seemed either sad or like they weren't feeling well. Others jumped on the gate of their cage as I passed by.

I didn't react. I stayed close to Katelynn. I'd seen this before. I knew I'd be put in a cage next to other dogs. She opened a gate, and I walked in. There was a bed and a bowl of water on the ground. She took the leash off me, walked out, and closed the gate behind her. I sat on the bed and watched her. "Don't worry, boy. I'm sure you'll get adopted," she said.

She took a paper from her pocket and did something to it. Before she walked off, she placed the paper on the outside of the cage.

I sat there for a while. I drank some water. There was nothing to do. Occasionally humans would walk by. Most of them looked at me and kept walking. One of them said, "Oh, he's too big."

Another said, "He looks mean."

One even said, "He's a pit bull. I don't want a pit bull."

I said something every time, but they always kept walking. No one ever stopped to see me except for the humans who fed me and walked me a couple times a day. I never did my business inside the cage. Some of the other dogs did, but they probably didn't know any better.

The boredom was killing me. One day, Katelynn and another human stopped by my cage and pulled the paper off the gate. They looked at it, and Katelynn said, "Poor Dudley, he's LOS, and nobody has taken an interest in him. I can't believe he's 'length of stay.' I sure hope he gets out of here. He's such a great dog. Aren't you boy?"

I knew she was talking to me, so I said something. That made them happy. They walked away. I went to my bed and sat down. The sun shone in from a window and warmed me. It felt good.

CHAPTER 26

I heard two humans walking and talking. I got off the bed and walked to the gate to see them. They were further down, but I could hear them coming toward me. One of them sounded familiar. When they drew closer, I could see them. One stopped walking. He looked at the other and said, "Check out that Blue Heeler and Red Heeler. Aren't they beautiful? I wonder if they're brother and sister? Should we have a look at them?"

The other human said, "No, those are working dogs. And from what I've seen, you don't really care for work. Besides, those kinds of dogs really need a lot of exercise, and I don't think you like that much, either."

The other human laughed and said, "You're right about that. But it sure would be cool to have a Red Heeler or a Blue Heeler."

"We'll find you a dog. Let's get out of here and come back another day." They both turned and walked away. I remembered one of the humans from the pipe yard. He'd been with the human who brought me here.

I pressed my body up against the gate so I could see him better. The sun shone into my cage from the window, and the warmth felt good on my body. I waited and stared at him. One of them kept walking ahead. The one I was staring at stopped dead in his tracks.

Does he see me? Does he remember me?

I remembered him. Without saying a word, he looked back over his shoulder. Our eyes met. I didn't blink. Neither did he.

He turned and walked back to my cage. My tail spun in circles. I couldn't help it. I was so glad to see someone I knew. He reached his fingers through the gate and rubbed my back. He looked at the paper on the gate. I knew then that I wanted this human, and I knew he wanted me. The other human walked up to us. My human briefly looked at him and nodded. Then he looked back at me, and I nodded my head just like he did. His gaze was locked upon me, the likes of which I hadn't seen since I'd been with my mother, Juna.

He took the paper off the gate and clutched it in his hand. The other human said, "I'm sure he's a fine animal, and if you really want to adopt him, that's great, Careless, but the shelter receives tons of dogs every day. This isn't something you should rush into. Maybe we should think about it and come back tomorrow."

My human's name is Careless. I like that name. "Dudley's not an animal," my human said. "He's my friend, and I'm not leaving here without him."

I knew he was talking about me, and I said something. They both looked surprised. My human stared at his friend, who finally nodded. My human smiled, looked at me, and said, "You're mine now, Dudley. I'm springing you from here, and we'll be best friends."

That's all I needed to hear. I said something as my tail spun around even faster. Finally, I had my human.

Just as I finished saying something, two humans passed by and stopped. They looked at me and said something to each other. I liked most humans, but now I belonged to my human. I said something to let them know I wasn't for sale. My human must have understood because he said to them, "He's taken. Move along. Nothing to see here!"

I love my human. When I settled down, he and I stared at one another again. He reached for the gate and was about to open it and let me out. I was ready to go with him.

Another human walked up behind him and said, "Hold on, sir, what do you think you're doing?"

My human looked at her.

"Sir, if you want to take him outside or to one of our get-to-know-you rooms . . ." She stopped talking and held out her hand. My human remained still. But then he gave her the paper he'd pulled off the gate.

"The name's Careless."

"If you want to take Dudley out of his dog run, I'll take him out for you and let you two get to know one another. If you want to adopt him, you'll need to fill out an adoption form and pay the sixty-five dollar adoption fee."

My human pulled out something from his pocket and took some papers from it. He tried to give them to her. She shook her head and said, "I'll take Dudley's kennel card to the adoption desk where you'll fill out an adoption form, get interviewed, and pay the adoption fee. I'll make sure Dudley doesn't get adopted to anyone else while we're going through the process. In fact, I'll handle this adoption personally. Is that okay, Careless?"

"That's fine." He looked at me and said, "I have to leave for a few minutes, Dudley, but don't worry—I'll be right back."

I said something.

My human walked away with the other two humans. I didn't want him to leave. He wasn't like other humans, and I wanted him to be my human. After they went through a door, the only thing I heard were the other dogs. I slowly walked to my bed and curled up in the sunshine, waiting for someone to come back. I lay there thinking about my human.

A few minutes later, he came back to me. I stood up, walked over to the gate, and waited. I was ready to go with him. My tail spun around in circles. I couldn't help it. I was happy. I pressed my body up against the gate, and my human rubbed me with his fingers.

Another human quietly walked up behind him. I didn't recognize him, so I said something. I didn't want anything to happen to my human. *I will protect him.*

My human was confused and looked behind him. "Oh, that's just Birk. Don't worry about him. He's okay. Dudley, the good news is, you'll be coming home with me. The bad news is that they want to do a procedure on you called a *lopitoffame.* You're probably not going to like it much, but it's the only way they'll let you out of here. I'm sorry, boy. I'll come back tomorrow and pick you up."

I didn't understand what he said, but I didn't like the sound of it. "Goodbye, boy. I'll see you tomorrow." As they walked away, I sat down and sighed. I wanted my human to turn around and come back to me, but he didn't.

CHAPTER 27

That same day another human came to my cage. He put a leash around my neck. I walked with him, past the other dogs and through several rooms. He said, "Don't worry Dudley, everything will be just fine. You won't feel a thing."

We went into the room they'd taken me to when I first came here. It smelled bad, and I didn't like it. He lifted me up on a table and several other strangely dressed humans surrounded me. They made me lay down on my side. I didn't like it, but I am a dog and must do what humans tell me to do. One of them held my front leg, and I felt a little pain. Suddenly, I felt very tired, and I closed my eyes.

When I woke up, I found myself back in a small cage like when I'd first arrived here. I wasn't feeling great, and I had some pain in my backside. It wasn't as painful as what Doctor Washington had done to me before, but it hurt.

There was something around my neck, so I couldn't look back to see where the pain was coming from. I went back to sleep. When I awoke the next time, my cage door was open and several people were standing around me. I wagged my tail a little, and they picked me up and put me up on the table. I could feel them doing something with my backside, but I couldn't see because of the thing around my neck.

One of them said something and lifted me off the table. I wondered where my human was. I really wanted him to come back. I hoped he didn't leave me like Daddy did. I walked around and sniffed everyone. A human put a leash around my neck and took me to a larger cage. He petted me on the head, and I walked in. When he closed the door, he said, "Don't worry, boy, you'll be going home tomorrow."

I went to the bed and lay down.

The next morning, a human came and took me outside to do my business. "Today's your big day, Dudley."

I heard my name, so I said something. He smiled and patted me on the head. We went back inside, and I walked into my cage.

A while later, a human came up to my cage and said, "Are you ready to go home, boy? Let me take the e-collar off of you."

I jumped up on the gate and said something. I felt much better.

She laughed and opened the gate, taking the thing off my neck. "Your new owner is here to pick you up, Dudley. He said something about a jail break." She smiled. I knew my human was in the building. I could smell him. I was happy and started jumping around. "You wait here, Dudley, and I'll have someone bring you out." She closed the gate and walked away. I waited.

A different human strolled up to my cage. He looked at a piece of paper on the gate and said, "Okay, Dudley, it's time for you to go. You be good, and everything will be alright. You hear me, Dudley?"

I didn't like this human much. Dogs can tell when a human is comfortable around them. It's one of the things that protects us from bad humans. He slightly opened the gate and slipped a leash around my neck. I knew he was afraid of me. I could tell.

I was so anxious to see my human that I pushed the gate open with my body and ran forward to find him. I couldn't see him, but I followed my nose. "Slow down there, buddy," the human holding the leash said.

But I didn't slow down. Normally, I listen to humans, but my excitement took over, and my legs churned ahead. I pulled him to the door.

When he opened the door, the scent of my human was strong. I knew he was close by. I rushed to a set of doors, but they were closed. Still pulling the human behind me, I jumped up against the two doors with all my might, and they flew open to reveal my human. I saw him standing there with Birk and the other human who'd checked on me earlier. He was happy. I knew he wouldn't leave me like Daddy had.

I pulled even harder, and the human holding the leash struggled to keep up. As I charged ahead, the human behind me lost his footing and fell to the floor, but he continued holding the leash. I knew it was wrong, but I dragged him along. I ran full speed all the way to my human. I stopped right in front of him and sat down. The human behind me stopped sliding as well. He stood up and brushed his clothes off with his hands.

"Good boy, Dudley S. Robinson," my human said.

The other human asked, "Mr. Careless, what does the *S* stand for?"

My human looked at him. "Steamroller!"

Everyone laughed. I said something as I waited for a command. And he gave me one. "Let's go home, boy."

He walked toward the door I first came in with David. I followed by his side. People walked toward me to pet me as we were leaving, but all I could think about was going home with my human, so I said something. I didn't want to stay in this place any longer. Most of the humans here were nice, but I was ready to go home with my human. I left the building.

CHAPTER 28

It was great to be outside, and being with my human made it even better. I already knew he loved me. A dog can feel these things.

My human was watching me, and I couldn't take my eyes off of him as I walked by his side. We made our way to a truck. Birk pointed something at the truck, and it made a strange sound. I turned my head sideways and wondered what it was. My human smiled and said, "It's okay, boy, we're going home."

He opened a door for me, and I jumped in. I was more than ready to go home. He and Birk climbed in the front seat, and Birk started the truck. I didn't want to be separated from my human, so I moved forward and stood next to him with my front paws. The rest of my body was in the back seat. When I placed my head on his shoulder, he smiled and removed my leash.

Birk wasn't happy.

"Why don't you open the sunroof? It's a nice day," my human said.

A hole in the roof opened. I'd never seen this before. I stuck my head through it. I could smell everything around me, and the wind felt great against my face. When the truck started going fast, my human said, "His jowls are catching the wind like sails. This sure reminds me of *The Beverly Hillbillies*. You can be Jethro Bodine, and I'll be Jed Clampett."

He smiled, and I said something. Birk was not happy. All the humans we passed—and we passed all of them—smiled and waved at us. My human sure knows a lot of other humans. And they were all nice.

After a while, the truck came to a stop in front of a big building. This must be our home. I had never seen a home this large. Birk got out of the truck and opened the back door. I jumped right out, and he said, "Damn dog, watch it! You almost knocked me over."

I really needed to do my business. I walked around the back of the truck and waited for my human to exit. After he jumped out, Birk got back in his truck and started it. He turned on some loud music and drove off. I did my business.

My human and I walked up, and I watched as he took something from his pocket and pushed it into the door. It opened with a loud, strange, creaking sound. I looked at it and turned my head sideways.

"It's okay, boy, this is where we're going to live."

We walked in, and it smelled different. It wasn't bad, just different—and old. Several people had been here. I didn't recognize their smells, and I didn't see anyone. I walked right by his side. We plodded up to some things I'd never seen before. My human looked at me and said, "Dudley, I wonder if you've ever walked up stairs. Let's give it a try."

I followed him. It was not a problem for a dog of my stature.

I am Dudley, and I go where my human goes.

I watched him as we walked. Whenever he stopped, I stopped and sat by his side. I wanted him to know I am loyal and that he is my human. We left the stairs behind and passed through a long, narrow place. He took something from his pocket again and pressed it against a door.

He opened the door, and we walked in together.

My human said, "Go ahead boy, check it out. This is where we'll be spending a lot of time."

Since he'd commanded me, I walked ahead and sniffed everything. It smelled like home to me. Not like with Heidi and Juna or Daddy, but like home. I knew this was where I needed to be. Everything smelled just like my human. I walked up to my new bed and jumped up on it. I curled up and closed my eyes. My human smiled and said, "I see you've found the sofa."

I was tired, but I opened one eye and kept it trained on him. He picked up the telephone, pushed it with his fingers, and placed it next to his face.

"Yes, ma'am, I'd like to make an appointment for my new friend, please." He pointed at me while talking to the telephone. I knew he was talking about me, so I said something. He gave me a strange look. He knew I knew he was talking about me.

"This will be our first visit," he said. "I just picked him up from the shelter, and he needs his first checkup. Dudley would like to see Dr. L.D. Eckermann, who came highly recommended by the other inmates at the shelter. He's that busy? Wow! The thing is, Dudley is dead set on seeing him. May Dudley speak to him to request an earlier appointment?"

I heard my name, so of course, I said something. Then my human said, "Honey, the name's Careless, and yes, that is my correct number. Dudley and I will be anxiously awaiting your call." He put the telephone down and strolled to the sofa where I'd been watching and listening from.

He sat down on the sofa next to me. I stood up and turned around so my face was level with his. I could tell by the look on his face that he wasn't sure what I was doing. But I knew what I was doing. I lay down and pressed my body up against him, pinning my head against his chest. I could hear his heartbeat, and that comforted me. My whole body relaxed and shuddered. I sighed.

He put his hand on my head and started rubbing my ears. I was definitely home. I loved this. He grinned and said, "I've never been spooned by a dog before. It's really not that bad."

He put his arm around me, and I dozed off. This time, I dreamed about my human.

CHAPTER 29

When I awoke, my human was sleeping. I decided if I'm up, everybody's up. I licked his face nonstop to show him how much I loved him. He woke up right away.

"Dudley, enough!" He tried pushing me away, but I was having none of that. I stood over him and kept licking him. I just couldn't make myself stop. The more he tried to push me away, the more I pushed my body up against him.

"Thank goodness Birk isn't here to witness this." He finally wiggled out from under me, but I let him go because he said, "No, Dudley! Enough! I guess I picked out a dog with a Kung Fu grip. Don't worry, I'm not going to kiss and tell." I said something, and he pointed at me and said, "And you better not tell anyone either."

My human stood up and walked across the room. I leaped off the sofa and trotted toward him. There was something in my way, so I lowered my body and crawled underneath it. I thought I was in the clear, but obviously I misjudged it. When I stood straight up to trot over to him, my back brushed up against the thing. It raised up off the ground, but I didn't care. I just wanted to be by him. I continued moving forward.

"Dudley, stop!"

I stopped.

"Stay, Dudley! Let me lift that coffee table up so you can get out from underneath it." He lifted the coffee table up, and I bolted away from it.

My human is strong like I am.

I sat by his side, waiting for his next command. He smiled and said, "You know, Dudley, this would make a great story for a mystery novel, and I already have a title for it—*The Case of the Walking Coffee Table.*"

I said something as we looked at one another.

A strange noise broke my concentration. It was coming from the telephone. I turned my head sideways and watched it. I looked back at my human. Then I looked back at the telephone and said something at it.

It made the noise again, so I lunged, grabbing it in my mouth. It did not taste good. I shook it from side to side and then up and down. I heard a voice coming from it, and my human walked toward me.

"Dudley, give me the phone you big goofus."

I stopped shaking the telephone in my mouth and looked at him. He was holding his hand out. He wanted the telephone. I flipped my head toward him while opening my mouth. The telephone came flying out, and he caught it in his hand. He looked at me with a curious expression on his face, so I said something, sat, and waited for his next command.

He smiled and said, "Dudley, you're really going to have to work on your phone skills. And when we finish that, I'll teach you how to beer me from the refrigerator. You're one smart dog!"

He wiped the telephone off on his shirt and lifted it to his face. "Sure, honey. That will be just fine with me, but let me check with the big guy real quick like."

He put the telephone down. "Hey, does two o'clock sound okay to you for your first checkup?" he asked.

Since he was talking to me, I said something.

He put the telephone next to his face again. "He says yes. Oh, no problem. I'll find you. I've got GDS. Oh, you don't know about GDS? That's Global Dudley Systems. Please tell the doctor we'll see him at two." He put the phone down.

I smelled a human on the other side of the door. I trotted over and stared at it. The hair on my back went up. "Is everything okay, boy?" my human asked. "Do you need to go outside? I was just about to take you outside. How did you know that?"

I didn't move.

A knock sounded at the door. My human looked at me and placed his hand on my head. "You're a good boy."

I am a good boy. I looked at him for a moment and then back at the door. I would protect our home. He opened the door.

A female human stood there. My human was trying to talk to her, but he was having a problem giving her commands. She had golden-colored hair like my own. She smiled at my human and asked, "What's the matter, Careless, cat got your tongue?"

I remained still, but my human was acting strangely around her. She walked in, and he closed the door. She looked at me, and a huge smile broke out across her face. "Is that a dog, or did you get a statue? Why is there a huge animal in your loft?" She was staring at me, and I stared back, not moving a muscle.

"Honey, that's not a dog. That's Melvin, the rat. He lives in the building and travels from loft to loft, stealing cheese from the residents. Are you telling me you've never seen him before?"

She walked over to me, put her arms around me, and gave me a big hug. I like this human—a lot. She ambled past me and toward Careless. Some feelings came over me I had never experienced before.

I said something, not like I normally do. When she turned her back, I sprang into action and bolted toward her. I don't know what made me do this, but I couldn't stop myself. I lowered my head and slid to a stop underneath her dress. Her leg was just staring me in the face. I grabbed it with my front legs and humped it. I had no choice in the matter. Something had taken control over my body. Strange noises came from me, too. I'd never made noises like that before. My eyes rolled back in my head.

"Careless," she snapped, "better get your critter off of me, or you can be pretty sure you'll never get as far as he has."

"E.D., that's not what I call my critter. I call him Big Pete."

My human bent down and lifted E.D.'s dress just enough to see me. I knew I was being a bad boy. I didn't want to be a bad boy, but I couldn't help myself. Something about this human and her hair made me a bad boy.

"Dudley, you look like you have bitter beer face. Stop that right now! *Now*, Dudley!"

I am a dog, and when my human commands me, I must listen. This time it was harder than usual, but I let go of E.D.'s leg and stopped making noises. I slinked out from under her dress and sat by my human's side.

I don't like being a bad boy.

Neither of the humans spoke for a while. I didn't say something because it was so quiet. E.D. finally said, "Careless, it would be quite all right if you let go of my dress now."

He dropped the dress, and it fell back to its normal position. I needed to go do my business, so I walked over to the door and sat down. I wanted my human to know I needed to go outside. E.D. noticed I was waiting by the door. My human was too busy staring at her to notice.

"Careless, your animal needs to go outside," she said. She smiled, patted me on the head, and said, "I know it's not your fault. Living with him pretty much explains what just happened."

I liked her. She understood me.

My human said, "And how is that my fault?"

"It just is," she said.

I said something in agreement. They both laughed.

E.D. said, "I came over because I need a couple of heavy boxes moved around in my apartment. And seeing that your name is Careless, I would like you to take 'care' of that in 'less' time than you normally take to do things for me. You think you can handle that?"

My human said, "No problem, honey. I'll just take Dudley out back and let him use the facilities. Then I'll get right on it."

CHAPTER 30

We left our home and went downstairs. E.D. came with us. We walked through a door to a large, fenced, grassy area. I peered up at my human, and he said, "Go ahead, boy. Go do your business."

He pointed out into the yard, so I ran off to explore and do my business. I smelled that other dogs had been here. I looked around, but there were no other dogs. I also smelled other animals. I tracked them with my nose, but I didn't see them.

When I looked back at my human, he was busy talking to E.D. I walked the perimeter of the yard. Then I caught the scent of an animal just ahead of me and tracked it with my nose in the air. I moved my head from side to side as I honed in on my prey. After a moment, I came upon a bush. Even though I couldn't see my prey, my nose told me it was there. It was a rabbit.

I charged the bush, and the rabbit shot out. It was quick, but I am Dudley, and I am faster than my prey. I chased the rabbit across the entire yard. He was heading for the fence. I increased my speed and was about to grab his neck when he slipped through an opening in the fence. I slid to a stop. I was determined to not let him get away. My prey drive forced me forward. I paced the fence back and forth until I found a space between it and the building. It was small, but I managed to squeeze my body through it.

Once through, I began tracking my prey. I walked for a while, through streets and past several cars. Some of them were moving and made noises at me. I continued on, but the scent was getting weaker. The trail had gone cold, and this time, my prey had eluded me. *Next time, he won't be as lucky.*

Then I remembered that this was exactly how I'd gotten lost from Scott and Gayle's house and ended up in the pipe yard. I loved my human more than anything, and I didn't want to lose him. I knew I must make it back to him. He needed me.

Tracking my way back, I walked down several streets and followed my own scent. I also picked up the scent of the rabbit so I knew I was going in the right direction. I saw some people standing around, and they called to me, but none of them were my human. I didn't trust them, so I stayed as far away from them as I could. I came across several things with bad-smelling food in them. It reminded me of the time I lived in the pipe yard. I wasn't hungry, so I sniffed them and kept walking. The food my human gave me tasted much better.

I couldn't see the fence, but I knew I was getting closer. I could smell it. My nose was leading me back. Finally, I saw it. I only needed to cross the street, and I'd be home. Cars thundered down the road, but I needed to go home. I darted into the street. A car was coming right at me and skidded to a stop. It made a loud noise, and I ran in front of it to the other side of the street. A human inside the car yelled, "Get out of the street, you stupid dog! Next time I'll run you over!"

I didn't like him.

I ran to the fence, found the opening, and pushed my body through it. It was small, and I could barely fit, but I managed to get back into the yard. I ran to where my human and E.D. had been standing and talking, but I didn't see them. I picked up his scent, and it led me to the door we had come through earlier. I jumped up on it, but it didn't open. I sat and waited for him to come find me, but he didn't. I hoped he hadn't forgotten about me like Daddy had. Soon I got bored and decided to go exploring, so I ran around the yard looking for things to do. I ran from tree to tree and marked each one.

As I was running around having fun, the scent of my human became strong. I looked over at the door, and it opened. He walked out, Birk following behind him. My human looked at me, eyes wide.

"Do you need glasses," Birk asked, "or are you just a dumbass?"

My human responded, "Possibly both! I swear Birk, he wasn't here before. E.D. and I walked the entire yard, and Dudley was nowhere to be found."

I ran to him as fast as I could and jumped up on him. I rested my front legs on his shoulders and licked his face. I couldn't stop licking him. "I missed you too, boy. Don't you ever leave me again! I was so scared something happened to you."

"Hey, why don't you two get a room?" Birk snorted.

"Okay, Dudley, that's enough licking," my human said. Although I didn't want to, I let go of him and sat at his side. He wiped his face with his shirt.

"Careless, I have some things to do. Are you okay now?" Birk asked.

"It's all good in the hood, Birk. Thanks for coming by. I really appreciate it," my human said.

We all walked back inside, and Birk continued on and went through the front door. My human and I headed back up the stairs, and I heard Birk's truck start up. It made a new sound. I turned my head sideways because I was curious. "Oh, that's just Birk honking his horn, boy. He does that all the time. Don't worry about it."

We returned to our home, and I went to the sofa and lay down. After a bit, the telephone began making that noise again. I watched, curious. My human looked at me, pointed his finger, and said, "Don't even think about it."

He picked up the telephone. "Crisis Hotline, please state your problem. And for your protection, this conversation may be recorded." He was smiling. My human always seemed to amuse himself.

E.D.'s voice came from the telephone. "Carefree, did you ever find that serial molester you call a dog?"

My human said, "That's Careless, and I believe the term is serial thriller. I know you were really worried about him. He actually just came back from his sabbatical and is resting up to get ready for another go round. What time shall I tell him you'll be arriving?"

"Before I come back down there, you'd better learn how to treat a lady. Especially one of my stature. Do we understand one another?"

He smiled and said, "You can't teach an old dog new tricks."

His mood changed somewhat when she said, "I was referring to your new roommate. I feel certain you're beyond help at this point."

"I'll take this matter up with my superiors. Bye, E.D." He put the telephone down on his desk.

He looked at me. I'd been watching his every move. "There's still goober on the phone from the last time you answered it. I don't think it's a good idea for you to get the phone until you've worked on your phone skills. Okay, boy? I'm so glad you're back," he said.

I said something, and he smiled.

I stood up, circled around several times to get comfortable, and sat down in a position to best see him. When I did, a strange thing in front of the sofa lit up and started making noises. I turned to see what it was and saw animals moving around making all kinds of noises. I was confused. I didn't smell anything, and usually, I could smell animals before I saw them.

"So, you like the Animal Planet channel, boy? Maybe one day you'll teach me how to use the remote control you just sat on. We need to leave, so please turn the TV off, Dudley."

I heard my name, so I said something. I stood up, and as soon as I did, the animals disappeared, and the sounds stopped. I still couldn't smell them. "I don't know how you did that. Do you understand what I'm saying, Dudley?" my human asked.

I heard my name, so of course, I responded.

He laughed and said, "I thought so."

My human walked out of our home, and I followed him. I heard someone behind us say, "Yeah, heh, heh, heh."

I didn't like the way that sounded, so I said something to let my human know I would protect him. The hair on my back stood straight up.

My human said, "It's okay, boy. That's just my friend, Sarge."

He ran his hand down my back several times and smoothed my hair down. It felt good, and it let me know that everything was alright. We walked outside together to his truck. He opened the door, and I jumped in. I sat next to him, and he started driving. He opened the windows, and I stuck my head out. *The wind feels good in my face.* My human looked at me and smiled.

CHAPTER 31

"You like this music, don't you, Dudley?"

I heard my name, so I said something. I did like the music. It made my tail spin around in circles. The truck came to a stop in front of a building, and my human said, "Okay, Dudley, we're here. I hope you like the doctor. Don't be alarmed when he has to checkle your schmeckle."

He got out of the truck, and I jumped out right behind him. Lots of dogs had been here. One of them still was.

"Come on, Sam," a human in front of us said. She picked up a tiny dog and looked right at me. My human smiled and waved at her, but she just walked into the building. I followed closely because I wanted to sniff Sam.

A human said, "Hello, welcome to Westbury Animal Hospital. How may I help you?"

My human looked at her and said, "Dudley, party of one."

She told him, "Oh yes, we've been expecting Dudley. Please fill out these forms, and we'll get a weight on him." She gave him some papers. I heard my name, so, of course, I said something.

My human said, "Ma'am, my name's Careless, and I'll be glad to do that, but where's the scale?"

She pointed. "It's just around the corner."

We walked to the scale, and I smelled the dog I'd seen earlier. She was standing next to her human. I walked up to her, and we started sniffing one another. Her human was not happy with this. My human must have sensed it because he smiled and pointed toward me and the other dog.

"The doctor will see you now," another human said to her. The other dog and her human walked away. I stayed with my human. He took the papers and sat on a sofa. I joined him, circled a couple of times, and sat, pushing myself against him.

He was doing something with the papers and said, "Quit reading over my shoulder. You know I don't like that." I responded by licking his face. He laughed. "Let's see . . . patient's name. Huh? No place for the middle name. What is your middle name?"

I said something. I picked up my front leg and put it on his shoulder. Then I looked up into his eyes. *I love my human.*

"Excuse me, Mr. Robinson, do you two need a few more minutes to fill the forms out?" a human said behind us. I'd heard him walk up, but I was busy with my human.

"No, we're ready."

"Mr. Robinson, why don't you bring Dudley to exam room three, and we'll have a look at him?"

"Okay, Doc, but the name's Careless," my human said.

The other human said, "You can call me L.D."

"You got it, L.D." He got up from the sofa and began walking. As always, I followed.

"Careless, why don't you weigh Dudley before the exam? The scale is right there," L.D. said, pointing at the ground.

My human said, "Come, Dudley." I walked over to him, and he said, "Sit." I did.

L.D. said, "His weight's okay at eighty-eight pounds. He should probably be closer to ninety-five, but once he starts eating properly, that should take care of itself."

They both walked away, and I followed them. When we walked into another room, L.D. closed the door behind us. I could smell that other dogs had been here, but I also smelled things I didn't like. I thought back to the room I'd been in with Jen and how it smelled bad like this one. I didn't like this room, but I knew my human would never hurt me.

My human said, "So I see you're an Aggie, L.D." He pointed to something on the wall.

"Class of '73. Right after I graduated, I moved to Houston and started working here. And in 1976, I became a partner."

My human said, "Okay, you're hired." They both laughed.

"Dudley will need to go up on the table for me to examine him. I'll call a vet tech in to help us," L.D. said. I didn't know what he'd said, but from the look on my human's face, I was sure it wasn't good.

I smelled and heard someone behind the door, and I didn't like it. Another human walked in, and I didn't trust him. The hair on my back stood up. My jowls began to curl up, and water dripped from them. I gave him a soft warning growl. A dog can tell when he should trust a human—or not. And I didn't like this one. My human walked toward me. Then I felt better.

L.D. said to the vet tech, "Why don't you wait outside?" The human turned around and walked out of the room. The hair on my back flattened down.

"Careless, could you bring Dudley back here for his examination?" L.D. opened a door and strode into a bigger room. I liked the smells in this room even less. "Do you think you can lift Dudley onto the examination table?"

My human responded, "Yes," and put both of his arms underneath me and picked me up. I didn't mind. I knew he'd never hurt me. L.D. touched me all over, stretched my legs out, and looked in my ears, mouth, and eyes.

My human chuckled. "L.D., you are a brave man."

He laughed. "I'm not afraid of this ol' boy. He'd never bite anyone."

I said something.

L.D. put something in his ears and touched my chest with it. "I think Dudley is around two years old. He's a bit malnourished, but I'm sure you can fix that. He also has a heart murmur. It's probably nothing."

The color in my human's face changed. I didn't know humans could change their color.

"He's been a little overactive, and his stitches from his neuter are coming loose. We'll need to re-stitch him. I'll use steel stitches this time so they won't come out. You'll have to come back in ten days to get them removed," L.D. said. L.D. did something to my backside but it didn't hurt. "Let's just take a quick picture of Dudley's heart and see what's going on there. Why don't you bring him over here and have him lie down?"

My human said, "Okay, boy, let's go."

I said something, stood up, and jumped off the table. I followed him to another table, and he patted it with his hand. After jumping up onto it, I lay down and saw a light. "Step back for just a minute, Careless," L.D. said.

"Stay, Dudley," my human said as he backed away. I watched him as he held his hand out for me to stay.

"All done. Let's see what we've got here."

I jumped off the table to join my human.

"Well." L.D. pursed his lips. "Dudley is suffering from aortic stenosis. His aortic valve is malfunctioning, so he may not get the proper amount of blood flow he needs. Right now, it doesn't look too severe and doesn't seem to be affecting him. He should never be exercised to the point of exhaustion."

"Don't worry. I'm positive that will never happen." My human laughed, but I could tell he was nervous.

"Let's just keep an eye on him. If it gets worse, we can start him on medication. But I think he'll be just fine."

My human looked a little happier. "Thank you." He opened the door and turned to look at me. "Come on, my little heart patient." I followed him.

He stopped at a desk and said, "Ma'am, Dudley and I just finished up with L.D., and we're about ready to take off."

My nose alerted me to something on the desk that I wanted to eat. Water dripped from my mouth. I couldn't control myself. Jumping up, I grabbed the good-smelling stuff, ripped it apart, and started eating it.

The human at the desk asked, "Sir, what was that?"

My human looked around and then upward and asked, "What was what?"

I wondered what he was looking at so I looked upward to see what it was for myself.

"Sir, did your dog just eat a whole bag of treats?"

"Honey, the name's Careless, and no speaky English." I continued to chew up the good-tasting stuff while watching him.

"Okay, Careless, since this is your first visit with us and because Dudley was adopted from a shelter, we won't charge you for the doctor's visit. However, I will have to charge you ten dollars for that bag of treats he just inhaled," she said.

I finished the treats and noticed that everyone around us was laughing. Someone walked up behind us. It was L.D. I could smell him.

"Careless," L.D. said, "there will be no charge for the bag of treats. We'll see you in ten days."

I let out a huge belch. Everyone looked at me and laughed again. We left the building.

CHAPTER 32

When the truck stopped at our home, I saw E.D. getting out of her car. I was so excited to see her that I jumped out the window and ran toward her. She is my second-favorite human. I heard my human get out of the truck and say, "What's the word, Thunderbird?"

"Careless, I hope you and this serial thriller of yours had a nice, long talk and at least one of you knows how to treat a lady." I walked up and sat right in front of her. She bent down and began petting me and rubbing my head.

"What? You don't know how to handle dogs?" E.D. said. "They like it when you rub their ears. It relaxes them. Am I going to have to teach you how to care for your dog?"

"Yes, you will. And I have some other things I'll need your personal instruction on as well. Will you be available, say, around six o'clock tonight for some tutoring?"

"Nice try, Carwash, but you and I both know that's just not going to happen. But you can send Dudley over for a visit now that I know he can control himself." I heard my name, so I said something. Unfortunately, I couldn't control myself any longer, so I mounted her leg. I didn't know what made me do it.

E.D. and my human both said, "Never mind," at the same time.

"Bad boy, Dudley!" snapped E.D. I stopped what I was doing and slinked back to my human. He didn't seem angry. E.D. walked inside the building.

My human looked at me and said, "Come on, boy. Let's go inside." When we made it back home, I trotted to the sofa and sat down. He opened something and poured some good-smelling stuff into his cup. Then he opened another thing and took out a bottle. He looked at me and said, "What? I've had a long day, and it's time for a Careless Coffee." He opened something else and dropped some hard, clear things in his cup.

He started drinking and then put some food and water in my bowls. I got up from the sofa just as he sat on it. He drank from his cup, and I drank from my bowl. Then I ate my food, taking a mouthful at a time and dropping it on the floor.

"Quit playing with your food," said my human, yawning. "Somewhere in the world there's a starving dog."

I finished eating my food and walked over to him. He was sleeping, so I finished the good-smelling stuff left in his cup. He didn't seem to mind. I jumped up on the sofa, circled several times to get comfortable, and leaned into him. I never wanted to be separated from him. I went to sleep.

When I woke up, my human was still asleep. I stuck my nose in his ear and said something to wake him up. Then the door opened, and his friend, Birk, walked in. "Ha! Now that's rich. If only I had a camera," he said.

I stood up, and the hair on my back went up. I growled. I would protect my human.

"Good boy, Dudley. It's okay. You're a good boy." My human ran his hand down my back and smoothed my hair down.

"Man, that mutt sure is protective of you," Birk said.

"That's right, he's a good boy. Aren't you Dudley?" my human said.

I answered him.

"Birk, how many times have I told you to call before using the spare key to get in?"

"I did call. You never picked up the phone. Have you been hitting the Careless Coffee again? You probably put too much Jack Daniels in it this time—again," Birk said. "Anyway, since you don't have to go to work until tomorrow, I thought we could go eat a late lunch and then go to the bookstore. What do you say?"

"I say you're buying, and what are we waiting for?"

I jumped off the sofa and went to the door. I needed to go outside to do my business. "Birk, take Dudley outside. Just keep your eye on him. I don't want him ruining my day with one of his great escapes."

Birk opened the door and walked out. "Dudley, come on boy. Go do your business." I couldn't go without my human. I didn't want to leave him.

My human said, "Dudley, move your butt." I sat and watched him. I could wait a little longer to do my business.

My human got up and went to another room. He came back with different clothes on. "Birk, why don't you go and wait on the outside of the fence and see if our little escape artist tries anything?"

Birk left, and I followed my human outside and did my business. I also smelled my prey. It was back, and I zeroed in on it. This time it would not get away. I ran at full speed. It popped out of a bush and darted out in front of me. I was about to overtake it and grab its neck, but it escaped through the fence just like last time. I wasn't letting it go. I squeezed through the opening to give chase.

Just as I passed the fence, Birk grabbed me. "That's right, Dudley, we caught you this time. Careless knew you'd try to escape again. I'll fix that right now." He sent me back through the space in the fence and picked up something lying on the ground. He wedged it in the opening between the fence and the building and closed it up. My prey had gotten away from me again. But I didn't think it would be as lucky next time.

I am Dudley. I get my prey.

I ran back and sniffed around the yard just in case, but I didn't find anything, so I ran back to my human and pressed my head against his leg.

"You have a beautiful gait, Dudley," he said. "You are one handsome boy. I can't even imagine how you ended up at that shelter. I'm just glad I found you."

CHAPTER 33

"Let's go, Careless," Birk said. "I'm hungry."

My human looked at Birk and smiled.

"No way! He's not coming with us," Birk said.

My human continued to look at him and smile.

"Fine! He can come with us, but I don't want him goobering all over my truck," Birk said.

My human just laughed, and they walked back into the building and out to the front. I followed. My human opened the door of Birk's truck, and I jumped in.

"The usual?" Birk asked. My human nodded.

I was so happy to be in the truck, I licked Birk's face. He rolled his eyes. I guessed he liked being licked on the face, so I did it again. He turned and looked at my human.

My human said, "Don't start whining like a little girl. He obviously likes you. Besides, they say a dog's mouth is even cleaner than his butt." I sat down in the back seat and licked myself.

"China Garden it is," Birk said.

Birk stopped the truck in front of a building that smelled good. We strolled to the front door, and two men were standing there together. I could hear them talking. One of them looked at me and said, "How do you want him prepared? I'm thinking stir fried with a nice, hot dumpling sauce." All the humans laughed.

"Dudley, what do you think about that?" my human asked.

I said something.

One of the humans said, "Careless, go on inside and eat. I'll watch your friend for you."

"Okay, Richard." My human put a leash on me and tied the other end to something sticking out of the ground. "Dudley, you stay here next to the parking meter with Richard. I can't bring you inside, but if you behave, I'll bring you a fortune cookie."

I sat and said something. I didn't want my human to walk away. What if he didn't come back for me? My human and Birk went into the building.

The humans kept talking. "I'm really worried. I've been getting strange phone calls in the middle of the night and bizarre letters. I'm telling you, I think I have a fan who's a little loony."

"Don't worry, Jake. I've got your back. You know I'm a constable in my spare time. I'll keep an eye on you."

"I know. I get crazy fans all the time, but this one just feels different. We've got a big show at the Astrodome for the Houston Livestock Show and Rodeo. And Jake Harm and the Holdouts has never missed a gig. I'd like to keep it that way. But this one concerns me."

"I've got this! *Please* lose the fake beard and sunglasses. It makes you stick out like the last eggroll at a fat man's convention." They both chuckled.

Jake pulled at his face, and all the hair came off. He shook hands with the other man. "Thanks, Richard."

"No problem. What are friends for?"

Jake walked away, and Richard sat down next to me. "I know you heard that. I don't want you to repeat it to anyone. Okay, Dudley?" He put his hand on my head and petted me.

I said something, and he smiled. "I know you can understand me," he said. "You know, Careless has been coming here since he was a little boy. Our family has known him for a long time."

He stroked the hair on my back. It felt good. When he reached over and took the leash off, I lay down with my legs in front of me. "That was my friend, Jake Harm. He's been playing music with his band, Jake Harm and the Holdouts, for a long time. A crazy fan's been stalking him. He asked for my help. I bet you could help us, Dudley. Couldn't you, boy?"

I said something, and he just smiled.

A while later, I smelled and heard my human and Birk behind me. My tail spun around. The door opened, and they walked out of the building.

Birk said, "That was the best meal ever, wasn't it, Careless?"

My human looked at me and smiled. "I see you don't have a leash on. You look very handsome, my little Egyptian sphinxster. What in the world have you and Richard been talking about?"

I stood up and ran to my human, and he rubbed my head. He had something in his hand that made noise. He took paper off of it and pulled a paper out of it. It smelled good. He threw it to me, and I caught it in my mouth and chewed it up. It was crunchy. "That's a fortune cookie. Marian, the owner of this fine establishment, wanted you to have it. I knew you'd like it."

Richard walked up and gave him the leash. "He really loves you."

My human looked at me and said, "Let me read your fortune to you, Dudley." He glanced at a paper. "In order to make a friend, you have to be a friend."

I said something, and they all looked at me.

My human said, "Bye, Richard." He and Birk walked over to the truck.

"Really, Careless, I don't want your mutt drooling all over the Cowboy Cadillac."

My human laughed and opened the door for me. I jumped in, and Birk opened the sunroof and turned on some music as he drove. I stuck my head out through the roof, and my tail spun around.

Birk said, "My favorite author, Kinky Friedman, just released a new book."

My human nodded.

Birk said, "Hey, are you listening to me? Did you even hear a word I said?"

"I'm sorry, are you talking to me?"

"Well, I wasn't talking to your new soul mate in the back seat."

I said something and looked right at him.

"Dudley, what do you think? Should we go to the bookstore to get Kinky's new book?"

I said something.

"Let's pick up Sarge on the way to the bookstore. You know how he loves books," my human said.

"Okay, but he'd better make it snappy. I want an autographed copy of Kinky's new book. Do you know what it's called?"

"*The Hard Boiled Computer.*"

"How'd you know? It was just released," Birk said.

"It's really quite simple, Birk. You're hard boiled, and you don't know how to use a computer worth a damn. It made perfect sense." My human chuckled.

Birk drove to our home and stopped the truck. My human got out, so I jumped into the front seat and out of the truck. I was so anxious to stay with him that I ran into him and pushed him forward.

"Hurry up you two," Birk said. I stopped on the way to our home and did my business. A loud noise came from the truck, and I looked back to see what it was.

"Don't worry, that's just Birk honking his horn. It's okay, boy."

I followed him into the building. When we got to our door, I stopped and sat, waiting for him to open it, but he walked past me. I was confused. I stood up and followed him. He went to the next door, stopped, and hit his hand against the door several times.

Someone said, "Wow, how, how," and Sarge opened the door. He put a black thing on his face and looked at my human. "Let me just get these glasses on. Oh, wow, man, han, han, han. I'm so glad to see you man, han, han, han."

Before my human could say anything, Sarge bent down and started petting me. I wasn't sure about him, so I said something but wagged my tail to let him know I wouldn't bite him. Sarge stood straight up and walked back into his home. My human followed. So did I.

My human said, "Sarge, we're going to the bookstore. Would you like to join us?"

"Are you serious, man, han, han, han? Hell yeah, I want to go. Thanks, man."

I watched him as he walked to his bed and picked something up. He looked at it and then sniffed it. I was curious because I thought only dogs sniffed things. He shook it and sniffed it again. I couldn't quit watching him. He looked back at my human and me and said, "Yeah, heh, heh, heh. Smells okay to me." He put the thing over his head and pushed his arms through it.

"I like your shirt, Sarge. Give peace a chance." My human laughed and held up two fingers, just like the picture on the shirt.

"Right on, man, han, han. Right on," Sarge said.

Birk's horn sounded again. My human and Sarge turned their heads in the direction it was coming from. "Let's get a move on. Birk is getting impatient and probably won't stop honking until we get down there," my human said.

CHAPTER 34

My human and Sarge walked down the stairs and out of the building. I stayed by my human's side. Birk was in the truck and looked unhappy. He waved his hand at us and said, "Come on! You guys move slower than molasses."

My human chuckled. They walked a little faster, and I matched their stride. After we climbed in, Birk drove the truck away. Music was playing in the truck. I recognized the voice singing the music. It belonged to the human who was talking to Richard when I ate that good-tasting fortune cookie. Birk was making strange noises.

"Birk, what is that chicken cackle noise you're making?" my human asked.

"What? I'm singing," Birk said. "It's the new *Wild Turkey At Sunrise* album. You know, Jake Harm and the Holdouts' new one. Some people think I have a pretty good singing voice."

"Yeah, well some people need hearing aids," my human said. He and Sarge laughed. Birk looked unhappy, but he started making that strange noise again.

When Birk stopped the truck in front of a building, I brought my head back inside. Sarge was excited. My human looked at me and said, "Okay, Dudley, you have to wait in the truck. Dogs are not allowed in the bookstore. I'm sorry. Stay here, boy."

I said something. I didn't want my human to leave me. He closed the door, and I was alone in the truck.

Birk laughed and said, "Why don't you pretend Dudley's a service dog or a seeing-eye dog?"

"The only reason I'd need a seeing-eye dog is because you're so butt ugly, I'd go blind looking at you." Sarge and my human laughed.

Birk didn't look happy.

I didn't want to stay in the truck. My human looked back several times, and I stared at him. I wanted him to know I didn't want him to leave. They walked through some doors and into a building. I could no longer see them.

I knew my human had commanded me to stay. And a dog must obey his human.

But you never know when your human might need you.

I stayed for as long as I could. Then I jumped through the open window. Hitting the ground running, I bolted to the building.

I will find my human.

I waited at the door until a human opened it, and I walked right in. There were a lot of humans in the store. I immediately picked up the scent of my human and followed it. He was standing with a few other people with his back turned toward me, talking to a human behind a counter. I stayed back because I knew he'd commanded me to stay in the truck. I didn't want to be a bad boy. I sat and watched him.

"Yes, ma'am, I'd like a large, iced coffee, decaf of course, with a neat shot of Jack Daniels to take the edge off."

"Sir," she said, "I'm sorry but we don't serve alcoholic beverages. Would you like me to leave room in your coffee for some cream or sugar?" He pulled something from his pocket and took some paper from it.

He handed the paper to her and said, "No, Maria, I like my coffee like I like my women—strong and bitter."

She laughed.

"I'm guessing you're from Mexico City. About twenty years old and here on a student visa, is that correct? And how long have you been a Buddhist?" he asked.

She raised her eyebrows. "Do I know you?"

The other humans looked at him. I didn't like this. I was tempted to go stand by his side, but I didn't want to be a bad boy. I stayed where he couldn't see me. But I was ready to spring into action if he needed me.

"Well, I surmised your name is Maria from your nametag. Your hair, eyes, and complexion—along with your accent—led me to believe your origin is central Mexico. So, I assumed you're from Mexico City," my human said.

"What about the Buddhism?" she asked, the lines around her eyes relaxing a bit.

"Oh, the Buddhist thing? Well, when I paid for the coffee, I noticed a quite colorful tattoo of Buddha on your left wrist when your sleeve moved." She chuckled and shook her head. My human continued, "The name's Careless. Would you like me to rub your Buddha's belly for good luck?"

"Next in line!" she called. "That was amazing, though. Next!"

As my human walked away, a human I'd never seen walked up to him. My human said, "Hello, Mr. Manager, or may I call you Store?"

"Yes, I am the store manager," the other human said. "My name's Seth. And your name is?"

"The name's Careless."

The other human raised his eyebrows. "Sir, we have a serious problem."

My human smiled and said, "When you say *we*, who are you referring to? Is there a mouse in your pocket?"

I wanted to say something. And I did, just not very loudly. I didn't want my human to hear me.

"No, Mr. Careless, but I am going to have to ask you to remove your animal from the bookstore," Mr. Manager said. My human looked around. *Did he see me? I don't think so.*

"The name's Careless. Just Careless. I know my friend, Birk, is getting agitated because he's been waiting in line for so long to purchase his Kinky Friedman book. And I know he hasn't shaved in days, but there's no need to refer to him as an animal. Are we all not animals? Are we all not people? Can't we all just get along?"

Mr. Manager looked unhappy.

My human scanned the room.

Now I'm a bad boy.

"Dudley, get over here right now! I know you're in the bookstore," my human said. He pointed at a spot right in front of him. I ran to him and sat. He stared at me.

I know I am a bad boy.

But then he said, "Good boy. I missed you so much!" Now I was confused. He rubbed my head. "I'm sorry for leaving you in the Cowboy Cadillac."

"Can I get you guys a room, or do you want to take it outside? No animals allowed in the store," Mr. Manager said.

He sounded angry. I turned my head toward him to let him know I would protect my human. I said something, and water came from my jowls. Mr. Manager stepped back and said, "It's store policy. Do I need to get security, or are the two of you going to leave right now?"

My human looked at me and said, "Come on, boy, let's take our business elsewhere." He strode toward the door, and I followed him. He waved to

Maria behind the counter. She covered her mouth with her hand. I heard her laughing. She waved with her other hand. My human went outside through some doors, and I followed.

CHAPTER 35

I followed him to another building. He looked at me and said, "One dog or two, Dudley?"

I heard my name, so I said something.

"So, you want two," he said.

I responded again. I rubbed my head against his leg so he'd know I loved him and no other dog could claim him. He walked into the building and held the door open for me. This building smelled good. There were a few humans sitting at tables and eating food. A human stood behind a counter. *I hope this one is nicer than Mr. Manager. I didn't like him.*

My human walked up, and the human behind the counter said, "Welcome to James Coney Island. May I take your order?"

"I would like your finest hotdog, smothered with chili, cheese, and onions. Also, my friend will have two plain hotdogs."

"Oh, will someone be joining you?"

"You don't see my friend, Dudley," my human said while patting the counter with his hand. I knew he wanted me to jump up on the counter, so I did. I rested my front paws on it. The other human looked scared.

"I didn't see him down there, sir," he said.

My human laughed and said, "Don't be nervous. He doesn't normally eat people if he gets what he wants. In this case, he wants two plain hotdogs. Right, Dudley?"

I said something.

"Better make those with cheese," my human said, smiling and placing his hand on my head.

"Sir, I'm sorry, we don't allow dogs in the restaurant unless they're service dogs. Your total is eight dollars and forty-five cents. Your order is number fifteen," he said.

My human took something dark from his shirt and placed it on his face. It covered his eyes. "Do you happen to have a copy of my bill in Braille?" he asked.

He pulled out something from his back pocket and took some paper out of it. "Dudley, how much is this," he asked. He held it in front of my face.

Even though it didn't smell good, I decided to taste it. I took the paper in my mouth. Then I said something.

"Oh, it's ten dollars? Thank you. Please leave it for this nice young man." He patted the counter with his hand, so I spit the paper out on it. It looked better than it tasted. "Keep the change."

My human sat down on a chair next to a table, and I sat by his side. He looked at me and said, "Dudley, you're now my service dog. How does it feel?"

I said something and leaned against his leg.

The other human called out, "Fifteen and twenty-one, your orders are ready for pickup." My human stood and walked back to the counter, with me trailing at his side. The other human asked, "You can really see, can't you, sir?"

"Actually, I have an excellent memory and sense of smell, so it was easy for me to find my way back to the counter." My human looked at me and smiled. He was happy. The other human didn't look happy, so my human took some more paper from the thing in his back pocket and handed it to him while asking, "How much is this?"

The other human looked at it, smiled, put it in his pocket, and said, "Have a nice day, sir."

My human and I walked back to the table, and we both sat down.

"I'm glad that worked out, Dudley. I didn't really feel like getting kicked out of another fine establishment today. There's nothing like taking a friend to lunch, right, boy?"

I wanted to say something, but I was concentrating on what he'd received from the other human. It smelled really good, and my mouth watered. I managed to say something but not with as much vigor and enthusiasm as normal. He placed some of the food on the ground next to me. I got very excited and ate it quickly.

He started laughing and said, "This place has sure gone to the dogs."

My human had almost finished eating his good-smelling food when I heard Birk's truck. As it got closer, it made a loud noise. My human made a face and waved his hand toward the window. "Can you believe this guy, Dudley? He can't even let us digest our food."

I said something, and my human took a white thing off the table and rubbed it against his mouth.

"Look at me, Dudley," he said, while rubbing the same thing against my jowls. "I don't think Birk would like it too much if I didn't napkin off your wet mouth. He likes his truck like he likes his bourbon—neat. Let's go, before he has a heart attack."

When we got outside, Birk said, "Let's go, grandma!"

My human smiled and started walking very slowly. I thought he was playing a game, so I walked slowly next to him. Birk looked even more irritated than before. When we reached the truck, my human opened the door, and I jumped in and stuck my head through the sunroof. The truck moved forward, and the wind blew through my jowls. My human looked at Birk until he asked, "What?"

"What the hell did you do with Sarge?"

"Oh, he wasn't ready to go. And since you and your hound-dog homeboy got thrown out of the bookstore and I'd already purchased my book, I told him I was ready to make like a tree and leave. He told me he would find a way home. He looked like he was really into the books he picked out, so I left him. He'll be okay."

I saw our home, and the truck stopped. My human got out of the truck, and I jumped out behind him and did my business.

Birk asked, "Can't you control that weasel dog of yours? He's starting to remind me a little of you."

I wanted to say something, but I was busy doing my business.

"Birk, you're a real wordsmith. Hey, isn't that Jake Harm and the Holdouts on the radio again?"

"Yep. And guess what! I have four tickets to see them play live this week at the Houston Livestock Show and Rodeo. Two for you and me and two for the lucky gals who'll be joining us," Birk said.

"Who're the lucky gals you're referring to? And I don't recall seeing Jake Harm and the Holdouts on the lineup," my human said.

"That's right, numbnuts. That's because he's not playing the main show. He's playing at the Hideout. And you need special tickets to get in to see him. It's very exclusive," Birk said.

"Well, see what you can do about rustling up some dates," my human said. He smiled and walked toward our home. I followed.

CHAPTER 36

"Dudley, why do you look like you're bobbing for apples when you drink water? You sure are funny."

I looked at my human and said something, but it was muffled because my jowls were wet. He got something to drink as well before plopping onto the sofa. His drink smelled good, and he really liked it. I joined him on the sofa, pressing my body against him as hard as I could. I wanted him to know how much I loved him, and I wanted to be as close to him as I could.

"Hey, I'm not that kind of a guy! Or am I?" my human said.

He pushed me away, but I wanted to be next to him. I stiffened my legs and pushed back with all my might. The more he pushed, the more I pushed. He finally stopped and grinned. "Okay, you win. I don't want you to keep Sir Isaac Newtoning me," he said.

He drank some of the good-smelling drink. I waited till he closed his eyes and went to sleep. Then I did the same.

When I woke up, my human was still asleep. I needed to go outside to do my business. I licked his face. "Good morning, Sunshine," he murmured.

I didn't know who Sunshine was, but I said something anyway. He stroked my face. Then he looked at something on his arm and said, "It's already after seven. I've got to go pick Sarge up from the bookstore. Want to go for a ride, Dudley?" We left our home.

E.D. was standing at the bottom of the stairs holding some papers in her hands. My human said something, but she didn't look at him. He waved both hands in front of her face. I wasn't sure what he was doing, but I walked over to her. I couldn't stop myself. Something made me do it. Something took over my body. I humped her leg, and my eyes rolled back in my head.

"What the hell's wrong with your mangy mutt?" she demanded.

"Well, for one thing, he has exquisite taste in women. You can't really fault him for that," he said.

"Well, he's about to get my foot up where the sun don't shine if he doesn't back off," she said.

My human called me, so I stopped humping her leg and walked over to him.

"Good boy!" My human placed his hand on my head. *I am a good boy.*

E.D. looked at the papers again. "I heard that, Witless," she said. I didn't know who Witless was.

"That's Careless, honey, and may I ask what you're doing?"

"Well, if you must know, I'm reading a letter. Is that okay with you and your serial thriller?"

My human asked, "Is it a good letter?"

E.D. stopped reading the letter and looked at him. "Let's just see how observant you are. Why don't you tell me if you think it's a good letter?"

"Okay, you're reading a letter you just received. Your boyfriend, who in fact lives in this very city, has just become your former boyfriend. In the letter he tells you he no longer wants to see you and is moving on. He hopes you will do the same. There is probably some generic reference about it being him and not you, and he is really sorry. In essence, he wishes you a nice life—just without him. If I'm not mistaken, it's a Dear John letter. If it's any consolation to you, I think he's a complete fool. How'd I do?"

She stared at him, and water streamed from her eyes. She was not happy. My human looked at me. For the first time, I didn't think he knew what to do. He looked confused.

She walked forward, put her arms around his neck, and placed her head on his shoulders, just like I do. I didn't like this, and I said something to let her know. I didn't want her taking my human. He looked at me and held his hand up. He wanted me to quiet down, and I did.

"You're one hundred percent right. It's a Dear John letter from my boyfriend, Burt. Or, I guess, my ex-boyfriend, Burt."

My human smiled and said, "Oh, I loved him in the *Smokey and the Bandit* movie."

She laughed and asked, "How in the world did you know all of that?"

"I have a keen eye for the obvious—and beautiful women, of course. He's obviously an idiot. You're better off without him. If it would make you feel any better, I'll take you out to dinner some time. Would you like that?"

"When?"

"I don't know."

"How about tonight?"

My human said, "Tonight it is. But right now, I have to go pick up Sarge. Birk left him at the bookstore, and I don't want someone to mistake him for a homeless person."

She put her hands on her hips and said, "No, you don't. I just saw him sitting on the sofa downstairs when I got the Dear John letter from my mailbox. What time did you say we're going out tonight?"

"Meet me in the stairwell at eight o'clock. I'll take you to a nice Italian restaurant."

"How romantic. You asked me out in a dirty, old warehouse stairwell." She was smiling now. "It's a good thing I love Italian."

"Kiss me, I'm Italian," my human said. He smiled. I didn't know what they were saying, but I said something anyway.

"We'll talk about that at dinner. And I'm going to want to know how you knew about the letter. Be on time. I don't like to be kept waiting!" She turned and walked up the stairs.

"Come on, boy," my human said, "let's go find Sarge and make sure he's okay. And I won't be telling her I saw the edge of the envelope she just got out of her mailbox, postmarked in Houston."

Sarge was sitting on the sofa next to the door, holding something with both hands. "Sarge, I'm glad you made it back. Dudley and I were just on our way to retrieve you from the bookstore. How did you get here?"

"Hey, man, han, han. This foxy lady asked me if I knew you. When she found out I did, she gave me a ride home after the bookstore closed," Sarge said.

"What are you reading? Did you buy a new book?" my human asked.

"Wow, how, how, man. I totally forgot to tell you something. That foxy lady handed me this book to give to you. So here you go man, han, han," Sarge said. He stood up and walked toward my human.

I said something.

"It's okay, boy. It's just Sarge," my human said, petting my head. Sarge gave my human the book. As he walked away, he patted me on the head.

My human held the book up and opened it.

He grinned. "Look at this, Dudley," he said. I was looking. I never take my eyes off my human. "She sent me a Sherlock Holmes book. Maria wrote a note on the inside cover. It says, 'To Careless, one of the most observant men

I think I shall ever meet. And also the most handsome.' Okay, she didn't write that last part, but I'm sure she meant it, don't you think, Dudley?"

I heard my name, so I responded. He smiled at me and kept reading, "Put your talents to good use. Until we meet again. Love, Maria. Interesting . . ."

He placed his hand on my head. "Come on, Dudley, let's go outside so you can do your business."

After we returned, my human went into a smaller room, took off his clothes, and got all wet from water coming out of the wall. Then he dried off with something and got dressed. "Dudley, I'm going to leave you for a while. I left food and water out for you. If you get tired, take a nap on that lovely yellow-and-orange sofa. If you really get bored, you can order a movie on cable TV. I left twenty dollars on the table for you to order a pizza. Oh, and don't order any inappropriate movies. I'll know if you do. Also, I don't have cable TV, so there's that."

I had no idea what he was saying, but I said something anyway.

"That's what I thought. Behave yourself. I'll be back soon."

CHAPTER 37

I didn't want my human to leave me. I said something, but he walked out of our home without me. I needed to be with him. I could smell E.D. on the other side of the door before I heard her.

"Careless, you clean up pretty well. Cat got your tongue? I know, I know, you're struck by my beauty. It's a curse, you know. Just nod your head up and down a few times to let me know you comprehend what I'm saying." Her voice faded as they walked off. *My human left me.*

I went to the window and watched as my human and E.D. walked to his truck and drove off. I pressed my nose against the window so I could be closer to him. I couldn't smell or see him anymore, so I drank all my water and ate all my food. Then I made my way over to the sofa and sat on it. The sofa smelled like him.

I sniffed a cushion. It was sticking up a little. I pushed it with my nose, and it moved. So I grabbed it with my mouth and pulled at it. It came up easily. Once it was up, I decided to chew it. I shredded it. I didn't know why. I really didn't have anything better to do. When I finished shredding it, I started on another. Before I knew it, all the cushions were shredded.

I still didn't have anything to do, so I started shredding the rest of the sofa. I was having a great time ripping its guts out. There was stuffing and pieces of sofa everywhere. I grabbed the remains of the sofa and pulled it across the room. If I had my way, there wouldn't be anything left of it. I dragged it all the way to the door. When it hit the door and could go no further, I left it. All that fun really made me tired. I meandered to my human's bed and fell asleep.

While I was still sleeping, I smelled my human. *He's home!* He called my name. I got so excited that I jumped out of the bed and ran to the door. I had to dodge sofa pieces to get to him.

My human stood next to the door. He didn't look happy. But I was happy. I was happy to see him and smell him. He didn't leave me like Daddy did. I jumped on him and rested my paws on his shoulder. I couldn't stop licking him.

He cracked a smile. "I know, I know, I missed you too, boy!" As I licked him, I heard footsteps outside of the door. I knew it was E.D. I could smell her. I stopped licking him and looked at E.D. She stood right behind us.

"Do you always leave your door open, Carwash?"

My human looked surprised. "So, you just couldn't get enough of me, is that right?"

"I have no idea why, but I was actually thinking about having a drink with you after that nice dinner we had. Thankfully, this scene just jarred me back to my senses. Now, your mutt better not be eyeballing my leg."

I jumped down and trotted toward E.D., but she glared at me.

My human said, "It's Careless, by the way."

She turned around and walked away.

He looked at me and said, "Well, it looks like we blew that one, huh, Dudley?"

I said something.

"I guess I can't leave you by yourself. You'll be going to work with me tomorrow."

He cleaned up the ripped pieces of sofa and pushed it back to where it had originally stood. Then he closed the door. I was tired. I went back to the bed and jumped in it. I heard my human walk close to the bed. He took off his clothes, and when he got in, I stood up, circled around, and came to rest with my head on him. He put his arm around me, and I watched him intently until his eyes closed.

In the morning, I heard the telephone on his desk making noises again. I turned my head sideways. He opened his eyes and yawned. "Being spooned by a dog all night isn't really that bad, Dudley." He patted my head. "I need to answer the telephone, big boy. You're going to have to let me up."

I said something because I wanted to answer the telephone. He tried to push me away. I didn't want to leave him, so when he pushed, I pushed back. He had a hard time pushing me away. But he managed to slip away from me. He picked up the telephone, and it stopped making noises. "House of Pies. Who the hell is this? Oh, Ross? No, I won't be coming to breakfast this morning. I'll meet you and Pappa at the office. I have a big surprise for you." He pointed his finger at me and grinned. Then he put the telephone down.

"That's right, Dudley, you're going to work today. And don't think you're going to be slacking off at the office."

I heard my name, so I said something.

A few minutes later, he walked out of our home before I could join him. As soon as I saw him leaving, I jumped up, but I was too late. I waited by the door and said something. I could still smell him.

He opened the door, and my tail spun around. *My human didn't leave me!* "I'm sorry, boy. I'm so used to running out of the door by myself, I completely forgot you. I may be a slow learner, but I eventually get to the picnic."

He bent down and hugged me. I love it when my human hugs me. We strode out of the building together and got into his truck. I sat next to him with my head in his lap. He drove to a place that smelled good. When he opened his window, a human said, "Welcome to Whataburger, may I take your order?"

I was confused because I didn't smell anyone.

My human responded, "Two potato and egg taquitos, please."

We drove to a window.

A human opened it and said, "That will be four dollars." She reached her hand out toward my human. I was intrigued. *What does she want?* I lunged forward until I was standing in my human's lap with my head out the window. The human inside the building frowned. My human pushed me back and took some green papers out of his pocket.

He handed it to her and said, "I'm so sorry. It's Dudley's first time at a drive-thru." She handed him a bag of good-smelling stuff, and we left. We drove until we reached another place. It looked familiar to me.

CHAPTER 38

"Welcome to the pipe yard, Dudley."

I remembered being in the pipe yard with the black female, and fighting and killing the big dog. Was my human going to leave me in the pipe yard? Would I have to live in the pipe yard again?

He stopped the truck, and we both got out. We walked into a building where an older human sat in a chair. He had something in his mouth, and smoke came from it. It was a cigar like the ones Scott and Paulito smoked. I turned my head sideways to study it. The smoke rose to the ceiling.

"Good morning," he said. I walked over to him, and he smiled. He placed his hand on my head. I didn't mind him touching me. A calmness emanated from him.

"Morning Pappa. Don't fall asleep with your cigar in your mouth," my human said.

He walked to another room and sat down. I followed him and sat next to him. He took the good-smelling thing out of the bag, and I watched it intently. It smelled so good that water dripped from my jowls.

He set it on the floor. I ate it like I'd never eaten before. It was so good I couldn't help myself. He began eating one as well. I placed my head on his leg and watched him. He smiled and gave me some of his good-smelling food. *I like this pipe yard.*

While he was busy doing things, I found a sofa and jumped onto it. I sat and watched him. Another human walked in and sat on the sofa right next to me. He seemed like a nice human. He looked at my human and didn't take notice of me.

"It's about time you got here," he said. He still didn't notice me. I decided to be nice to him. I licked his ear and his face. Jumping up, he said, "What the hell is that? Are you out of your mind?"

My human pointed at me and said, "Meet Dudley, our new silent partner."

I said something.

"I guess he's not always silent. If he plays his cards right, I was thinking of promoting him to collections. What do you think of that, Ross?"

"This is a place of business. Pets don't belong here."

"I'm not sure that's company policy, is it? Besides, I can't leave him at home. He ate my sofa last night when I left him alone."

Pappa walked into the room, still smoking the cigar. He looked around and chuckled. Ross saw this and started laughing as well. Pappa made more smoke, and it floated upward.

"You boys get back to work." I looked up at him, and he placed his hand on my head. He reminded me of my human. He turned and walked away.

My human said, "Well, it looks like you're in, Dudley."

I responded.

Ross stood up and walked away.

After watching my human awhile, I fell asleep. When I woke up, I needed to go outside and do my business. I jumped off the sofa and said something.

My human looked at me and asked, "What's the matter boy?"

I walked over to the door, and he opened it for me. We walked outside together, and I did my business. When I was finished, I came right back to him. *I don't want to ever leave my human. I love him too much.*

When we walked back in, I trotted up to Pappa, who was sitting in a chair and smoking a cigar. He petted me. Then I went back to sleep on my sofa and listened to my human with my eyes closed.

He said something, so I opened my eyes. He was holding the telephone against his head.

"Will you please move the forty-two inch pipe to a different pipe rack? I want to make a dog run where that pipe's at. Once it's moved, please have the crew fence it off and plant some grass and a tree for the newest member of the business team."

He waved at me, so I said something.

"Then please send Hammer in to see me." He stopped speaking, stood up, and walked away. I followed him.

He looked at me. "Stay!" He went outside into the pipe yard. I wanted to follow him, but he closed the door behind himself. I walked over and sat next to Pappa and watched the smoke rise to the ceiling.

My human finally came back, and I joined him in his office. Soon, I smelled another human approaching.

"You wanted to see me, boss," the new human asked.

"Hammer, meet our newest member of the team." My human pointed at me.

I said something. Hammer petted me, and I said something again. I wasn't going to bite him, but I only like certain humans petting me.

"I'd like to build a doggie door in the restroom leading out to the new dog run. Do you think you can do that for me?" my human asked.

"You got it, boss man. I'll get right on it." Hammer turned and walked away. I heard noises coming from another room, so I went to investigate.

Hammer was cutting a hole in the wall with something noisy. I watched for a little while. When he left, there was a hole in the wall with a clear, soft door hanging from it. I decided to check it out. It moved when I nosed it, so I shoved my head through it. Finally, I walked through it. It slammed shut behind me. I walked around and did my business. When I came back inside through the door, my human was standing there watching me.

"You are one smart boy. You've already learned how to use the doggie door. Now you can go in and out as you please." I went outside to do my business several times that day. It seemed to make my human happy.

When I was resting on the sofa, I smelled something good. My nostrils flared. Hammer came into the room. "Excuse me boss man, but some of the men and I went to lunch, and we brought back a little something for Dudley. Is that okay?"

"Sure. What, pray tell, did you get him?"

"What we have here is the Ultimate Cheeseburger from Jack in the Box." Hammer lifted something out of the bag, and the smell got even stronger. Water dripped from my mouth. He unwrapped it and placed it on the floor. I jumped off of the sofa and attacked it. It tasted as good as it smelled.

"Thank you, Hammer, it appears Dudley has a new favorite meal now," my human said. Both of them laughed. I left and went back outside. I liked it out there. I could chase trucks and bark at people. But I never stayed out long because I didn't like to be away from my human.

One time, I saw something that looked interesting. Some white paper hung in a roll on the wall next to the doggie door. It smelled strange. I nosed it. It moved, and some paper rolled off of it. I grabbed it in my mouth and pulled. More and more strange-smelling paper appeared. The more I pulled, the more paper appeared. I grabbed it with my mouth and took it outside with me through the doggie door. I was having fun. Finally, the paper stopped coming, so I went back inside.

I saw Ross sitting on something, and he screamed when I walked in on him. *He must think I am a bad boy.* I ran to my human. I didn't want to be a bad boy. Ross approached us. "Your dog just scared the crap out of me. Literally! I was on the toilet when he popped his head through the doggie door. That's just not right. A man needs a little privacy on the throne. And when did you install a doggie door in the restroom?"

My human smirked. "That was the only place it could be safely installed without cutting through brick. You do look like someone just scared the crap out of you."

Pappa walked in and started laughing, and then everyone started laughing. I said something. *I am a good boy.*

"Well, go check out what your boy did with the roll of toilet paper, Careless. I bet you won't find *that* too funny," Ross said.

My human walked over and looked at the paper on the ground. He smiled.

"Dudley, if this wasn't so funny, I'd be mad at you. How on earth did you manage to get that toilet paper trail outside? I'll go clean it up, but don't do it again. Next time, it's coming out of your paycheck."

I said something, and he hugged me. *I love my human.*

I watched as he cleaned up the paper. He moved the rest of it up high on top of something. I could still get it if I jumped, but I knew my human didn't want me to do that. So, I left the paper alone.

After I went to sleep on the sofa for a while, he said, "Alright Dudley, not bad for a first day. Let's go home."

I followed him out to his truck and got in. Pappa and Ross got in a car and left. My human drove off but stopped. "I have to shut the gate. You stay here. I'll be right back." He left, and I watched him sliding something toward the truck. I moved over to his seat to see him better.

When I did, my paw landed on something, and the truck moved backwards. My human yelled and bolted toward the truck. He opened the door and jumped in. I quickly moved to my seat. He did something, and the truck stopped. "Dudley, you bad boy. You just drove the truck into a fire hydrant," he said.

I said something. I was a bad boy.

He got out of the truck, walked around, and climbed back in. "It's okay, boy. It's just a small dent in the bumper. The fire hydrant's fine. You're a good boy but a terrible driver. I bet you don't even have a driver's license, do you?" I licked his face. *I am a good boy.* My human smiled at me.

"Dudley, let's make a quick pit stop. I want to go see Maria at the bookstore and thank her for the book she gave me. Is that okay?"

I said something and lay down with my head in his lap. After a while, my human stopped the truck. He looked at me. "Oh no, you don't. This time, stay in the truck."

He looked serious. I licked his face. He left the truck and closed me in. I said something. He turned and looked at me. He pointed two of his fingers at his eyes and then pointed one back at me. I knew he was watching me. He kept walking but occasionally looked back. I didn't want to stay in the truck without him. I said something again, but he went into the building.

When I saw him walking back to the truck, my tail spun around. I couldn't help it. I pressed my nose up against the window. He opened the door and sat down, and I collapsed in his lap. He was happy, and I licked him.

"It's a good thing you didn't go back inside the bookstore. I'm not sure the store manager could handle another visit from you," he said.

I responded.

He laughed. "She was gone, Dudley. She went back to Mexico. Can you believe that? She left me a note. Want me to read it to you? You'll appreciate it."

I said something.

"Okay, here goes. 'Careless, once I see you again, I'll know just how intuitive you really are. Until then, Maria.' That's all she wrote. She does have nice handwriting, but still, I can't believe she left."

That night, just before I was about to go to sleep, I smelled someone. It was E.D. She was outside our home. My human didn't smell her. I jumped off the sofa and walked to the door. She didn't come in.

My human looked at me. "Do you need to go do your business, boy?"

I said something.

He walked over and opened the door. E.D. stood there. She looked happy to see me.

"How'd you know I was here, Carwash? I didn't even knock on the door. I was just debating whether to knock or turn around and go back upstairs. But now that I see my handsome boy, I know I made the right choice."

My human said, "Well, thank you . . ." He stopped talking when she bent down and hugged me. E.D. loved me, and she smelled almost as good as my human.

"Be a good boy," she said, "and go get that box I brought over there."

I said something. *I am a good boy.*

"Careless, I'm talking to you. Go get that box I brought for you," she said.

My human walked over and picked something up.

"I saw what Dudley did to your sofa last night, and since you were somewhat nice to me, I decided to help you out. It's obvious someone needs to care for the dumb animal living here. And I wasn't talking about Dudley."

My human said something.

Then I said something.

"Dudley dismantled your sofa because you left him alone for too long, and he didn't have anything to do. He got bored. You're lucky he stopped at the sofa. I purchased some items at the pet store that should keep him busy the next time you're away. That should stop him from chewing up any items in your loft, although most of them needed to take a one-way trip to Goodwill anyway."

"You're such a sweetie, E.D. Oh, I like the way that sounds. I should call you *E.D. Sweetie* from now on," my human said.

E.D. pulled something from the box. She ripped at it until she was holding something that smelled good. She held it out. "This is a Greenie."

I grabbed it with my mouth and ate it. It tasted as good as it smelled. My human was happy.

"Here's a squeaky ball," she said. She threw it toward me, and I caught it in my mouth. It didn't taste good like the Greenie. I spit it out.

"I guess he didn't like the ball," my human said.

I watched E.D. She pulled something else out of the box. I couldn't take my eyes off of it. Something about it caught my interest. "I call this one Baby," E.D. said.

She threw me a soft, white thing. It had two legs, two arms, and a head. I caught it in my mouth. It didn't have much taste. It didn't smell good. But I liked something about it.

My body took over, and I dropped it to the floor. Then I grabbed it with my front paws and humped it. I don't know why. I had no control over myself.

E.D. started laughing, and my human said, "Dudley, cut that out."

I finished what I was doing and grabbed Baby with my mouth. I tilted my head back and let go of it. I watched it go up in the air and land on floor. All this wore me out, so I went to our bed and curled up in a ball.

"Thank you, E.D. That was kind of you. I'm sure Dudley will really enjoy the gifts."

"Well, I do love big handsome dogs," she said. "And I guess I'm becoming fond of you as well. I'll head back upstairs now. I'll see you around the building." She kissed him on his face.

CHAPTER 39

The next morning, we drove to a house I'd never been to before. When we went inside, Pappa and Ross were sitting at a table. It smelled good. My human sat down and said, "Morning Pappa. Morning Ross."

I lay down under the table and waited for my human's hand to come down with food in it. I didn't have to wait long. Then Ross's hand came down with food, so I took it from him as well. They finished eating all the good-smelling food. "Well, gentlemen, let's go to work. Thank you for breakfast, Pappa. Delicious as usual."

Pappa and Ross laughed.

We left the house, and my human and I got back into our truck. When we got to the pipe yard, Ross opened the gate. I smelled something strange. I stuck my nose up to the spot where the air was coming into the truck.

My human laughed. "You're crazy, Dudley. Why do you have your nose against the vent? I bet you smell the hops and barley. The Anheuser Busch Brewery brews their beer early in the morning. They're just across the street. Isn't that a great smell?"

I said something.

Ross walked further into the pipe yard. We followed Pappa into the office, where he sat in a chair and smoked a cigar.

He looked at me and said while smiling, "What? It's my morning cigar." Smoke wafted from the cigar in his mouth. This always made me curious. I couldn't quit watching him.

My human chuckled. "Pappa, those cigars are going to be the death of you."

"The only thing keeping me alive are cigars and coming to work," Pappa said. I watched the smoke for a while and then went outside through the doggie door.

While outside, I saw big trucks in the pipe yard. *I'm glad I don't live in a pipe yard anymore. I like living with my human in our home.* People climbed out of the big trucks and walked into the office. I decided to go in and investigate. I wanted to make sure my human was okay. I went to him and sat by his side at his desk. Without looking at me, he placed his hand on my head and rubbed my ears.

I saw something move outside of the window.

I growled.

My human looked at me. "Dudley, what are you going on about?"

I walked over to the window and watched.

"It's probably just a truck driver, Dudley. Don't worry," my human said.

I saw someone walk by, and my hair stood up. The door to the office opened, and I ran over to see who it was. I didn't recognize this human. I passed Pappa, who was still smoking the cigar. When I saw the truck driver, I growled again. *I must protect the humans in the office.*

My human walked up behind me, but I didn't move or take my eyes off the truck driver. "Simmer down, Dudley." My human set his hand on my head. I went quiet. He slid a window open. "Good morning, how may I help you?"

"Your Black Mouth Cur sure is protective. He must really love you." I remembered when I was living with Heidi, Juna, and my brothers and sisters that Heidi called us Black Mouth Curs. *I am Dudley. I am a Black Mouth Cur.*

My human looked down at me. "I didn't know what he was. I adopted him from the shelter. I thought he was just a mutt."

"Oh, no, he's definitely a Black Mouth Cur. They make great hunting dogs. And they can track anything. They have great noses. Anyway, I'm here to pick up a load going to El Paso."

"Just one moment." My human walked to his office and came back with some papers. He gave it to the truck driver on the other side of the window. "Just see Ross in the pipe yard, and he'll get you taken care of."

"Thank you." The truck driver waved at me. "See ya later, boy."

I said something.

He left, and we went back to our office.

I lay down on my sofa and closed my eyes, but not for long.

Something in the office smelled really good. I got up and followed the smell until I saw Pappa with many humans I'd never seen before. They sat at a desk with small papers in their hands.

I sat next to Pappa, and he gave me some of the food. My human walked in and said, "Pappa, don't give Dudley too much pastrami. I don't want him getting an upset stomach."

Pappa and the other humans didn't say anything. They were eating, smoking cigars, and looking at the papers in their hands. "Alright, you boys have fun with your card game. And don't forget to clean up when lunch is over," my human said.

He walked back to his office, but I stayed with Pappa. *I like him, and I think I can convince him to give me more good-smelling food.* Pappa did give me a little more. When they all left, I went back to my human's office and relaxed on my sofa. "Welcome back, boy. I hope you can get some work done while on your executive sofa," my human said as he laughed.

When I woke up, my human said, "Okay, boy, it's closing time. Let's go home."

I leaped off of the sofa and followed my human, Pappa, and Ross outside. He opened the truck door, and I jumped in. This time, when he stopped the truck at the gate, he turned the truck off. "I'm taking the keys this time, mister. I'm not going to have a repeat of yesterday's fire hydrant adventure. I bet your driver's license has expired, hasn't it?"

I said something and lunged forward to lick his face. He smiled and said, "That's what I thought."

When we got home, Sarge was sitting on a sofa inside. He was holding a book in front of his face, but he reached his hand out and patted my head.

I said something. I only like to be touched by my human and sometimes Pappa and E.D. I followed my human past him.

"How's it going man, han, han?" Sarge said.

"Fine, we're just going upstairs to grab a bite to eat and relax."

"Right on, man, han, han."

When we reached our home, my human gave me some food and water. He sat down on a chair, and just as he did, the telephone on his desk rang. I stopped eating and turned my head sideways to look at it. "Oh, no you don't! You are not getting the telephone again. Forget that!"

I said something.

He got up and talked to the telephone. I could hear his friend Birk talking. I looked around but didn't see him. "Careless, I need a lift. The Cowboy Cadillac won't start, and I'm getting it towed to the shop. Can you meet me there? It's the Ford dealership off Loop 610. I'll catch a ride to the shop with the tow truck driver. And Careless, you are never going to believe this. I have a friend who's a detective in the Houston Police Department, and he just told me that Jake Harm, of Jake Harm and the Holdouts, is missing. He has a concert scheduled at the Hideout tonight, and nobody's seen him in days. Isn't that strange?"

"I think you're strange, Birk. I'll head out to get you now."

"Dudley, I have to go pick up Birk. Stay here. I'll only be gone a few minutes. Okay, boy?"

I said something. It was not okay.

He put some of the things E.D. had brought over on the floor. "Be a good boy." He hugged me and left.

I carefully watched the door for my human. I wanted him to come back. *He probably forgot I'm supposed to go everywhere with him. He must not remember.*

I watched for a while, but my curiosity got the better of me. I nosed all the things my human left on the floor. Some of them smelled like I needed to eat them. I ripped into a paper box. I couldn't help myself. My human left me a lot of good-tasting things. I ripped them all open and ate every last one of them. I couldn't stop. I had no control over myself.

When all the good-smelling things were gone, I felt really tired. I went to bed. I hadn't been sleeping long when I heard and smelled my human walking up to the door. I jumped off the bed and ran to greet him. Before I got there, I found the soft, white thing called Baby. I grabbed it with my mouth and began chewing on it. My human came in. When I turned around to jump on him and lick him, he looked upset. "Holy crap, Dudley, are you okay?"

I looked around to see what was upsetting him, but I didn't see anything. Maybe I was a bad boy. I didn't like being a bad boy. Maybe he still missed his sofa.

I said something, but not very loud. *I must be a bad boy.*

My human started wiping my face with his hand. "Why is your face all green?"

I licked his hand and said something. He still seemed worried. "You don't look so hot. I better call the vet," he said, holding my head with both of his hands. He walked over to his desk and picked up the telephone.

I heard someone say, "Westbury Animal Hospital, how may I help you?"

He spoke quickly. "Yes, is L.D. in? My dog's face is all green, and I don't know what to do."

I heard the telephone say, "Sir, it's after hours. We don't have a vet here right now."

"Well, can I have his number?"

The telephone said, "Maybe I can help you. What seems to be the problem?"

"Dudley's face is all green. I think he may not be getting any circulation to his head."

"Has he eaten anything green?" the telephone asked. My human looked around and picked up the papers I'd shredded when I ate the good-tasting things. He looked at me, laughed, and kissed my head. *I am a good boy now.*

"Thank you. I believe I know what the problem is now," he said to the telephone. He put it back on his desk, and hugged me. "Well, you'll be a big hit at the next Saint Patrick's Day celebration."

CHAPTER 40

I was thirsty after eating all of those good-tasting things. I walked to my water bowl.

"You know boy, you almost drink water like a horse," my human said.

I turned my head, water dripping from my jowls, and said something. Then I went to the bed and jumped up on it. I circled around a few times and lay down. I watched my human as he made one of his good-tasting drinks. He sat down in a chair, and the box with noise and light came on. He watched it, and I was about to close my eyes when the telephone rang. I turned my head sideways. I was going to jump up and investigate when my human turned to me, pointed, and said, "Oh, no, you don't. You stay right there, young man." I stayed, even though I didn't want to.

He walked over and picked up the telephone. He held it to his ear and said, "Ciro's Pizza, may I hava your order please?"

He was talking in a funny way. I heard E.D.'s voice on the telephone.

"How's that mutt of yours? Is he behaving? Did he like the toys I brought him?" she asked.

"I think he may have liked them a little too much. Right now, his face is all green."

"Please tell me you didn't give him the whole box of Greenies at one time. You didn't do that, did you Carwash?"

"No speaky English." He grinned.

"Is he okay? Does he have an upset tummy? Is he comfortable?"

"Well, I think he makes a living," my human said.

"Okay, I'll just come by and check on him tonight before the Jake Harm and the Holdouts concert at the rodeo. I ran into Birk earlier, and he asked me if I wanted to go with you guys. I told him yes because someone needs to keep you out of trouble. I'll be down in forty-five minutes. Get yourself ready to go."

I didn't hear E.D.'s voice after that and my human put the telephone on the desk.

"I can't believe I forgot about the concert. I better go shower up and get ready," my human said.

He walked toward the other room but stopped and looked at the box with noise and light coming from it. "Hey, that's Richard from China Garden. What's he doing on TV? And why is he dressed up as a constable?" He looked at me and said, "Things are beginning to make sense now."

I said something.

He went into the room where water comes from the wall. He put some good-smelling stuff on himself and washed it off. *I like his smell better.* When he finished, he opened a bottle and rubbed something on his face. He saw me watching him, so he called me over. I walked to him and sat. He rubbed his hands on my face and left the good scent on me.

"There you go, Dudley. Now you have some smell good on your face. Women love that Aqua Lavanda. That was Frank Sinatra's favorite. What do you think?"

I said something. Now I couldn't smell anything except the smell good my human rubbed on my face. It overpowered my nose. But it wasn't bad.

I heard someone walking on the other side of the door. I couldn't smell them, but somebody was definitely there. I turned and walked to the door, staring at it so my human would know someone was there. He was getting dressed. He finally looked at me and asked, "Is there someone at the door, boy?"

I said something.

He walked over and opened the door to find E.D. Now I could smell her. She looked at me, and my tail spun around in circles. She bent down and kissed me on my head.

She looked at my human. "What? Nothing to say, smartass?"

My human looked at her and said, "Save a horse, ride a cowboy?"

"Very funny. Let's get a move on. I don't want to be late for the concert. And don't think that I didn't see Dudley's face was all green. I know you gave him too many Greenies."

My human hugged me and looked into my eyes. "Now Dudley, you can't come with us. We'll be back soon, and I'll leave some toys out for you. There's food and water in your bowls. You be a good boy, okay?"

I said something. I wanted to walk out with him when he left, but he told me to stay. So, I did. He closed the door behind them. I turned around and picked up the soft, white thing they call Baby. I put him in the bed, circled around a few times, and lay down with my head on top of him.

I woke up when I heard the truck outside. I jumped out of bed and ran to the window. My human was outside. I could hear him talking. I could see him. My tail spun around in circles. I pressed my nose against the window. My human, E.D., and Sarge walked into the building. I ran to the door and waited.

Why is he taking so long? I could hear them walking up the stairs and talking.

E.D. said, "What do you think happened to Jake Harm? I can't believe they rescheduled the concert for tomorrow! Why do you think he didn't show up?"

My human said, "I think I know what happened to him. We must act quickly if the show is to go on."

"Well, what happened? Where is he?"

"Not just yet. I have a few things I need to take care of. All in good time. All in good time."

I said something. I couldn't wait any longer. I said something again.

"I'll get it out of you, Careless. One way or the other."

I listened as she walked up the stairs.

Sarge said, "Later man, han, han."

The door opened, and my human walked in. I couldn't control myself. I hadn't seen him in what seemed like a long time. My tail spun around. I jumped on him and bent my front legs over his shoulders while licking his face.

E.D. walked up behind my human. He didn't know she was there. I watched her while licking my human. "I just came down for a nightcap," she said, "but I can see you boys are busy." She turned and walked away.

My human looked at me and said, "Foiled again, Dudley."

I said something. Then I continued licking him. He took me outside where I did my business. When I was finished, we walked back to our home. He took out a good-smelling thing and said, "Dudley, you've been a good boy so I have a Greenie for you. Sit!"

I sat and took the Greenie in my mouth. I never let my teeth touch him. I only use my teeth on my prey or when I defend myself. As I ate it, I watched him make his drink. He drank it, took his clothes off, and lay down in our bed.

I finished eating my Greenie and jumped in bed with him. I circled several times to find just the right spot and lay down next to him, resting my head on his chest.

He put his arm around me. "Dudley, tomorrow, we'll find Jake Harm. And I'll need you to help me. What do you think about that, boy?"

I heard my name, so I said something.

"Yeah, we're going to find him alright. I don't know how I made it this long without you, but I'm sure glad I found you!"

In the morning, my human woke up. I watched him carefully until his eyes opened. "Come on Dudley, let's get ready for work."

We went to Pappa's house. Pappa and Ross were there. I walked up and sniffed them. Ross petted me and I said something. Pappa petted me. I didn't say anything. *I like Pappa.*

I sat under the table and waited for food. As always, my human handed me something good. After we finished, we all left. My human and I went in the truck to the office. We met Pappa and Ross there.

CHAPTER 41

I walked into the office with my human. Pappa walked in and sat in his chair. He started smoking a cigar. I followed him. The smoke went up above him. I don't mind the smell, and I like watching the smoke. Then, I went outside to do my business and walk around for a bit.

When I got tired of that, I went back inside to be with my human. He was sitting at his desk holding the telephone next to his ear. I walked over to him and sat. He put his hand on my head. "Detective Present, we'll need at least four or five of your undercover guys at the concert tonight. Birk and I will be there to help. If all goes well, Jake Harm's kidnapper will be revealed. Very good. Then I'll see you tonight. Thank you."

I walked over to my sofa and jumped up on it. My back was itching so I lay down, turned upside down, and wiggled around. It felt good. I decided to stay in that position, but I kept my head pointed at my human so I could see what he was doing.

Ross walked in. "The twenty-four inch beveling machine just broke. It needs to go to the repair shop."

"Well, you want Dudley to run it over there? He can do it, but he's a pretty crappy driver."

My human was happy. Ross was not.

"I was hoping you could do it," Ross said.

"No problem, I'm on it."

"Okay, thanks," Ross said as he left the room. *He moves fast and doesn't stay in one place very long.*

My human stood up and looked at me. "Dudley, I need to go somewhere. You have to stay here and hold down the fort. Can you do that for me, big fella?"

He rubbed my belly. When he walked away, I rolled over and followed him. We walked to where Pappa was. He was sitting in his chair with his eyes closed. I thought he was sleeping, but he made a loud grumbling noise every time he breathed. He had a cigar in his mouth that was still smoking.

My human looked happy and slowly pulled Pappa's cigar from his mouth. He placed it in a round thing on the desk. He looked at me and said, "You have to stay here, boy. I'll be back soon. You be a good boy."

I fell asleep, but shortly after, my nose picked up a mixed scent that caught my attention. I smelled my human and something else that smelled almost as good. I stood up and waited for him. He walked into our office, and my tail spun around in circles.

"How's my sweet boy?" he asked.

I said something.

"Well, since you were such a good boy, I brought you something special. Here's the Class Clown hamburger from Bernie's Burger Bus. It had your name written all over it. I bet it'll be your new favorite."

He took something out of a paper bag and held it in front of my mouth. I couldn't wait any longer. I took it from his hand. I chewed it quickly and swallowed it. *Delicious.*

My human smiled and said, "I knew you'd like that, boy. Don't get used to it. Frankly, I'll probably need to have your cholesterol checked." He patted me on the head and went back to his desk.

Ross walked in and sat on a chair in front of my human's desk. My human was busy and didn't see him. "What are you doing?" Ross asked.

My human seemed startled, so I perked up and came to attention. Dogs can feel what a human is feeling.

"You seem preoccupied today. What's going on?"

"Well, some friends and I went to the Jake Harm and the Holdouts concert last night at the rodeo. It went great until Jake Harm didn't show up to perform. He's just completely vanished. One of Birk's friends, Detective Present, with the police department, told us they were searching for Jake but didn't have any clues. But I figured out he's been kidnapped, and I know who did it. I've been working on a plan with Detective Present to catch the kidnapper and find out what happened to Jake. Can you believe that?"

"Well, why don't you take the rest of the day off? I've got everything under control here," Ross said.

I smelled Pappa's smoking cigar, so I decided to walk over and investigate. He was holding it in his mouth, watching the smoke go up in the air. I decided to join him. I sat by his side, and every time he put the cigar in his mouth, smoke came out and drifted upward.

He put his hand on my head, and I said something. *I like Pappa, and I like watching the cigar smoke go up in the air with him.* As I watched the smoke, I heard and smelled my human coming toward me.

"Pappa, I'm taking the rest of the day off. I'll see you tomorrow." Pappa nodded his head, made more smoke, and waved to my human.

CHAPTER 42

When we got home, I drank a bowl of water.

"I don't know where you learned to drink like that, boy, but you're giving me whiplash just watching you," my human said. I was tired so I went to our bed and lay down. I watched my human as I rested. He made one of those good-smelling drinks and sat down at his desk. He held the telephone to his ear. "Birk, I need you to be on time tonight. Okay?"

I heard Birk say, "Okay, I got this."

"And no need to share this with anyone. Understand?"

"Understood, Careless, understood."

My human put the telephone back on the desk and said, "I know damn good and well he's going to tell everyone about this." A little while later, he changed clothes and walked toward the door.

I hope he doesn't leave me by myself again. I watched him and waited. He looked at me and said, "What are you waiting for? Let's get a move on. I'm going to need you tonight." He slapped his leg with his hand and called me. I leaped off of the bed and ran to him.

We hurried out of our house and down the stairs. I could smell E.D., Birk, and Sarge ahead of us. My human seemed to know they were there before we could see them. *Maybe humans have a good sense of smell, too.*

They were all waiting for us at the bottom of the stairs. All of them leaned against the wall, their arms folded over their chests. I didn't know what they were doing, but I didn't like it. I stepped between them and my human.

"You most certainly didn't think you were going to the concert and trying to solve this mystery without us, did you Clueless?" E.D. asked. They unfolded their arms and stood straight, as if they were going with us. I relaxed my stance.

My human looked at E.D. "Honey, if I didn't want you all here, I wouldn't have told Birk to come alone and to tell no one. Besides, this mystery's already solved. And the name's Careless." He grinned.

We all walked out of our house and climbed into Birk's truck. There wasn't enough room for me in the front seat, so I sat in the back with Sarge. I wanted to sit next to E.D. and my human, but Birk was already there.

I stuck my head through the sunroof even though the truck bounced up and down a lot.

"I got the Cowboy Cadillac back. Good as new. Just needed a new starter," Birk said.

"Birk, do you have to hop over those curbs? It's almost painful," my human said.

"That's the way I roll, son," he said to my human. We drove to a big, round building surrounded by all kinds of lights and smells. I was curious.

The truck stopped at a gate, and a human said to Birk, "Welcome to the Astrodome. Do you have a parking pass?"

Birk showed her a piece of paper, and we moved forward.

When the truck came to a stop, we all got out. We walked past a lot of lights and big, moving things. People were everywhere. But I stayed by my human's side. There were a lot of good-smelling things around me. I turned my head from side to side to take them all in. Water dripped from my mouth.

I hope my human gives me some of this good-smelling stuff to eat.

My human looked at me and said, "Don't worry, Dudley, I'll buy you a turkey leg or maybe a corndog. But first, we have some business to take care of."

I said something.

We strode up to the round building and stood behind a lot of people. They crept forward one by one.

Birk said, "Okay, everyone put on the gold badges I gave you last night. Does everyone have a badge?"

All the other humans answered, "Yes."

My human turned to E.D. "Want me to help you pin your badge on, honey?"

"No, thank you, Careless. I don't think I need to be felt up from the belt up."

Everyone chuckled. The people in front of us continued to move forward.

My human pulled a dark thing from his pocket and placed it on his face. I could no longer see his eyes. He reached down and grabbed my collar. He held it as we walked forward. "It's alright, Dudley. You're a good boy."

I said something. *I am a good boy.*

The human at the front of the line looked at my human. "Sir, no pets allowed." My human didn't look at him.

He looked in another direction and said, "I'll have you know that Dudley isn't a pet. In fact, he's my seeing-eye dog. Would you like to explain why we can't go in to my friends who are all recovering, high-powered attorneys?"

Birk, Sarge, and E.D. all raised their eyebrows. The human silently raised his hand and waved toward the round building. My human lifted his hand and waved in another direction where no one was standing.

I was confused, but we walked forward and into the building. My human said, "Dudley, sit."

I sat.

"Dudley, stay." He and the other humans walked forward. I stayed. It took all my might because I wanted to be at his side.

I stayed for what seemed like a long time. Many people passed by me. Some looked happy and tried to pet me, but I said something and warned them off because I only like certain humans to pet me

I heard a lot of noise ahead, and then some music. Someone said in a loud voice, "Ladies and gentlemen, what you've all been waiting for. One of our very own, please welcome Jake Harm and the Holdouts!"

The noise crescendoed. My ears perked up. I wanted to make sure my human was okay. I waited for him. He would never leave me like Daddy did. My human loves me.

I heard a whistle. I could wait no longer. I was sure my human needed me. I followed the sound until I picked up my human's scent, then I ran at full speed to be with him.

I found him quickly. He was with other humans, some of whom I'd never seen or smelled before. I sat by his side waiting for a command. One human stared at me, a grimace on her face. I didn't like her. A dog can tell when a human is no good. This human was no good.

I'd been running so fast and was so excited to be with my human that water dripped from my jowls. My human put his hand on my head.

I said something and fixed my gaze on the human I didn't like. I wouldn't let her hurt my human. I said something again. I wanted her to know to come no further. A dog will gladly protect his human with his life.

"No, no, moist, keep him away. I hate moist. No moist! Keep him away," the bad human said in a loud voice.

I growled.

Water came from her eyes.

"Young lady, I won't be able to keep my friend, Dudley, away from you for much longer. He doesn't like you, so if you don't tell me what I want to know he will stick his moist face in yours, and I won't be able to control him. Is that what you want?"

"Okay, okay, my name's Sherri. Jake is mine. He only wants to be with me because I love him so much. And he loves me! Only me, and no one else! We're going to get married. You'll see. Moist! I hate moist! Keep that thing away from me," she said. She was looking at me. I didn't like her.

I said something. It scared her.

My human patted my head a few times. I looked up at him and then back at her. "Good boy, Dudley," my human said. *I am a good boy.* "Now, young lady, tell us where Jake Harm is."

"Jake's mine! He loves me. He sang it in his song. I heard it. He loves me, and only me." She crossed her arms.

"That's fine, honey. No problem. I'm just going to turn you over to my friend, here. He's going to want to have a face-to-face conversation with you. You won't mind that, will you?" my human asked.

He lifted his hand off my head and walked toward the bad human. I didn't like this, so I stood up and walked with him. I didn't take my eyes off her. I wouldn't let my human get hurt.

I growled to let her know I meant business. My jowls curled, and water flowed from them.

"No! Moist! Moist! I hate moist! Keep him away! The storage closet in the back of the food court. That's where Jake is. Please make him stop," she begged. *She's afraid of me. She should be.*

My human stopped, and so did I. I sat by his side, watching for her to make a move. Luckily for her, she did not.

Another human walked up and slapped something on her wrist. "I'm Detective Present, and you're under arrest for the kidnapping of Jake Harm. You have the right to remain silent. You have the right to an attorney, and if you don't have one, one will be appointed for you. Do you understand? You'll remain handcuffed to this pole till we get back. And when I get back, we'll be taking a trip downtown."

She said nothing. I didn't like the way she looked at my human.

My human said, "Let's go." He walked away with me by his side. The other humans followed.

As we got further away from the bad human, I heard her shout, "Jake is mine! No one else can have him! He only loves me!"

All of the humans looked at one another with their eyebrows raised. We walked ahead to a place that smelled good. People were making food behind a counter. Water flowed from my jowls.

My human looked at me and smiled. Detective Present pulled a shiny thing from his pocket. He held it up and showed it to the people making food. "HPD."

A human behind the counter said, "How can we help you?"

Detective Present said, "We need to get to that storage closet in the back." He pointed. A human opened the door, and we all walked in. We passed a man holding a hot dog. I snatched it from his hand and wolfed it down. It was good.

He was not happy. My human chuckled.

"Hey, that's seven dollars for the hot dog," the man said.

My human pulled some paper from his pocket and said, "Keep the change." Then he turned to Birk. "He might want to check and make sure all of his digits are still there."

All the humans looked at me and laughed.

CHAPTER 43

We walked to a door in the back of the room, and everyone stopped. My human moved some boxes that blocked our way and opened the door.

"Wow, how, how, how," Sarge said.

E.D. looked at my human. "Jake's not in there."

I looked in the closet. It was empty, but the bad human had been here. I smelled her scent. My human walked into the closet, and everyone followed. At the back of the closet stood two doors.

"Who would put an elevator in a closet?" E.D. asked.

"Judge Roy Hofheinz, that's who," Detective Present said. My human pushed some round things on the wall, but nothing happened. The other humans turned around. I stayed with my human.

"I guess this was a dead end, boy," my human said. He patted me on the head.

I said something.

"Let's go find the others," he said. He began walking away from the two doors, but I heard a noise behind us and turned to look. My human stopped and looked at me. Both of the doors opened to reveal a small, dark room, but I could see there was no one inside.

My human bent down and kissed me on the head. "Good boy, Dudley."

I am a good boy.

He called to the other humans who had walked away. They ran back.

"That's amazing," Birk said.

"Since it's a small elevator, only four people can go up at one time. The first ride up belongs to me, Dudley, Detective Present, and E.D.," my human said.

Birk crossed his arms over his chest. "How come I have to wait?"

"Simple. Dudley and I found the elevator, so we should go first. It's Detective Present's case, so he needs to go. And E.D.'s hot, so there's that. Any more questions?"

"No, that sounds about right," Sarge said.

E.D. smiled. My human was happy.

148

We walked into the small room behind the doors, and my human pushed something on the wall. The bad human had been in here. I smelled her scent.

The doors closed, and it was dark. We began to move upward. I'd never seen anything like this. But then I got distracted because I was standing between my human and E.D. I couldn't help myself, so I pressed my nose against E.D. and sniffed her. She smelled good.

"Careless, that better not be your hand on my backside," E.D. said.

"Honey both my hands are well accounted for."

"That's an understatement."

My human and E.D. both said at the same time, "DUDLEY!"

I said something and backed away. The room stopped moving, and the doors opened.

We stepped into a large, well-lit room. I smelled the bad human and someone else, but I didn't see anyone. The doors closed on the little room, and a few minutes later they opened. Birk and Sarge emerged.

"What in the world is this place?" E.D. asked.

Detective Present said, "This is Judge Roy Hofheinz's private living quarters in the Astrodome."

Birk said, "I always heard rumors about this place, but I never thought it was real."

I walked with the humans as they looked around.

"Where is he?" E.D. asked. "Where is Jake Harm?"

My human pulled something from his pocket and commanded me to sit. I did. He placed something soft in front of my nose. It smelled like the other human I'd smelled a few minutes earlier.

"Go get him, Dudley," my human said.

He wanted me to find someone. *I am Dudley. I can track his scent.*

I said something and began tracking. I walked with my nose in the air and my tail straight behind me. I strode right up to a wall with lots of things on it. The scent didn't stop there. It came from behind the wall. I sat and stared at the wall.

My human said, "I got one of Jake Harm's bandanas from his drummer. He uses them in his concerts. I'm sure Dudley can track him."

CHAPTER 43

My human looked at me, and he knew what I knew. Dogs can sense these things.

Detective Present sighed. He looked at me and my human and said, "I thought you could find the kidnap victim. I don't see him anywhere. I knew this was a bad idea."

My human looked at him and said, "He's here."

All the other humans watched my human. He walked over to me and placed his hand on my head. "Good boy," he said.

I am a good boy. I said something.

"You see, there happens to be a secret room behind this bookcase. Dudley tracked Jake Harm to this very spot," he said while moving several of the things on the wall. The last thing he moved made a loud clicking sound. The wall moved.

I turned my head sideways, waiting to see what would happen. My human swung it wide open. I walked in first. I wanted to make sure it was safe for him, and I smelled the human he wanted me to find. His scent was strong.

There he is. I'd found the human.

Detective Present walked up to him and said, "I'm Detective Present with the Houston Police Department. You're safe now. Hold still, and I'll untie you and take the tape off of your mouth. He pulled something from the other human's mouth.

"Thank God you're here! That crazy little blonde must've drugged me. How long have I been here? What day is it?"

Detective Present said, "Everything's fine. You're safe, and we have the kidnapper in custody." When Jake was untied, he looked at me and started petting me. Normally, I say something, but this time I didn't. *I like Jake.*

My human said, "Yeah, we tricked the kidnapper into showing her hand when we hired a Jake Harm impersonator to play with your band."

Jake nodded, a grin spreading across his face. He looked at my human and said, "Is the concert still going on?"

My human nodded.

"Son, I've got a show to put on. Let's shake a leg." He walked out of the room and toward the elevator.

Detective Present said, "Jake, I need to ask you a few questions."

"We'll talk after the show," Jake said. "My fans are here to see the real deal." He looked at me and my human. "You boys coming, or what?"

My human walked over to him, and I matched him stride for stride.

"And bring that pretty little filly with you." Jake pointed at E.D. She joined us in the small room. The doors closed, and we moved downward. When they opened, we were back in the closet. I smelled the bad human, but when we got back to where we'd left her, she was gone. Everyone stopped walking.

My human picked up a paper. "It says, *I'll get you, my puppy!*" Everyone looked at one another. My human gave the paper to Detective Present, who had walked up behind us.

"Son, let's go," Jake said. "We've got a performance to put on. And since you helped me out, I want you and your boy over there to come backstage and watch the show."

We hurried toward the music. Jake jogged up to some people on a stage, and the music stopped. They all started hugging one another. He picked something up, and the music started again.

"It's a good thing Jake made it back during a break. No one even noticed the real Jake Harm and the Jake Harm impersonator change places," my human said to E.D.

I sat by his side while the music played. *I like the music.* My tail spun around in circles. E.D. and my human looked at me and smiled.

When the music stopped, Jake walked over and said to my human, "Thanks for your help, partner. I won't soon forget it. And you're a good boy, Dudley." He patted me on the head.

I said something. I know he is a good human. He left with his friends.

Detective Present came up and said, "Careless, I don't know how you found Jake Harm, but I sure am grateful. You may want to look into consultant work for the force, if you're interested. Just let me know."

My human said, "Perhaps I will. Thank you." When Detective Present left, my human said, "Come on, let's go home. You're such a good boy, Dudley. And a hero."

I am a good boy.

When we got home, I sat waiting for my human to open the door. E.D. pressed her mouth onto my human's face.

"Thanks for showing a girl a good time," she said when she released him. "And you, Dudley, you will always be my boy!" She bent down and kissed the top of my head. I liked the way she smelled. I stood up, and my tail spun around in circles.

"Want to come in for a nightcap?" my human asked.

"As tempted as I am right now, Careless, I think I'll pass. You keep playing your cards right, and we'll see." She was happy and my human was as well. She walked up the stairs.

My human opened our door, and I walked over to my food and water. I ate my food and drank all the water. I was tired.

"Moist," Careless said. "Moist saved the day, Dudley."

I heard my name, so I said something.

"It's a good thing your mouth is moist." He laughed. I watched him as he made his good-smelling drink. When he went to bed, I jumped up, circled around several times, and lay next to him. My head rested on his chest. He placed his hand on my head and closed his eyes. *This is my favorite time with my human. I love my human.*

CHAPTER 44

The next day, Ross came in and sat on my sofa in my human's office. "Did you find your man?"

"I didn't, but Dudley sure as heck did. I'll tell you all about it later. I have to finish up a few things," my human said. When the day ended, we left.

At our house, I jumped out of the truck and did my business. My human and I walked up the stairs together and into our house. He gave me food and water in my bowls, but I didn't eat or drink. I was preoccupied because I heard something on the other side of the door. I smelled E.D., Sarge, and Birk. I walked over to the door and stared at it.

"Dudley, what are you doing? Go eat your food. You know, somewhere, a dog is starving in China," he said.

I didn't take my eyes off the door.

"Open up, Careless, we know you're in there," E.D. said from behind the door. My tail spun around in circles. My human opened the door. Birk and Sarge were holding a sofa like the one my human and I used to sit on, before I shredded it. They carried it in and put it where the other one used to be.

My human looked confused. E.D. brought something else in. I didn't know what it was. I walked over to the sofa and smelled it. There were many scents on it, most of which I'd never smelled before. I did smell Detective Present on it. He'd definitely been on this sofa. I looked at my human.

He pointed his finger at me and said, "No, Dudley, this one is not a chew toy." I sat on the sofa and watched him. Sarge took the thing from E.D. and put it next to my human's desk.

My human walked over and sat on the sofa next to me. I immediately stood up and repositioned myself so there was no space between us. I knew my human liked this because he looked happy, and it gave him a place to rest his hand.

"Where on earth did you guys get this lovely sofa?"

"Oh, it's not from us, Careless," Birk said. "I told Detective Present about the demise of your sofa. He's had this sofa for twenty years in his house

153

and his wife thought it was the ugliest thing she had ever set eyes on. So, I thought it'd be perfect for you. Besides, she was going to make him haul it to the dump, so I did him a favor and hauled it to you instead. He wanted you to have it for helping solve the case."

"Well, free is my décor," my human said.

Everyone laughed.

"What's under the blanket," my human asked while pointing at the thing Sarge had left next to the desk.

"We'll tell you what's under the blanket if you tell us how you solved the case," E.D. said.

My human grinned, stood up, and walked over to make another one of his good-smelling drinks. "I'll be happy to tell you how I found Jake Harm. I found my first clue when I visited with you at the downtown library, E.D. Do you remember that?"

E.D. nodded.

My human said, "One of the photographs in your exhibit caught my attention. It was of the Astrodome. There was one small detail I couldn't reconcile in my mind. The top of the Astrodome is made up of many small windows to let light in. All of the windows reflected the sunlight exactly the same way in your photograph, except for one. One was slightly darker than the others. That led me to believe there was something different behind that window."

He took a drink. "My next clue was when you, Dudley, and I ate at China Garden restaurant, Birk. Do you remember that?" he asked.

"Yes," Birk said.

"I saw Richard talking to a strange-looking, bearded man in front of the restaurant. He looked familiar to me, but it wasn't until later that I realized the man talking to Richard was actually Jake Harm. I remembered that Richard was also a constable and concluded Jake probably went to Richard for help—and possibly some Lemon Chicken."

Everyone laughed, so I said something. They laughed even more.

"My next clue was when we all went to the Jake Harm and the Holdouts concert at the Hideout. Everyone was streaming in and excited to see Jake Harm and the Holdouts perform except for one person. I noticed a young blonde woman fighting against the crowd to get out. Now, why would she be leaving if the sold-out concert was just about to start? She obviously knew something no one else did. She knew Jake wasn't going to be at that concert. There was no reason for her to remain. I suspected then that she was our kidnapper. E.D., do you remember when I took you to dinner at Lucio's?" he asked.

E.D. smiled at him. "I sure do."

"That night, the doorman mistook me for Damian Mandola, a local restaurateur. It got me thinking about how everyone probably has someone who looks like them, so I hired a Jake Harm impersonator to fill in at the concert."

"Is that why we got such special treatment at the restaurant?" she asked.

"Indeed it is, E.D. I probably shouldn't have told you that," he said, smiling.

"Detective Present and the Holdouts were in on the plan. I wagered that her curiosity would get the better of her, and it did. She showed up. There were too many people at the concert for her to get to Jake without being discovered. She was waiting until it ended to go see him. Anyway, I figured out the last clue at my office. Dudley nabbed a roll of toilet paper and took it through his doggie door. He brought it outside where he shredded it."

I heard my name, so I said something.

"That's right, Dudley, without you, we would have never found Jake Harm. Dudley left a toilet paper trail leading to the outside. Had the doggie door not been transparent, it would have looked like the trail stopped right there. In the Astrodome, Dudley led us to the bookcase, and that's where it appeared the trail ended. I recalled Dudley's toilet paper caper and noticed a very small circular wear pattern in the carpet. Almost as if the bookcase opened outward. That's when I realized there was a secret room behind the bookcase," he said.

He drank more of the good-smelling stuff. Quiet settled on the room.

E.D. stood up and walked over to the thing next to the desk. I watched her. She pulled at something, and it fell to the ground. Underneath was a big thing.

"Careless, we bought this file cabinet for you to keep track of your cases. We want you to take more cases, and if you don't include us, there's going to be trouble. Do I make myself clear?" she said.

"Roger that," he said. He walked over to the file cabinet and took something from his desk. He pressed it against the file cabinet and said, "I think I'll label it, *The Dudley Files*. That has a nice ring to it. Doesn't it, boy?"

I said something, and my tail spun around in circles.

CHAPTER 45

Everyone left, and my human and I went to sleep in our bed. We went to Pappa's and the pipe yard almost every day after that. It was our routine. At the office one day, my human walked over to Ross and Pappa and said, "I'd like a few days off next week. I want to go to Mexico to see if I can find a girl named Maria. I met her at the bookstore several months ago, and she invited me to come find her in Mexico."

Ross and Pappa looked at one another, and Pappa said, "Go ahead."

That night at our house, my human picked up the telephone. I heard E.D. talking, but I didn't see or smell her.

"Can you come over?" he said. "I need to ask you something." He put the telephone back on the desk. "You don't mind staying with E.D. for a couple of days, do you, Dudley?" he asked.

I heard my name, so I said something. Then E.D. came to the door. I could smell her. I ran to the door and waited. My tail spun around in circles. When my human opened the door, E.D. kissed me on my head and walked in.

"So, what do you want to ask me?" she said.

"I'm thinking about going to Mexico for a couple of days, and Dudley really needs a place to stay. He seems to love you, so I was wondering if you wouldn't mind taking care of him."

"Of course I'll take care of my big boy. It will be fun, won't it, Dudley?" I said something.

"Great, can I drop him off in the morning? I have an early flight," he said.

"See you in the morning, Dudley. Why are you going to Mexico?"

"Oh, I'm working on a new case," he said.

She said, "Okay," and left.

"Don't worry, Dudley, you'll be fine. I'll be back soon. I sure am going to miss you."

I went to sleep in our bed with him, my head resting on his chest and his hand resting on my head. In the morning, my human got dressed and took me outside to do my business. When I was finished, I walked to the truck just as I do every morning. This time my human called me back, and I went to him. We walked up the stairs, past our home, and stopped at a different door. He made a noise on a door with his hand. E.D. opened it, and I wandered in.

"All his food, treats, and bowls are at my place. I really appreciate you taking care of him," he said.

"No problem, Careless, you know I love him. Have a great trip." He bent down and grabbed my head with both of his hands. He held my face next to his. I licked his face.

"I'm going to miss you, boy. I love you. Don't worry, I'll be back soon." He kissed me on the head. Then he stood up and left. I tried to follow him, but E.D. closed the door before I could get out. I was confused. The last time someone left me was when Daddy took me to the woods and dropped me off. I hoped my human wasn't doing that.

I stayed with E.D. and stared at the door. *I love her but I must be with my human.* I waited at the door for him to come back. She walked to the window and called me. I didn't want to leave the door because I was sure he'd be coming back.

"Come on, Dudley. Come wave goodbye to Careless."

I heard my human's name, so I walked to her. I saw him next to his truck. He looked at me and waved. I pressed my nose against the glass so I could smell him. But I couldn't. I said something, but he didn't hear me. He got in his truck, and I said something again.

He must have forgotten that I was supposed to always ride with him in the truck. He left as I waited by the window. I went to E.D.'s sofa, sat, and waited. My human would never leave me. *I will wait for his return. I am a dog. That's what we do. We wait for the return of our humans.*

E.D. sat next to me and rubbed my ears. That made me feel better. But still, I waited. "Don't you worry, Dudley. He'll be back in a couple of days. You and I will have a lot of fun."

I sighed and rested my head in her lap. Then I closed my eyes and waited. She got up from the sofa, and I heard her moving around. I opened one eye and watched her. She put on different clothes. "Oh, I see you're awake, sleepy-head. I'm going to get your bowls, food, and treats. Want to go with me?" I stood up and walked by her side as we went to our home.

I looked all over for him. His scent was strong, but he wasn't there. E.D.

gathered up some things and said, "Let's go, Dudley." I went to the sofa and waited for my human. E.D. called me again. "I've got a treat for you, Dudley. How about a nice Greenie?"

She made a noise with a bag, and that caught my attention. I could smell she had something good. I am a dog, and I can be bought off with treats. I leaped from the sofa and joined her. I walked by her side until we got to her home. She gave me the treat. It was good, but it didn't last long. She put food and water down for me and even had my favorite toy–Baby!

"Now Dudley, I have a meeting I have to go to. I have to leave you for a little while, and I want you to behave. You will behave, won't you, boy?"

I said something and walked to her. She kissed me on the head and left. I heard her going down the stairs and closing the front door. Then I went to the window and watched her leave. For a long time, I waited there, watching for my human. He didn't come, and I got bored. I ate my food and drank my water. I picked up Baby in my mouth and sat on the sofa with him. I lay down and put my head on Baby. I waited some more.

Finally, I heard footsteps walking toward the door. It was *E.D.* I could smell her. I left Baby on the sofa and ran to the door.

"Hi, big boy," she said as she opened the door. My tail spun around in circles. "Were you a good boy? Let me check," she said.

She walked around and looked at everything. I followed at her side. "Okay, you were a good boy. Here's a treat."

I am a good boy. And I get a treat.

She reached in her pocket and pulled out something that smelled good. I ate it, and it tasted good. "I've got another surprise for you. Today we're going to the dog park," she said. "Are you ready?"

I followed her to her car and jumped in when she opened the door. Not long after, she stopped in front of a place where a lot of dogs were running and playing together. I'd never seen anything like this. When she opened the door, I jumped out and walked by her side as we entered a gate. She looked at me and said, "Go ahead, Dudley. Go have fun with your brothers and sisters."

I ran ahead, and as soon as I did, a lot of dogs fell in behind me and followed. I turned, and they turned. I sped up, and so did they. I even jumped in some water. I looked back at E.D., and she was happy. She waved at me and smiled. I finally got tired and lay down with the rest of my new friends.

E.D. was talking with several humans I'd never seen before. When she saw me lying down, she called me. I ran to her side.

"Okay, it looks like you've had enough for one day. Let's go home," she said.

When we got to her home, I drank my water and went to her bed to go to sleep. I watched her as she went into the room where water comes from the wall. When she dried off and put some clothes on, she got into bed with me. "Move your big butt over, Dudley," she said.

I stood up, circled around, and came to rest with my head on her chest. She laughed and put her arm around me. We went to sleep.

In the morning, she woke up and fed me. She let me outside to do my business, and when we got back to her home, she said, "Let's call your boy, Careless, and see how he's doing in Mexico. What do you say, Dudley?"

I said something.

"Good, then that's what we'll do." She picked up the telephone. I could hear it making noises.

The noised stopped, and I heard someone say, "Bueno!" It was my human. My tail spun around in circles.

"Careless, is that you?"

"Si, zees is Carlos. How may I assist you?"

"Your homeboy wants to talk to you. So wake up and start talking sweet nothings into his ear. It'll make him feel better," she said.

I decided that was a good moment to hump her leg. She pursed her lips. "Stop humping my leg, you serial thriller, and talk to your partner."

I heard my human laughing and stopped humping her leg. E.D. held the telephone next to my head. "Hey, big boy. I miss you so much. You're such a good boy. I'll be home soon," he said.

I said something, and E.D. looked happy. My tail spun around in circles.

E.D. put the telephone next to her head and said, "When are you coming back? I don't mind taking care of Dudley. In fact, I kind of enjoy having him here, when he's not trying to hump my leg."

I heard my name, so I said something. I also licked E.D.'s face. That made her happy. "It's just that he's missing you, Careless. I take him out back and let him run around, but it seems like he's always looking for you. He's just not the same when you're not here. There's no accounting for taste." She chuckled.

"Put Dudley back on the phone."

She held the telephone next to my ear, and my human said, "You behave, boy. E.D. will take good care of you. I love you, Dudley."

He stopped talking, and E.D. took the telephone away.

I said something. *I miss my human.*

"Goodbye, Careless."

My human said, "I'll see you soon."

E.D. put the phone down on a table. *I love E.D., but she is not my human.*

CHAPTER 46

That night I went to sleep with E.D. When she got into the bed, I circled around a few times and lay right next to her. She kissed me on the head and said, "Goodnight, Dudley. Don't worry. Careless will be back tomorrow." She closed her eyes and went to sleep. She didn't rest her hand on me like my human did every night. I pressed my body against her and went to sleep.

In the morning, I heard my human's truck. My ears perked up. I couldn't smell him, but I knew that sound. I opened both eyes and jumped off the bed.

E.D. woke up and said, "What's the matter, boy? Do you need to go outside?"

I didn't say anything this time. I ran as fast as I could to the window. He was there! He was outside. He climbed out of his truck. I pressed my nose against the window to see if I could get his scent. He must have been too far away because I couldn't smell him.

My tail spun around. I finally said something. He looked at me. Our eyes locked. He waved. I said something again. He walked toward the front door of the building. I ran to E.D.'s door and said something. I kept saying something until E.D. got out of bed.

"Okay, boy, you need to go outside? Let's go." She opened the door, and I bolted down the stairs. E.D. ran after me, but I'm much faster than she is. I wanted to be with my human. I stopped at the door. It was closed. E.D. finally caught up to me, and I pawed the door to let her know my human was outside and I wanted to join him.

"Okay, boy, here you go." She started to open the door, but I couldn't wait. I hit it with my two front paws, and it flung open. I bolted to him. Just before I reached him, I jumped into the air and landed on him. He fell down on his back, and I was on top of him. I licked his face. *My human is my favorite smell.*

He tried to push me away, but I used my muscles to stay on top of him.

"Dudley, save room for Jesus."

I heard my name, so I said something. Then I resumed licking him.

"Are you two going to take a break, or shall I come back later?" E.D. asked as she strolled up.

"I sure missed you, boy," my human said. He squeezed out from under me and stood up. He walked toward E.D. and held his arms out.

"You know, Careless, I'm not sure I want to hug you after what I just witnessed. I mean, really, it's just unnatural," she said.

A feeling just came over me right then. I was just so happy to see my human, but I couldn't control myself. I walked over to E.D. and humped her leg.

"Careless, I trained him up nicely while you were away. You're back, and in less than a minute he's already reverted to his obnoxious ways."

"Dudley, stop that right now," my human commanded. I stopped.

"Get your bromance over with, get cleaned up, and then call me so we can catch up," she said. She turned and walked away.

I looked at my human, and he was happy. "Come on boy, let's go home." I did my business and followed him back to our home. We walked inside the building together, and Sarge was sitting on the lobby sofa, holding something up to his face.

"Hey Sarge, is that a good book?" my human asked.

Sarge pulled the book down from his face and said, "Hey, man, han, han. It's good to see you." He patted me on my head. I said something. I wasn't going to bite him. It was just a warning.

"Sarge, I missed you," my human said.

"Did you go somewhere, man, han, han?"

"Yeah, Sarge, I was in Mejico. And I brought a little something back for you." My human pulled something out of his bag and held it up.

Sarge looked happy and said, "Wow, how, how, man! What a cool tie-dye t-shirt. Thank you."

My human gave it to him and said, "I found it in a nice little coffee shop called The Core. Wear it in good health."

We walked back to our home, and when my human opened the door, I went to my bowl and drank water. I smelled E.D. She must have brought my bowls back from her home.

My human laughed. When I looked back at him, he was watching me. "Dudley, you are the funniest dog I have ever seen," he said.

It was great to be back in our home. I had fun with E.D., but I liked my home better. It smelled like my human. It also smelled like me. He put food in my bowl, and I ate it. He also made one of his good-smelling drinks. "Ah yes, there's nothing like a good Careless Coffee after a long trip. Good till the last drop."

He walked to the sofa and sat down. I walked over and plopped next to him. Right next to him. He wore something around his neck. I'd never noticed that before. *Do humans wear collars like dogs?*

It smelled like someone I didn't know. He placed his hand on my head and said, "My friend Maria gave it to me. It's a key. At first I thought it was the key to her heart. But her heart belongs to someone else. Just like my heart belongs to you. I'm just so thankful you didn't eat the sofa like you did the last time I left."

I said something. I liked it when he rested his hand on my head. We sat on the sofa together for a while. I could sit with him all day.

He dozed off for a minute and started talking in his sleep. "I missed you boy. Let's ride, Eagle."

He stopped talking, and I watched him until he woke up. He looked at me and said, "Morning Sunshine." He tried to get out of my grip, but I didn't let him. The harder he pushed me away, the harder I pushed back. And I can push hard.

"Dudley, my eyes are starting to float," he said. He finally got away from me, went into the little room, and did his business. Then he got dressed in some different clothes, and we went outside.

I ran around and did my business. I smelled everything. There had been other dogs here, but I didn't see them. When I was finished, my human called to me. I said something, ran to him, and sat by his side. He placed his hand on my head.

I smelled Sarge behind us and heard his footsteps. My human didn't. I turned and waited. I finally saw him, and he said, "Hey man, han, han, any chance you'd give me a lift to the zoo?"

"Well, Sarge, we were just on our way out to get something to eat."

Sarge said, "Perfect, can you help a brother out? I volunteer there on Saturdays."

My human said, "Okay Sarge, let me just go park Dudley upstairs, and I'll give you a ride to the zoo."

I heard my name, so I said something. I walked back to our home with my human. When we were inside, the telephone began making noises. I found this curious, so I turned my head sideways.

"Dudley, don't you dare . . ."

But I couldn't help myself this time. I snatched the telephone up in my mouth. I said something, and I heard Birk talking from it. "Dudley, give me the phone right now," my human commanded.

I turned my head and opened my mouth, and it flew into the air. He caught it and said, "You really must work on your phone skills, boy." He smiled at me.

He put the telephone next to his head and said, "House of Pies, may I take your order?"

I heard Birk say, "That's really funny, Careless. I know you're back in town. You want to grab some lunch? I can come pick you up?"

My human said, "Okay, Birk, but first we have to drop Sarge off at the zoo. Is that okay with you?"

"No, but I'll do it anyway. And you're buying. I'll be there in five minutes."

"Come on, boy, it looks like we're going to lunch," he said. My human and I walked downstairs to meet Sarge. "Okay Sarge, Birk is on the way, and we'll take you to the zoo."

Sarge grinned and said, "Thanks man, han, han." We all walked outside. Birk's truck was already there.

"Dammit, Careless, do you always have to bring that animal with you everywhere you go?" Birk asked.

"I feel like that's a trick question," my human said.

Sarge said, "I'm not an animal. I'm a person."

CHAPTER 47

I stuck my head out the sunroof. *This is my favorite spot.* When we came to a stop, I smelled all kinds of animals. Most of them I'd never smelled before. Sarge said, "Hey man, han, han, have you been on the Hermann Park train since they redid it?"

My human and Birk looked at one another. Then they looked at me.

I said something just as my human and Birk both said, "No."

"Oh, man, you've got to ride on the train. Now it's longer than before and even nicer. Come on, I'll ride it with you." My human and Birk exchanged glances.

"Sarge, don't you have to go to the zoo? You don't want to be late," my human said.

"It's a volunteer job, man, han, han. What are they going to do, fire me?"

"He does have a point," Birk said. My human looked at Birk with an annoyed expression on his face.

Sarge said, "Come on man, han, han. It'll be fun."

My human said, "Sarge, you've done me a lot of favors. Let's go ride the train."

"You won't be sorry man, han, han."

My human looked at Birk and said in a quiet voice, "I already am." Sarge didn't hear it, but I did.

We got out of the truck and walked up to a small building. I followed by their sides. An older, unhappy-looking woman was seated inside the small building.

"Four tickets, please." My human held up his hand with four fingers sticking up.

The woman scowled. "Four tickets? I only see three of you. Why do you need four tickets?"

My human pulled something dark from his pocket and put it on his face. They covered his eyes. "Ma'am, Dudley's a service dog. I need him to ride the train with me."

She looked at him. Then she looked at me, standing by his side.

He put his hand on my shoulder.

"Read the sign. No animals allowed on the train." She pointed.

"Well, I wasn't going to bring my friend Birk on the train." He gestured at Birk.

Birk rolled his eyes. "That's really funny, Careless. Ha ha ha."

The woman said, "I'm sorry sir, I don't make the rules. Your dog can't ride the train. Next in line!"

My human said, "Okay, we'll have three tickets please."

He pulled some papers from his pocket and gave them to her. She handed him some smaller papers.

We walked away, and everyone stopped by a fence. A loud sound blared. I turned my head sideways and looked for the thing making the sound. Then I heard another sound.

My human said, "That's the train, Dudley."

The train pulled up with a lot of people on it. When it stopped, the people got off of it. My human bent down and looked at me. "Dudley, stay!"

I said something, but I sat and stayed. *I am a dog and must listen to my human.*

The humans waiting in line hurried to the train and got on. My human sat at the very back. Sarge went to the same spot and my human said, "Sorry this seat is taken."

Sarge briskly walked to another place on the train and sat down. The train started making that noise again, and I watched as it pulled away with my human.

I said something.

I could no longer see the train, but I heard it and smelled it. I had to stay because my human had commanded me. Then I heard something. My human called me. He needed me.

I jumped up and followed the train at full speed. My nose led me right to it. It was in a dark place. I caught up to it.

I am Dudley, and I run fast.

My human patted the seat with his hand. He wanted me to sit next to him. I jumped onto the train and scrambled up to him. He put his arm around me, and I licked his face.

The train emerged from the darkness, surrounded by trees. "Did you like the tunnel, Dudley? I know you did. Maybe we should call it the tunnel of love," my human said.

I saw some water. Ducks waddled next to it. I wanted to shred and eat them, but I stayed with my human.

I picked up E.D.'s scent. She was somewhere nearby. Then I heard her say something behind us. She was walking between the trees. My human heard her as well. We both turned our heads. She was holding something up to her face and smiling.

"Oh, great," my human said. "Now she's got a picture of me with my arm around you on the train. I'll never hear the end of this."

I licked his face. E.D. still had the thing in front of her face. She lowered it, laughing.

When the train stopped, my human asked me, "How'd you like the train ride?"

I said something. I did like it.

I jumped off the train, and my human followed. The human in the building looked at us and pursed her lips. My human waved.

Sarge walked up and said, "Thanks, man, han, han."

He walked away toward the place where all of the animal smells were coming from.

E.D. came up to us. "Now, why am I not surprised that you and your mangy mutt are acting like newlyweds on a honeymoon train trip through Europe? And you better stop Dudley from creeping over here and humping my leg. Or the next thing you'll see is my backside leaving you both standing here."

I understood she didn't want me to have my way with her leg, so I stopped and sat in front of her. She kissed me on my head and rubbed my ears.

"So, what are you doing out here, E.D.?" my human asked.

"I'm on assignment for a morning TV show called Positively Houston. What are you doing here? On a love connection with your boy there?"

"Not that there's anything wrong with that, but no. We just decided to take Sarge on a train ride. Because that's the way we roll. Right, boy?"

I heard the word roll, so I rolled over. When I got back up, I said something.

All the humans laughed. I didn't know why.

"E.D., we're going for lunch now. Would you care to join us?" Birk asked.

"Sorry, boys, I have to finish up my assignment. It's due today."

My human waved. "Okay, we'll see you later."

She pointed at me. "Are you sure you'll be able to break yourself away from your true love?"

"Honey, don't you worry. I've got plenty of love to go around."

"Great!" she said. "We'll be taking Dudley to the dog park today. Your friend could use some socialization skills." She pointed at me again, so I, of course, said something.

"Sounds good. Stop by later. We'll get Dudley socialized."

"Maybe while we're there, you'll get practice, too." She grinned.

We returned to Birk's truck. My human opened the door, and I jumped in.

As Birk drove the truck, he said. "You know, Dudley has a better shot with E.D. than you do."

"I may just wear her down with my boyish charm."

Birk looked at my human and chuckled. "Yeah, like that's going to happen. Where do you want to have lunch?"

"Keep your eyes on the road. Let's just go to Kenny & Ziggy's. Best deli in the city."

"I'll fly if you buy."

My human shrugged. "Whatever. I can't *remember* the last time you bought."

Birk was driving fast, and I poked my head out the sunroof. I could smell everything. And some people waved to me when we passed them. And we passed everyone.

CHAPTER 48

The truck stopped, and my human turned around to look at me and pat my head. "Dudley, you wait in the truck."

I said something. *I don't want to stay.*

"We'll be right back, and if you behave, I'll bring you a doggie bag."

I said something again and sat down.

Birk and my human left. I stood up and watched them with my head sticking out of the sunroof. My human looked back at me for a moment. I thought he was going to call me, but he didn't. He saw me watching him and waved.

I said something. I wanted to let him know I was watching him and that I was ready to protect him. He entered a building with Birk.

I stayed vigilant, standing with my head sticking out of the truck. I smelled and watched many humans pass by. Finally, my human came back with Birk. My tail spun around in circles.

As my human approached the truck, I smelled something good. When he got in, I pushed my body up against him and licked him. The smell wafted up from inside a bag he was holding. My jowls watered. "Don't worry, boy, I brought you a doggie bag. A doggie bag for my number one doggie," he said.

I said something.

Birk scowled. "Careless, your mutt is goobering all over my truck."

My human laughed and said, "Spit happens."

I licked him.

When we got home, Birk stopped the truck. "I'll send you the cleaning bill, Careless."

"Just put it on my tab." My human and I both said something at the same time. Birk was not happy.

Before we went inside, I did my business. My human said, "Good boy, Dudley." *I am a good boy.*

We walked inside and up the stairs. I smelled E.D.'s scent further up ahead. My human didn't smell her yet. I waited for her. I heard her walking toward us. "Come on boy, let's go," my human said.

E.D. came around the corner. "There's my boy! Come give Mamma a hug. And I said hug, not *hump*. I know your tricks."

She walked over, bent down, and hugged me. She was the only human I liked almost as much as my own. She smelled almost as good.

"Careless, it's time for Dudley to work on his socialization skills. And we'll work on yours as well." She nudged him. "Dudley likes a nice dog park I took him to while you were in Mexico. By the way, you never did tell me about that case. And I *will* want to hear all about it. But that can wait. Right now, I'm ready to go. And so is Dudley."

"Great idea, E.D. But first, I need to feed Dudley this half of a Swiss & Shout sandwich from Kenny & Ziggy's. It was too big for a person to finish, and since, technically, Dudley is not a person, I'm going to let him give it a try. Or are you a person, Dudley? Sometimes, I wonder."

I responded by saying something.

We walked into our home with E.D., and my human opened something that smelled good. He put it in my bowl, and I wolfed it down. It tasted as good as it smelled.

My human said, "Who's driving?"

"I'll drive, Careless. I think Dudley will be much happier in the back seat of my car than that old hunk of junk you call the Power Wagon. Besides, I've seen your driving, and it's nothing to write home about."

CHAPTER 49

When we reached the dog park, I pressed my body up against the car door. It didn't open. My human and E.D. got out of the car, and she said, "I sure hope he behaves himself, but that's probably too much to ask."

My human said, "He'll be fine, don't worry."

She opened my door. "I wasn't talking about Dudley. I was talking to Dudley about you." She smiled. So did my human.

I jumped out of the car and ran to the gate to join the other dogs. My tail spun around in circles.

My human opened the gate, and as I ran ahead, other dogs fell in behind me. *I am Dudley, the leader of the pack.*

I ran into the water, and the others followed. When I stopped, they stopped. Sometimes we wrestled. We liked to grab one another with our mouths. It helps us remember that we're part of a pack.

When I got tired, I lay down. The other dogs wandered off. Except one. A large yellow female lay down next to me. I sniffed her, and she sniffed me. When I got up, she followed me.

I like her. Sometimes I do things I can't help. This was one of those times. I started humping her. She didn't like it, and she let me know.

Just as I was about to stop, a human ran over and shouted, "Scout, stop that right now!" She looked at me, then at my human. "Can you control your dog, please?" Scout turned and snapped at my jowls. I stopped what I was doing.

E.D. looked at my human and said, "Do something."

"I didn't answer her because I thought it was a trick question," my human said.

E.D. crossed her arms.

My human said, "I'm sorry, Suzie. I must apologize for my overactive friend. Sometimes he has a mind of his own."

"Do I know you?" she asked.

"Yes, we met on an airplane trip from Cozumel. I sat next to you and your family."

"Of course. I'm sorry. I've had a lot on my mind lately." She reached out and shook my human's hand. I found this curious.

When they stopped, Suzie reached her hand out to E.D. "Hi, I'm Suzie."

"My name's E.D., and I'm sorry for the way Dudley acted. I blame it on his owner, who has not trained him well."

They both looked at my human, who didn't look happy. I walked off, and Scout followed me.

As I walked away, I heard E.D. say, "You know, Careless recently solved a big kidnapping case involving a country singer named Jake Harm. It was in all the newspapers."

Scout and I walked around in a big circle that led right back to our humans. When we were close to them, I heard my human say, "Of course I'll help you. Let me know when you're available to give me the details. My trusty sidekick and I will take your case. I warn you, however, you may not like what we find."

"How'd you know something was wrong? I don't remember telling you anything," Suzie said.

E.D. looked at my human. "You don't even know if she needs help?"

My human said, "Your great-uncle was recently called home, and there's a mystery surrounding his estate. You have great concerns. Isn't that right, Suzie?"

E.D. and Suzie looked strangely at my human. Suzie nodded. "Oh my gosh! That's exactly right. He did just recently pass away. And no one seems to know anything about his estate, or anything else for that matter. I just find it odd that no one's told anyone about anything. We received an email from one of my sisters while we were on vacation in Mexico with the kids. Once we learned he was deceased, we cut our trip short and came home. I met you on the plane ride back. Since then, I've reached out to her and my other sisters and brother. I've only heard back from my brother, and he doesn't know anything either. It just doesn't feel right."

My human nodded.

"Are you sure you want to help us after hearing all of that?" she asked.

"Of course he'll help you. Won't you, Careless?" E.D. asked.

"You bet. Dudley and I will get to the bottom of it." My human extended his hand to Suzie. This time, instead of shaking his hand, she hugged him. I wasn't okay with this, so I moved closer and said something.

My human looked at me. "It's okay, boy." So I sat by his side.

She backed away from him.

"Right now, we're going to take Dudley home and rest up. He's had a busy day," my human said. He pulled a paper from his pocket and gave it to Suzie. "Here's my card. Call me tomorrow, and we'll set up a meeting." My human started to walk away, but Suzie hugged him again. Water streamed from her eyes.

Before I walked away with my human and E.D., Scout sniffed me and licked my muzzle. After that, she sat by her human's side. *I like the dog park, and I like Scout.*

My human opened the door of E.D.'s car, and I jumped in. I was tired from all the running, so I lay down. E.D. looked at my human. "You know, it would've been nice if you'd opened my door for me before you opened Dudley's for him."

"I'm sorry, honey, age before beauty."

This made her happy, and I said something.

E.D. drove us home.

CHAPTER 50

When we got to our home, I did my business outside. E.D. and my human walked together.

"Careless, how on earth did you know Suzie needed help? How did you know what kind of trouble she was having? Are you some kind of stalker?"

"Just keen intuition, my dear."

She shrugged. "Well, I don't know whether to be scared or impressed."

He grinned. "Perhaps both."

She rolled her eyes. "You will tell me what I want to know. And don't even think about taking this case without my help. Let's face it, you need all the help you can get." My human was happy.

I walked up the stairs to our home with E.D. and my human. E.D. bent down and kissed me on my head. Then she rubbed my ears. She always made me feel good. My tail spun around in circles.

She stood up, and my human raised both of his arms and held them out toward her for a hug. She grinned and shook one of his hands.

He pouted. "You're not going to leave me hanging are you?"

She smiled. "You will tell me everything. Men are weak. You'll spill the beans." She walked up the stairs to her home. My human stood there with his arms outstretched. I guess he was waiting for me to hug him. So, I did.

Later, my human joined me on the sofa. "Dudley, you're watching entirely too much TV, young man. Don't forget to turn it off when you're finished."

I said something as I stood up to reposition myself to be as close to him as I could. I pressed my body up against him, and he put his arm around me.

"I guess I could have told E.D. that Suzie probably didn't remember telling me on the plane about her great-uncle passing away, but where would the fun be in that? What do you think?" my human asked.

I said something and licked him.

"Okay, time for bed. Let's go." He tried to push me away, but I stiffened my legs and pushed against him even harder. He finally got away from me and walked over to his bed and lay down. I followed him and jumped up in the bed. I circled around several times to find the most comfortable spot.

I placed my head on my human's chest. He rested his hand on my head. He was happy. "Now, let's say our prayers, Dudley. Repeat after me. Now I lay me down to sleep. I pray Jack Daniels is my favorite drink. If I die before I wake, I'll miss Dudley, for goodness sake."

I said something.

"Amen, Dudley."

When my human closed his eyes, I closed mine and went to sleep. I dreamed of my mother, Juna. I'll always remember her. I dreamed of Heidi and how nice she was to me. And Red, my horse friend. The whole time I slept, I felt my human's touch. So, I knew he was always there. And every time I woke up, he was.

I woke up before he did, but I didn't move. When he woke up, he looked right at me. "Good boy, Dudley. You are a good boy."

I am a good boy. I said something. He patted my head and slipped out of the bed. I didn't make it easy for him. My favorite place is next to him. He walked into the small room where he does his business and went into the small space where water came from the wall. It sprayed him. I watched him closely. I stuck my head in with him and got wet.

Later that morning at the office, I smelled someone I'd never smelled before. I was laying on my sofa when I heard footsteps. A large man walked toward my human. The hair on my back raised up, and I said something.

"It's okay, boy, it's just Big Kenny," my human said. I quieted down but watched intently. Big Kenny sat in a chair in front of my human's desk. "Big Kenny, how many years have you been driving for me?"

"'Bout ten years, Mr. Careless."

"I got a call from the refinery where you made a delivery this morning. They told me they found a bottle of Jack Daniels and a naked woman in the sleeper cab of your truck. Now, what makes you think that's all right?"

Big Kenny's eyes widened. "Well, Mr. Careless, I know I screwed up. I'm sorry," he said.

My human rubbed his temples. "Big Kenny, you know I love you, but I can't have my truck drivers doing things like this. I'm going to let you off with a warning this time, but you are on probation. Do I make myself clear?"

He nodded. "Yessir, it won't happen again."

"Next time, Dudley may have some words with you. Right, boy?"

I said something.

Big Kenny tightened his jaw. He left, and I watched him the whole way.

That afternoon, I smelled something tasty. The human named Hammer walked in. "I have a cheeseburger I picked up for Dudley at lunch. We wouldn't want him to go hungry." He smiled and put the cheeseburger on the floor. I scarfed it down. Hammer and my human grinned. I licked my chops.

The telephone made a noise, and when my human talked to it, I heard Scout barking. "Tonight would be fine, Suzie. Do you mind if I bring my sidekick, Dudley, with me? Super. We'll see you then."

He put the telephone down and looked at some papers on his desk. When it was time to go home, we left the office. My human gave me food at our home and made one of his good-smelling drinks. When we finished, he said, "Okay, boy, I'm going to visit Suzie, and you can visit Scout—as long as you promise to behave yourself. Do I have your word?"

I heard my name, so I said something.

"Okay then," he said.

I walked out with my human and jumped in his truck when he opened the door. We drove away, and when we stopped, I could smell Scout. I knew she was nearby. As soon as I jumped out of the truck, my tail began spinning around in circles. I heard her barking.

Then I saw her sitting behind a window in a house. My human didn't hear her. We walked up, and Suzie opened the door. Scout ran out and sniffed me. I did the same to her and said something. Then I followed her into the house.

Susie clasped her hands. "Thanks for coming, Careless. We didn't have anyone else to turn to. Come inside. We're about to eat dinner. Why don't you join us? I insist."

My human said, "Well, if you insist. Thank you."

I roamed around the house with Scout and found two small humans. She walked up to them and sat down. I did the same. One of the small humans hugged her. The other hugged me. I liked the small humans. A dog can tell when a human is nice.

"Zach, Sam, Jack, time for dinner," said Suzie.

The two small humans dashed to another room. Scout followed them, and I followed Scout. My human was sitting down at a table with Suzie. Another human walked over and sat down.

Suzie said to my human, "This is my husband, Zach. And these are my guys, Sam and Jack." They waved at my human.

My human nodded. "Pleased to meet you." Scout walked under the table and sat down, just like I did at Pappa's house. I followed and sat next to her.

"Tonight we'll be having the house favorite—Hawaiian chicken. I just took it out of the oven," Suzie said.

My human took a bite. "Honey, this is delicious. You should start your own restaurant."

Suzie, Zach, Sam, and Jack smiled when my human said that.

"So, I noticed some beautiful art in your house. Are you guys collectors?" my human asked.

Zach said, "Actually, I made most of the artwork in the house. I'm a graphic artist and sculptor."

Suzie touched Zach's arm. "Zach's being modest—he designs floats for most of the New York parades and some parades in New Orleans and Galveston."

The small humans' hands began creeping toward me and Scout. They had good-smelling food in them. Scout and I gently took the food from their hands.

"So, tell me what the problem is and how you want me to help?" my human said.

Suzie sighed. "I'm not sure you'll be able to help us. I've never been through anything like this before, and I'm really confused."

Zach cleared his throat. "Are you two boys finished with dinner?"

They both said, "Yes."

Zach nodded. "Why don't you clear your plates, get a cookie, and go upstairs and play? When I finish here, I'll come up and you'll both get *the claw!*"

They squealed and took the good-smelling food to another room.

"I'm sorry, I just have to ask—what is *the claw?*" my human asked.

"Oh, it's just a little game I play with them. I make my hand into the shape of a claw and then tickle them while saying *the claw.* My father used to do it to me. It's a lot of fun." Zach chuckled.

Suzie said, "My mother and father died in a car accident ten years ago.

We don't have much family. I have two sisters, Burtha and Wanda, and a brother, Chuck. We were very close with our great-uncle. His name was Ike Swift. He and his wife, Linda, never had children."

My human looked very interested. "You mean Ike Swift, the local World War II hero? I remember reading newspaper articles about him. Wasn't his nickname Smoke Swirl Swift?"

Suzie nodded. "Yes, that was him. He was pretty famous around here. He believed in hard work and discipline. He also believed in helping others in need. My sister, Burtha, said she was taking care of his affairs. She followed him around like his shadow and rarely let him out of her sight.

"When his health worsened, she didn't want to take care of him anymore. The rest of the family pitched in and helped out, but she always stayed just close enough to manage his affairs, especially when others were around. We stayed in contact until Ike passed away."

My human furrowed his eyebrows.

"After that, she dropped everyone in the family like a hot potato. She won't return phone calls. We do know she's still going to his house because when we pass by, her car is there." She frowned.

My human said, "I find this intriguing. I'll need as much information as you can provide. Does that sound okay?"

"Sure." She tapped her hands together. "Ike's wife, Linda, passed away several years ago from Alzheimer's. During that time, Ike complained that things were going missing from the house. Burtha told everyone that Ike was imagining things. We had no reason to doubt her.

"When Linda was still alive, she walked me around her house and told me she wanted me to have a mosaic art piece after she was gone. It was an image of a fruit bowl. She told me Burtha was taking everything in the house and she specifically told Burtha this was for me and not to take it. I thanked her and thought it was a nice gesture. She also told me I was their favorite niece. I don't think they made a secret of that, either. We visited pretty often, but Burtha always managed to know when we were there and made her way over. She never wanted anyone to be alone with them."

She wrung her hands. "I knew there was a problem when Uncle Ike's longtime housekeeper spotted Wanda's husband, Dick, leaving with Uncle Ike's gun collection after he passed. He had an extensive gun collection, some that he brought back from his World War II tour of duty in Europe. The housekeeper was concerned because Uncle Ike never liked Dick. Dick was somewhat like Burtha–never really held down a job. And Uncle Ike promised those rifles and pistols to Zach. Zach was the only family member who ever showed an interest in them. In fact, Zach would visit Uncle Ike almost every weekend. They'd clean and oil the guns together. I think Uncle Ike really enjoyed that," Suzie said.

My human narrowed his eyes in thought. "So, you became suspicious there was something funny going on with your uncle's estate the day he was called home, is that correct?" my human asked.

She nodded.

"And then your brother-in-law, whom your uncle despised, made off with some guns that weren't meant to go to him?"

She nodded again.

"And many items in your uncle's house went missing when your sister was present? And your sister refuses to return your phone calls?" My human leaned back in his chair.

She nodded again and said, "Well, neither Burtha nor Wanda will return phone calls now."

"I've heard enough. It's very clear to me what's going on. Dudley and I will take it from here. Now, we must leave. We'll contact you shortly. By the way, I'll need your uncle's address. And do you happen to have a key to his house? And by chance, did he have an alarm? If so, do you know the code?" my human said.

"I do have a key, and I'll email you the address and alarm code." She took something from her pocket and gave it to my human. "Thank you for helping us. There's one more thing. We don't have much money. I know we never talked about your fee . . ."

"It's our pleasure, Suzie. We'll work something out for my fee. Don't you worry about that. If you think of anything else, please let me know. Let's go, Dudley. We have a lot of work to do."

I heard my name, so I said something.

"Hold on, Careless, I want to send you and Dudley home with a Hawaiian chicken doggie bag," Suzie said. She walked away, and when she came back, she handed something to my human that smelled good. Scout smelled it as well. Her nose twitched. So did mine. Suzie hugged my human.

I said something. I was a little jealous. Scout said something too.

My human patted my head. "Come on, boy. Let's go."

He began walking, and I joined him.

Scout walked over to me and licked my snout. She was my mate. Dogs like to have a mate. Then she wandered over to Suzie and sat by her side. As my human and I left, Suzie and Scout watched us from the window.

CHAPTER 51

I rested my head on my human's leg as he drove. "What do you think, boy? You think we can solve this one?"

I said something.

"That's what I think, too. I know that, with your help, we can get this done," he said. We got to our home and walked in. Sarge was there.

My human said, "Hey Sarge, what's the word, Thunderbird?"

Sarge looked up and petted me.

I said something to let him know I belong only to my human.

"Hey man," Sarge said.

"I may need your help with a new case. Can you help a brother out?"

Sarge grinned. "Right on, man. You can count on me."

I followed my human into our home. He made one of his good-smelling drinks, and I sat on the sofa waiting for him to join me. But he didn't join me on the sofa like he normally did.

He walked over to his desk and pushed a button on the telephone. A voice came from it, "Hey, Careless, it's Rod. I have a bit of a problem out here. My prized miniature donkey Eddie has gone missing. I can't find him, and I've looked everywhere. I'm really worried about him, and Chico's been down in the dumps since Eddie's been gone."

I was confused. I heard someone talking, but no one was there. I didn't even smell anyone. I turned my head sideways. My human pushed something on the telephone again.

"Don't worry, Dudley. It's just my friend Rod. He lives on a ranch with his pet donkey, Eddie. His dog, Chico, is unhappy because his friend, Eddie, is gone. Let's listen to the rest of it," my human said.

I said something.

He pushed the button again and Rod said, "I know you and Dudley have solved some mysteries, and you told me he can track anything."

I heard my name. I said something. My human smiled.

"I was wondering if you wouldn't mind driving down to help us find

Eddie. There have been several mountain lion sightings. And if cubs are around, well, that always makes me nervous. Can you help me out? Call me," Rod said.

I still didn't see anyone. The voice stopped talking.

"Well, it looks like we might be going to the Texas Hill Country, Dudley. What do you think about that?" my human said.

I said something.

He drank his good-smelling drink and went to his bed. As always, I joined him.

I woke up later and watched him until his eyes opened. He was happy when he saw me. He got out of bed and did his business in the little room. Then he got dressed, and we left our home.

Just like always, he drove me to Pappa's to eat breakfast. After everyone ate, we left. I followed my human, and he drove his truck to the pipe yard.

When we got there, I went outside. When I came back in, Pappa was smoking a cigar. I sat with him until he fell asleep. Then I went into my human's office. He was talking to the telephone.

I lay down on my sofa and watched him. He looked at me and put the telephone down with a smile on his face. "I'm glad you're here, Dudley. You've been with us for a while now. I'm thinking of promoting you to CFO. That's Chief Fido Officer. Of course, that will come with a pay raise and benefits. What do you think?"

I said something.

"Perfect. I'll alert the media you've accepted," he said.

The telephone made a noise, and my human picked it up and held it to his head. "What? You have to be kidding. He did what? Alright. Thank you," he said.

Ross walked in. "What happened? I heard you on the phone."

My human shook his head. "Shorty, the truck driver, delivered a load of pipe to NASA but forgot it's a government agency. He also forgot to leave his concealed handgun at home and was taken into custody."

"Good lord. What an idiot," Ross said. "How did it turn out?"

My human tapped his fingers on the desk. "Well, they held him in a jail cell for a couple of hours, took his gun away, and turned him loose. He's also banned from entering NASA ever again. Would you mind having a little chat with him about his job security when he gets back?"

Ross nodded. "I got this."

"I may have another case to solve in the Texas Hill County. Would you and Pappa be okay with me taking a few days off? My friend's pet donkey's gone missing, and they're worried about him," my human said.

Pappa walked in, yawning. Ross looked at him, and they both nodded.

Pappa said, "Go solve the case. But when you get back, we want to hear all about it."

My human pointed at Pappa. "You got it."

Pappa and Ross left, and my human said, "It looks like we're going on a Texas Hill Country adventure, boy. It should prove interesting."

I said something.

He pushed some buttons on the telephone and put it next to his head. "Birk, I need to go on a little adventure tomorrow. Are you in? You have to do what? Can't it wait? Okay, I'll have to solve this one without you. Sorry, buddy."

He pushed the telephone again and said, "Sarge, are you busy tomorrow? Dammit! Okay, I'll talk to you later."

When he pushed the telephone for the third time, he said, "E.D., I have another case. How about you, me, and Dudley head down to the country and take care of business? Yeah? Terrific! We'll drive down tomorrow. I'll fill you in when I get back tonight."

He put the telephone down and looked at me. "Looks like it's you, me, and a beautiful blonde, Dudley," he said.

I said something.

He picked the telephone back up and pushed it. "Rod? How's it hanging? Guess what? We're coming down tomorrow, and we're going to find Eddie. It's going to be me, Dudley, and our friend, E.D. Sure, I can pick something up for you and bring it to the ranch. Just email me the details. No problem. We'll see you tomorrow."

We left the office, and I jumped into the truck. When we got home, my human gave me food and water. He ate something and made his good-smelling drink. I took my food and nosed it around on the ground.

"Dudley, quit playing with your food. Somewhere a dog in China is starving . . . if he hasn't been eaten yet," he said.

I said something and ate my food. The telephone made a noise, and I turned my head sideways.

I trotted over to investigate it, but my human said, "Oh no you don't. I'll get the telephone. Just until you work on your phone skills." He smiled.

I returned to my food.

I heard E.D.'s voice coming from the telephone. My ears perked up. My human said, "We'll leave at seven. Let's try to miss the traffic. No, I won't be late. You can't wait to see Dudley? Got it. See you tomorrow."

CHAPTER 52

When my human woke up the next morning, he went straight into the little room to do his business. I followed him. Being curious, I stared at him, and he said, "No weiner!"

I didn't know that command, but I said something. *I'm sure I will learn it.* He got dressed and gave me food and water. I saw him take several things and put them in a bag. I cocked my head. "I'm just packing some things we'll need for the trip. Finish your food so we can get going."

I said something and finished eating.

He opened the door, and we walked out together. I heard someone jogging down the stairs. It was E.D. I smelled her.

My tail spun around in circles.

"I knew you'd be waiting for me, Dudley. I wasn't so sure about you, Careless," she said.

I walked to her and sat in front of her. She hugged me and kissed my head. *She is my second-favorite human.*

"Who's my good boy?" she asked me.

I said something.

"Well, let's go, boys. Careless, be a dear and take my bags down to the truck." She handed some bags to my human. He took them, and we walked outside. I did my business, and then he opened the door, and I jumped into the truck. I sat in my seat and waited for them.

My human looked happy. E.D. did not.

"Move your butt, mutt," she commanded.

I jumped into the back seat. E.D. sat in my seat and closed the door.

"E.D., we have to make one stop before we hit the road," my human said.

"Where are we going?"

"My friend wants me to pick up a wooden Indian and bring it to his ranch. It's only a few minutes out of the way. We're just going to throw him in the back of the truck and keep on going," he said.

He drove to a building, and we all got out. We walked in and found a woman waiting for us.

"You must be Careless. I'm Anne, and I can't thank you enough for coming to pick up Kaw-Liga. I've wrapped him up in a tarp to keep him safe for transport. Rod's doing me a big favor by taking him," she said.

My human furrowed his brow. "What do mean?"

She leaned toward him. "Well, I think Kaw-Liga is a stalker. His eyes always seem to follow me. One morning, I forgot he was in the antique shop, and when I came in and turned the lights on, he gave me such a fright! Sometimes I'm in the shop by myself and forget he's there. It scares me when I glance over at him. He just looks so darn real. I almost called the police once. My nerves can't handle it anymore. He's made of solid teak wood, so you'll need a dolly and some help to get him in your truck."

I smelled Kaw-Liga. It smelled like a tree. My human and E.D. put it in the truck. There was still room for me. My human started talking in a strange voice, *"On the commode again, I just can't wait to get on the commode again . . ."*

E.D. groaned. "What the hell are you singing?"

"What, you don't like Willie Nelson? Who doesn't like Willie Nelson? That's un-American."

"Shut up and drive, Careless."

I went to sleep.

I felt the truck slowing down, so I opened my eyes. I heard a sound coming from behind us. A car with flashing lights was parked there. I watched but remained quiet, and the truck stopped moving.

E.D. said, "Way to go, lead-foot."

A human with a hat and something dark over his eyes got out of the car and walked to the truck.

My human said, "Good morning, officer."

The officer said, "License and registration please."

My human gave him some papers from his pocket. I stuck my head out the window.

The officer smiled. "That's a fine-looking dog you have there. Everything appears to be in order. I'm going to give you a warning this time, but I want you to slow it down."

My human nodded. "Yessir, officer, I sure will. Thank you."

The officer patted me on the head and gave back the papers.

I said something.

The officer walked away but stopped at the back of the truck. He looked in the window at Kaw-Liga and narrowed his eyes. He rested his hand on something on his hip and walked back to my human. "Sir, what do you have in the back of your truck?"

"Oh, don't worry about that. It's nothing," my human said.

The officer raised his eyebrows. "Sir, I'm going to have to ask you to step out of the truck and open the tailgate for me," he said.

He stepped back with his hand on his hip. My human got out of the truck. I followed him.

"It's just a wooden Indian I'm hauling up to my friend's ranch," my human said.

"Sir, open the tailgate and take the tarp off the item in your truck for me," the officer said, his voice low.

My human pulled something off Kaw-Liga.

The officer looked at it and said, "Sir, you do realize it looks like a wrapped-up body in the back of your truck? You need to be a little more careful." He took his hand off of his hip. "Drive safely."

He strode back to his car, and my human closed the tailgate. I did my business and jumped back in the truck.

E.D. sighed. "Next time, I'll drive."

My human said, "Yes, dear."

She said, "Just start driving before you make me really angry." I went to sleep. Traveling in the truck for a long time always makes me tired.

I woke up when the truck starting jumping up and down. "We're almost there. Rod's house is just over this hill," my human said.

The smell was different here. I smelled all kinds of animals and another dog. It smelled like the place Daddy left me by myself. My human would never do that.

When the truck stopped, my human opened the door, and I jumped out. He opened E.D.'s door for her, too. We walked away together, and a big dog and his human came up to us.

I smelled the dog. He watched me, and I watched him. I wasn't sure about him. I licked his nose to show him I was friendly. We both relaxed. His human hugged my human.

"Rod, this is my friend, E.D., and you already know about Dudley," my human said. He pointed his finger at E.D. and then me.

"Pleased to meet you. This is my boy, Chico. Careless, you didn't tell me how beautiful your friend is," Rod said.

"Oh, I thought I sent you pictures of Dudley. You didn't get them?" my human asked while smiling.

"Well, finally someone with some class," E.D. said as she frowned at my human.

Rod hugged her. Then he patted my head.

I said something.

Chico said something as well.

"Did you have any trouble picking up Kaw-Liga?" Rod asked.

E.D. scowled. "He damn near got us arrested! That wooden Indian looks just like a dead body when wrapped up in a tarp. When that state trooper stopped old lead-foot here, he thought there was a dead body in the back of the truck." Rod burst out laughing.

My human didn't say anything. Neither did I.

"Come on, let's get Kaw-Liga inside. Then I'll tell you his story," Rod said. My human opened the truck, and he and Rod carried Kaw-Liga into a house. Chico and I followed. My human and Rod put down Kaw-Liga next to another tree-smelling thing and unwrapped it.

"Wow, you have two wooden Indians right next to one another. Pretty sweet, Rod," E.D. said.

Chico lay down on something soft that smelled like an animal. I followed suit.

"Well, let me tell you the story of Kaw-Liga. Legend has it that Kaw-Liga was a wooden Indian made from a knotty pine tree. As he stood in the doorway of a shop, he fell in love with a wooden Indian maiden in an antique store close by. They could see one another, but he never let her know his true feelings. One day, someone purchased the wooden Indian maiden and took her away. But Kaw-Liga stayed, as lonely as can be. He was so lonely he wished he was still a tree. But now Kaw-Liga can stand right next to his Indian maiden. In fact, I wouldn't be surprised if they end up holding hands," Rod said.

E.D. laughed. "That's a silly legend."

"Hank Williams didn't think so. He wrote the song, *Kaw-Liga*, and it was a popular hit."

"They do look happy together," my human said.

Everyone sat on a sofa. I stayed with Chico and watched for my human to give me a command. "That's a heartwarming tall tale, Rod. What I really want to hear about is Eddie. Give me all the details," my human said. He stood up and walked to another part of the room. He made one of his good-smelling drinks.

"Well, I purchased Eddie several years ago from a farmer who didn't want him anymore. It was the best eight-five bucks I ever spent. Chico just loves that little donkey. Two days ago, Eddie went missing. We haven't seen him since. I'm very worried, Careless," Rod said.

"No problem. I'll get our things out of the truck, and we'll get busy," my human said. He walked outside, and I followed him. He hauled some bags out of the truck and returned to the house. I stayed by his side.

"Okay Rod, do you have anything that smells like Eddie?" my human asked.

Rod nodded. "I have an old blanket that we sometimes wrap him in during the wintertime to keep him warm. Will that work?"

"That'll do," my human said.

Rod went outside, and we all followed him into a house that smelled like animals. He picked something up and gave it to my human. I was curious, so I walked to him and smelled it. It smelled almost like Red, the horse from Daddy's farm.

"Good boy, Dudley. Go get him," my human commanded.

He wanted me to find the horse. *I am Dudley. I can track him.*

I lifted my snout into the air and picked up his scent. I left the house following his smell. Chico walked next to me, and the humans trailed behind.

"Good boy, Dudley. Good boy," my human said. *I am a good boy.* I walked up to a tree and sniffed it. The horse had been here. I stopped. His scent was strong here.

Rod said, "This is an old pistache tree Eddie scratches his back on. You can still see some of his coat stuck to the bark."

My human said, "Well, we're on the right track. Go get him, Dudley."

I began to trot. I smelled his tracks. I stopped and looked at my human.

"There's your problem, Rod. Someone cut your fence down. I'm sure that's where Eddie got out," my human said.

"I can't believe I missed this. Who would do such a thing? I'll get my ranch foreman to mend the fence when we get back. Let's move on," Rod said.

"Go get him, boy," my human commanded. I walked forward and up a hill.

"I can't believe Eddie climbed this hill," Rod said.

I smelled something I'd smelled a long time ago. It was the same smell of the animal that tried to kill me when Daddy left me in the woods. Chico didn't smell it yet. The hair on my back went straight up. The animal was near. I didn't hear it, but I could smell it. I was ready for it.

I will kill it this time. I am bigger and stronger now.

My human patted my head. "What's wrong boy?" I didn't look at him. I stared at some bushes.

"Stop!" Rod said.

He bent down and looked at something on the ground. "We've stumbled into a mountain lion den. Everyone walk slowly backwards and we'll circle around this area." The humans walked backwards. I remained and guarded them.

"Come on boy, let's go," my human commanded. I did not want to go. I wanted to kill the animal. I snarled, and water dripped from my jowls. "Dudley! Let's go now."

I had to obey him, but I didn't want to. I slowly walked backwards, watching the bushes where the animal was hiding. I joined the humans where the animal smell was not as strong.

"We were probably being watched by a mountain lion. I found some fresh scat on the ground up there. We were lucky. They're fierce, especially when they have cubs," Rod said.

E.D. frowned.

"Good boy, Dudley. You protected us," my human said.

He rubbed my ears.

I said something.

"Okay, go get him, boy," my human said.

I began tracking the horse again. I led my human away from the animal in the bushes but still followed the scent of the horse. I walked downward, and the smell of the horse got stronger. I trotted ahead. I was getting close.

The land flattened out, and I knew the horse was up ahead. I saw a house and smelled a human. I stood still. The horse my human wanted me to find was right in front of me. He was with bigger horses. I stared right at him. Chico was next to me but didn't know what to do. The humans caught up with us. "There he is! There's Eddie! Dudley, you good boy, you found him," Rob said.

"Good boy, Dudley," my human said.

I walked ahead and into a building. There was a human moving some things around. She bent over with her back turned toward us.

I said something.

She stopped what she was doing and stood straight up. She still had her back turned.

I said something again.

She turned around. She didn't look happy. "What on earth are you doing in here, dog? Where did you come from?"

She had the same color hair as me. I said something and walked over to her. I don't know what happened, but something made me grab her leg with my front two legs, and I made a noise I normally don't make. My eyes rolled in the back of my head, and I humped her leg. "What the hell!" she exclaimed.

She shook her leg so fast and hard, I forgot what I was doing and let go. She banged her hand against the building and said, "Git going."

I ran back to my human and sat by his side. I was probably a bad boy.

She walked out and saw us. "Is this your dog?"

"Good afternoon. My name's Careless. These are my friends E.D. and Rob. I believe you've already met Dudley. I'm sorry if he bothered you," my human said.

"No bother, but he did just hump my leg."

E.D. softly slapped my human's arm. "Chalk another one up to your serial thriller," she said with her eyebrows raised.

Rod laughed.

"I'm Shelley O'Neal. I work at this ranch camp for boys and girls. I'm the head wrangler. What can I do for you good folks?"

"Well, we were looking for Eddie, my donkey. He's right over there," Rod said. He pointed at Eddie. Rod made a funny sound with his mouth, and Eddie walked over to him. Chico and Eddie smelled one another. I smelled Eddie, too.

"He just showed up a couple of days ago. The children started feeding him, and he stuck around. They didn't know his name, so they call him Jewford. The kids really love him," Shelley said.

"Thank you so much for taking care of him. We all really miss him. I'll come pick him up tomorrow with my trailer if that's okay. I live just over that hill at Highland Ranch," Rod said.

"Oh, you live just past Echo Hill? Would you folks like a ride back? It's a long way, and I've got plenty of room in my truck," she said.

"We'd love a ride back," E.D. said. The humans walked to a truck and got in. I followed, and so did Chico. I sat between Shelley and my human.

"And about that little incident with Dudley," my human said.

"That's alright. If he has another episode, he's most likely gonna wind up with a boot in his ass," she said.

"Well, nobody wants that. Especially Dudley." They both laughed.

The truck got bumpy, and we made it to Rod's house. The humans got out, and Chico and I followed. "Goodbye," said Shelley. "See you tomorrow, Rod." She drove away in her truck.

Another human walked up to us. I stood between the newcomer and my human.

"Emitt, I need to get our fence mended," Rod said.

"Already done, Mr. Keith. I found the damaged fence just after you left. A neighbor of yours, Mrs. DeSoto, decided she didn't like your fence and took it down. I called the Sheriff. She won't be bothering you again, Mr. Keith," Emitt said.

Rod nodded. "Thank you, Emitt."

"Well, I guess you and Dudley solved another case, Careless. I can't thank you enough. Dudley sure does have a keen nose," Rod said. The humans returned to the house, and Chico and I followed. "Here's your reward, Dudley—a nice big antler horn," Rod said. He gave me and Chico each a hard thing that smelled good. We took them outside and chewed on them. The humans stayed inside.

When Chico and I finished chewing the antler horns, we walked inside and lay down. I was tired. The humans were sitting at a table and eating. My human got up and gave us food and water. Chico ate his right away, but I took my time.

When the humans finished eating, they went to different rooms with beds. My human took his clothes off and lay in bed. I joined him.

I woke up the next morning and waited for my human to awaken. When he saw me, he was happy. He got out of the bed. I tried to stop him, but he slipped away. He went to a little room to do his business. After that, he went into a smaller room where water came from the wall. I could see right through the door. I pressed my nose against it to see if I could smell him. The water made it hard for me to pick up his scent, but I did.

When the water stopped flowing from the wall, he tried to open the door. "Dudley, you need to move so I can get out."

I moved.

He opened the door and stepped out. I watched him. He looked at me and said, "No weiner! No weiner! Sit!"

I said something as I sat. I waited for his next command. He wrapped himself in something, and that's when I smelled E.D. I stood up, and my tail spun around in circles. I couldn't help it.

"Sheesh, do you guys do *everything* together?" She walked into the room.

"I feel like that's a trick question. Who wants to know?" my human asked with a chuckle.

She pursed her lips. "Certainly not me. Now, if you two bozos don't mind giving a girl some privacy, I'd like to take a shower."

"Do you need any help? It's really no bother," my human said. He grinned. She did not.

"That won't be necessary. Now, both of you run along." She waved at us. My human walked away, and I followed him. He put his clothes on and went outside, where we found Rod and Chico.

"Morning, Sunshine. How'd you and your soul mate sleep?" Rod asked.

"Just fine, Rod. Nothing wrong with being spooned by your soul mate, right Dudley?" my human said.

I said something. I walked over to Chico and sniffed him. Then I sat and watched my human for a while. Soon, I heard and smelled E.D. coming toward us. She carried three cups of good-smelling stuff like my human always drinks. It was a little different, but it was still the good-smelling stuff.

"Thanks for the coffee, E.D.," my human said. When they finished drinking the coffee, my human clapped his hands once. "Rod, we're going to need to shove off. I've got a lot of work to catch up on, and I have what I think will end up being a big case. I'm so glad we were able to find Eddie."

Rod nodded. "About that, Careless. I've thought more about Eddie. It seems like he really likes it at the camp. The kids love him, too. I think I'm going to let him live his life out as Jewford and bring joy to the boys and girls at the camp. Chico and I will go visit him regularly. What do you think about that?"

My human smiled. "I think it's a grand idea."

"Okay, then. It's settled. Eddie is now Jewford. I'll send you a check for your expenses, Careless. And sorry about that mishap with Kaw-Liga." Rod grinned.

My human stood and walked into the house. He picked up some bags and put them in the truck.

"Let's hit the road, E.D.," he said. She hugged Rod. My human shook Rod's hand, and I licked Chico's snout.

"Did you have a good time, boy?" my human asked.

I said something. I did have a good time.

He and E.D. climbed in the truck, and I followed them.

My human opened the window, and I smelled many animals and trees on the bumpy way down. "*On the commode again, I just can't wait to get on the commode again . . .*" my human sang.

"Shut up, and turn on the radio," E.D. snapped. He pushed something, and music filled the truck.

"Hey, listen, it's Jake Harm and the Holdouts' new hit single, "Wild Turkey at Sunrise." Isn't this a great song?" my human asked.

I said something. I like music.

E.D. said, "This is one of my favorites." When the truck was not bumpy anymore, I lay down and closed my eyes. I listened to my human and E.D.

"Careless, you sure know how to show a girl a good time. You know, if you didn't have such a silly name, I'd almost consider dating you."

CHAPTER 53

We made it back home. It smelled a lot different than the ranch. I liked it better at home. My human stopped the truck and said, "E.D., I hate to leave you, but since it's still early, and I've missed a lot of work, I think I'm going to drive to the office. Thanks for coming. We couldn't have solved the case without you."

"Oh, I highly doubt that. But thanks for letting me tag along." She picked up some bags, jumped out of the truck, and walked into our home.

"One day, Dudley, I'm going to tell her how much I love her. One day. Now, let's go to work."

When we walked into the office, Pappa was smoking a cigar. The smoke was curling up toward the ceiling. He looked at me, and my tail spun around in circles. He was happy. I sat by him, and my human went to his office.

When Pappa fell asleep, I went outside to do my business. After I finished, I went to my human's office and lay down on my sofa. A while later, Pappa and Ross walked in together.

"So, tell us how the case ended up," Ross said.

"Well, Dudley tracked down the donkey. He escaped through a fence a bad neighbor had pulled down. We almost got eaten by a mountain lion. The donkey was at a camp with other horses and boys and girls who loved him. When my friend, Rod, saw how happy he was there, he decided to let him stay. Case closed," he said.

Pappa smiled. "That's amazing. Now, get back to work."

My human stayed at his desk the rest of the day. He spoke to the telephone several times. Once I heard him say, "Sarge, I've got a job for you. Will you meet me at the loft at seven o'clock? Great, see you then." A minute later, he said, "Birk, I need your help tonight at seven. Can you help a brother out? Terrific, I'll see you then." I watched him for a while. Then I went to sleep. But I listened to him while my eyes were closed.

When it got quiet, everyone left the office, and we drove home. Once we got inside, my human gave me food and water. While I ate, he made one of his good-smelling drinks. He sat on the sofa, and when I finished eating, I joined him. Just as I got comfortable with my head on his shoulder, I heard two humans behind the door.

Sarge and Birk. I jumped over the back of the sofa and stared at the door, waiting for a sound.

I said something.

My human stood up and said, "Good boy, Dudley."

Someone knocked on the door.

My human opened it. Sarge and Birk walked in. "Come in, gentlemen. Have a seat," my human said.

They lowered themselves onto the sofa. I stayed next to my human, who was walking back and forth.

"I met a family on my flight back from Cozumel. The mother's great-uncle, Ike Swift, was recently called home. He was a local World War II hero."

Sarge said, "You mean Smoke Swirl Swift? Wow, man, I remember reading newspaper articles about him."

My human nodded. "That's the one. My clients are concerned because, since his passing, two of her sisters no longer talk to any family members. It's as if they've just disappeared. My clients just want to make sure their aunt and uncle's wishes are respected. Also, certain family heirlooms were promised to certain family members. Everyone in the family is aware of this. So, they want to make sure everything ends up in the right place."

Sarge and Birk stared at my human.

"Gentlemen, we need to get inside Ike Swift's house and inside Suzie's sister's mind. Her name's Burtha, and she seems to be controlling everything. I feel certain I already know what's going on, but we need to find out for sure. Do either of you have any ideas?" my human asked.

It was quiet. Sarge and Birk looked up into the air, searching for something like Pappa does when he watches the smoke rise from his cigars.

My human watched them. "Okay, I have an idea. What if you two pretend to work for the alarm company that monitors his house and say you're checking the alarm system, when in reality, you'll be nosing around? How does that grab you?"

Sarge and Birk stopped looking up and nodded.

"I hate to ask a stupid question," Birk said, "but how do we know the house has an alarm?"

"There are no stupid questions," my human said. "The house has an alarm system. It was installed and is monitored by Home Lock Security. And I happen to have the key to the house. Although, if I guess correctly, it will not be useful to us."

Birk nodded.

My human clasped his hands. "Here's what's going to happen. You'll call Suzie's sister, Burtha. Tell her there's trouble reported in one of the alarm zones and that it'll need to be repaired. Make an appointment with her, dress up as Home Lock Security repairmen, and meet her at the house. Sarge, I'll need you to remember the alarm code when she deactivates it so we can enter it later on. Both of you will walk around the house and pretend to check the alarm contacts, but you'll really be checking things out. Are you with me so far?"

They stared at him.

"There's a problem," Birk said. "Caller ID. When we call Burtha, she'll know right away we're not with Home Lock Security. What are we going to do about that?"

My human picked up a paper on his desk and handed it to Birk. "Great question. Here's the address of Home Lock Security. It's not far from here. Written below that is Ike's address and telephone number. I want you to pretend your car broke down. Walk in to the Home Lock Security office. Then ask to use the telephone to call a tow truck. You must be convincing. Most of these offices have telephones in their lobbies. Birk, once you have access to their telephone, I want you to call Burtha. She'll be at Ike's house. Make the appointment just as described. Sarge, while he's doing that, I need you to distract the receptionist so she doesn't hear what Birk's doing. Talk to her about books or pretend to become violently ill. That shouldn't be hard for you. I want you both to shave, wear khaki knit shirts, black slacks, and nice shoes. Are you with me?"

"You got it, Careless. We can do this," Birk said.

"Terrific, make the appointment, and call me when it's done. Okay, Dudley and I need to eat dinner and go to sleep. We've had a long day. I'm counting on you both."

CHAPTER 54

When my human woke up, he slipped away from me and went to the little room to do his business. He got dressed and walked outside. I followed him and did my business. I jumped in the truck with him, and he took me to Pappa's house. He fed me as I lay under the table, just like always. When they finished eating, we all left, and my human drove me to the pipe yard.

I watched Pappa smoke his cigar until he fell asleep. Then I went outside for a little while and wandered back in to flop on my sofa.

My human spoke to the telephone a lot. The telephone rang, and when my human lifted it to his head, I heard Birk talking, but I didn't see him. "Careless, you're not going to believe this. The plan worked like a charm. We have an appointment with Burtha at the Swift house this afternoon. Can you believe that?" He was talking fast.

"Great! You and Sarge come to my office during lunch and wear the appropriate clothing," my human said.

"Okay, Careless, see you in a little while."

My human pushed the telephone and said, "Hammer, can you come to my office when you have a free moment?"

A few minutes later, Hammer poked his head into the office. "What's up?"

"Can you cut some vinyl decals with our stencil machine? I need it to say *Home Lock Security*. And I need four of them. Two to fit on the back of some shirts and two for a van."

Hammer nodded. "Sure thing, boss."

He was walking out when my human said, "Oh, and Hammer, one more thing. I know it's a big favor, but could we borrow your van and put the decals on it?"

"No problem, boss. I'll bring it up front for you."

I went outside, and when I came back, Sarge and Birk were sitting in my human's office. "Okay, Hammer has the Home Lock Security van ready to go.

If you boys will turn around, I'll apply the Home Lock Security decals to the back of your shirts," my human said.

Sarge and Birk stood up and faced me. My human put something on their backs.

"Now, I want you both to drive the van to your appointment. When you see Burtha, you need to get her to activate and deactivate the alarm. Just tell her your office is doing an internal test on it. Sarge, I need you to remember the code. Can you do that?" my human asked.

"Yeah, man." Sarge held his fist out with his thumb up.

My human drummed his fingers on the desk. "All I need you guys to do after that is to pretend to check all the contacts on the windows and doors. Just inspect them and tell each other they check out. Do it quickly, and try to be professional. If you get into trouble, call me on the phone, and I'll pretend to be your supervisor."

"We got this," Birk said. They both left the office.

"What do you think the chances of this going right are, Dudley?" my human asked.

I said something.

"Yeah, that's what I think, too," he said.

My human continued to talk to the telephone. I barked at some truck drivers who came in the office and went outside to play. Before we left the office for the day, Sarge and Birk came back into my human's office. They were talking fast.

"What are you two laughing about? What happened?" my human asked.

"You wouldn't believe it, Careless. We pulled up to the house, and there was a car in the driveway. We rang the doorbell and a rather large, unpleasant woman answered. We got everything done, but she sure wanted us out of there. And Careless, there's almost nothing left in the house, except in one room upstairs. And it looks like a tornado hit it."

Sarge and Birk looked at each other and laughed.

"What are you two laughing about?" my human asked.

"We named her Big Nasty. Because she's big and nasty," Sarge said.

"Okay you guys, nice job. I knew you could do it. You've provided me with valuable information. Go home, and we'll regroup later."

"Uh, there's one more thing, Careless . . ." Sarge said. He stopped talking and looked at Birk.

My human rolled his eyes. "Spit it out, Sarge. I'm not getting any younger."

"We're never going back to that house," Sarge said. "Ever! Careless, that place is haunted. There were noises coming from empty places in the house. Once I even heard a door slam in the corner of a room. No one was there but us and Big Nasty. And we just felt like someone was watching us the entire time. Isn't that right, Birk?"

My human scoffed. "You guys are crazy. There's no such things as ghosts."

"Well, you weren't there," Birk said. "That place *is* haunted. And we're not going back."

"Okay, simmer down. Go home and we'll talk later," my human said.

Sarge and Birk left.

"Can you imagine that, Dudley? What's wrong with those two?"

I said something.

"Exactly," he said. "Oh, guess what? I called Suzie. You're going to see your girlfriend, Scout, tonight. What do you think about that?"

I heard Scout's name, so I said something.

Ross and Pappa left together, and my human drove me in the truck to see Scout. I saw her lying behind the window. She stared at me and wagged her tail, then she stood up and barked. *I can smell her. I like Scout.*

When we reached the front door, my human pushed a button that made a noise. I heard footsteps, and the door opened. It was Suzie and Scout.

"We're just about to sit down for dinner. Won't you and Dudley join us?" Suzie said.

She led my human to the table where the rest of the humans were already seated. I scooted under the table with Scout to wait for our food. We didn't have to wait long. Lots of hands holding food snuck down toward us. Scout ate from the young human's hands. I ate from my human's.

When the food stopped coming, my human said, "Okay, Suzie and Zach, I need to know everything. Start at the beginning, and tell me everything you can remember."

Suzie said, "Boys, why don't you clear your plates, get a cookie, and run upstairs and play?"

The young humans darted into the kitchen and then ran to the stairs.

"Well," Suzie continued, "my grandparents died in a plane accident when we were young. I remember going to Uncle Ike's and Aunt Linda's a lot. They were always around helping my parents. Ike was a hard-working man. He spent most of his time at his office. He was a little rough around the edges. But he was a good man who cared deeply about his family. Linda was an angel. Anyone who knew her would tell you that. She was always thoughtful and kind. She helped anyone in need, including me and my siblings.

"Many years later, we lost our parents in a tragic car accident. Uncle Ike and Aunt Linda moved in with us to help raise us. When we were all old enough and went to college, they moved back into their house, and we all lost touch, for a while. After college, we became close again.

"When Zach and I got married, they were like parents to us. In fact, Ike walked me down the aisle. Zach became close with Ike. He loved hearing all the war stories and looking at the antique guns."

Zach nodded. "Ike and I would take the guns apart on weekends and clean and oil them. I loved spending time with Ike. He had quite a collection. Most of them were World War II guns. He called his favorite one the Burp Gun. He said when the Germans opened up on them with it, it sounded like someone burping. He also said that when they heard that noise, they hit the dirt."

"It's really a Schmeisser MP 41. He always got a crooked little smile on his face when he pulled that one out to be cleaned. It was almost as if he wanted to tell me something about it, but he never did. I found that endearing," Zach said. He stopped talking and looked straight ahead like he was dreaming about something.

He shook his head and continued. "He told me on several occasions that when he was gone, he wanted me to have his gun collection. He said I was the only one in the family interested in guns, and he told everyone in the family that all his guns were to go to me after he passed away. I think he knew his time was running out. He already gave me his officer's model M-1 Carbine. I have it in the other room," Zach said.

"I'd love to see that," my human said.

Zach stood. "I'll go get it."

"Ike was a very secretive man," Suzie said. "When he didn't want you to know something, you didn't."

Zach walked back in. "Here it is. Check out this pristine World War II M-1 Carbine." He handed it to my human.

My human looked happy. "What a beautiful rifle. It's in such great shape." He held it up and looked at it.

"You should see the Burp Gun. It's just as nice as his carbine. He was in the process of transferring it over to me before he passed away. It has to be registered with the government. He kept the registration hidden in a big file drawer in his desk. I don't think he wanted anyone to find it, but I know where it is. He showed it to me several times. It's strange, later on in his life, near the end, he took great delight in pulling out the Burp Gun. He kept his gun collection in a locked closet in an upstairs room he used as his office. Nobody had the key except for him," Zach said.

"Once we were married, Linda referred to us as her own kids. Family was really important to Ike and Linda," Suzie said.

Zach folded his hands on the table. "Ike was a fair man, but he believed in hard work and honesty. He thought it was important for people to take care of themselves and then others."

Suzie glanced at Zach and then at my human. "When Linda came down with Alzheimer's, my two sisters started spending a lot of time at my aunt and uncle's house. We're not sure what they were doing over there because we hired a nurse to care for Linda. Ike was older and having problems of his own at the time. That's right when my aunt and uncle said things were going missing in their home. Even some of their furniture vanished."

"And their toilet paper," Zach said.

My human raised his eyebrows. "Their toilet paper? Who would steal toilet paper?"

"That's what we'd like to know," Suzie said.

"Okay, I've heard enough. Dudley and I will take care of the rest. Right, Dudley?"

I said something.

"Just one last thing. Have either of you seen a copy of your late uncle's will, or do you know where it is?" my human asked.

Suzie shook her head. "No, as I said, my uncle was a secretive man. We never asked because, frankly, we never thought about such things. I know Burtha asked him once. She told me he became angry when she did. I don't think she or Wanda ever brought it up again with him. My best guess is that it's upstairs at his house, in the room he used as an office."

"So, he never gave you any documents of any kind?" my human asked.

"Not that I recall."

"Very well. Dudley and I'll be leaving now. I believe I have a plan of action. Come on, boy, time to go."

I stood up and licked Scout on the nose. Then I walked by my human's side on his way toward the door. He stopped, so I stopped.

He looked at something on the wall.

"Do you like that print?" Suzie asked. "Uncle Ike gave it to Zach. One day, Zach helped him and Aunt Linda hang up a beautiful blanket on the wall. They purchased it on one of their trips. He had to take this print down to make room for the blanket. The frame was in disrepair, and since Zach's an artist, Uncle Ike told him to take it with him and to keep it. Zach fixed the frame."

"I didn't have to do much. I didn't even have to take it apart. I just put some wood glue on it and pushed it back together," Zach said.

Suzie frowned. "In fact, before Ike passed away, my sister confronted me about the print. She wanted to know where it was. When I told her Ike had given it to Zach, she got very upset and told me it was *very* expensive. She just kept repeating over and over how expensive it was. Isn't that strange?"

"Indeed it is," my human said. "Well, it's a lovely print. It really catches the eye. I'll be in touch."

CHAPTER 55

"Birk," my human said into the telephone after we got home, "I have a job for you tonight. Are you in? Great. Be at my place in twenty minutes."

He pushed some buttons on the phone again and said, "Sarge, are you busy tonight? Perfect. Come over in twenty minutes."

He pushed it again and said, "E.D. would you like to help out with another case? It's for the girl you met at the dog park. Super. We're all meeting here in twenty minutes. Bring your A-game."

He drank his good-smelling drink and looked upward, just like Pappa does when he watches the smoke swirling up from his cigar. I heard humans outside the door, so I finished my food and stood at attention.

"Good boy," said my human. He walked over and opened the door. Sarge, Birk, and E.D. stood in the hallway. They walked in.

"Have a seat," my human said. They lowered themselves onto the sofa, and he sat at his desk.

"Tonight, we'll be visiting Ike Swift's house. We need to nose around and see if we can find a copy of his will. I have the key, and Sarge knows the alarm code," my human said.

He held something up for them to see.

Sarge and Birk frowned.

"Okay, what is wrong with you two?" my human asked.

Birk crossed his arms. "Well, we didn't really enjoy our time with Big Nasty."

E.D. raised an eyebrow. "Who's Big Nasty?"

Birk said, "She's the plump, unpleasant woman at the house."

Sarge nodded. "Yeah, she was frumpy, dumpy, and somewhat lumpy."

Sarge and Birk chuckled and high-fived, but then they frowned as Birk said, "But we would rather face her again than be around that ghost who haunts the house."

"Look, you two, there's no such things as ghosts," my human said.

"I'm telling you, that house is dark and eerie," Sarge said.

"You two Nancy boys need to butch up." E.D. pursed her lips. "I'm going in there, and you are, too. Careless needs us. It's going to look really bad when a woman will walk in the house and you won't. Besides, we'll have Dudley with us. He'll protect us. Won't you, boy?"

I said something and walked to her. She kissed my head. My tail spun around in circles.

"What's it going to be, boys?" she asked.

Sarge and Birk looked at each another.

Birk sighed. "Okay, fine. We'll go, but if anything happens to us, we're coming back to haunt you."

"Perfect," said my human. "Birk, how are you at picking a lock? I have the key to the house, but if the lock's been changed, we may have a problem."

Birk grinned. "There's not a lock made I can't open."

My human said, "Well, what are we waiting for? Let's roll. Birk, you drive. You know the way. I have flashlights. We'll use them in the house so we won't need to turn on lights and draw attention to ourselves."

My human drank more of his good-smelling drink, and we all walked out of our home. We went to Birk's truck. My human opened the door, and I jumped in. I stuck my head out of the sunroof. I could smell everything from there.

We stopped at a house I'd never been to. Birk turned the truck off.

"There's a car in the driveway," my human said. "Let's stay in the truck for a few minutes to make sure no one's home."

I jumped in the front seat and sat with E.D. and my human.

A little while later, my human said, "Okay, it looks like the coast is clear. Let's go check it out." We all left the truck. It was dark outside. They walked to the door of the home and stopped.

My human raised his hand. "Let's be quiet. We want to make sure we're the only ones here."

Sarge looked at Birk and said softly, "We definitely won't be the only ones here."

My human knocked on the door. I waited for someone to open it, but no one did. He took something from his pocket, put it in the door, and tried to turn it. It made a noise but didn't turn. He pulled it out and tried again.

"Okay, Birk, just as I thought, Burtha's changed the lock. Come work your magic. And Sarge, when the door opens, I need you to deactivate the alarm. Are we good?"

Sarge and Birk both said, "Yes."

Birk walked up to the door and took something from his pocket. He put it in the door and moved it around. The door made a noise and opened.

Birk nodded. A beeping noise came from inside, and Sarge walked in and pushed something on the wall. The noise stopped. Sarge smiled.

The humans all walked inside the house and closed the door. My human took something from his pocket and pushed it with his hand. Light came out of it. "Here's two more flashlights," he said.

He gave one to Sarge and one to Birk. Light came out of all three flashlights.

"It's just as I suspected. Burtha left a car in the driveway to scare people off. There's no one here but us," my human said.

"We'll see about that," Birk muttered.

The humans walked around. My human said, "You guys are right. There's almost nothing left downstairs. Let's go upstairs." They walked to the stairs. I followed them. I saw something on the stairs above us. I'd never seen anything like it. I could feel it. It was cold. But I couldn't smell it. I didn't like this.

I walked in front of my human. *I will protect him.* The humans did not see the thing. The hair on my back rose up, and I snarled. I looked at my human and looked back at the thing. It looked like a human, but it wasn't.

"It's okay, boy. It's okay. We're going upstairs now," he said.

I didn't say anything because I was watching the thing on the stairs.

"Come on, people, let's get this over with," my human said.

Sarge and Birk exchanged glances.

When I looked back up, the thing on the stairs was gone. The hair on my back flattened back down.

The humans walked up the stairs. I followed them. "It seems like nothing much is left up here either," my human said. They went into a little room, and he shined his light on the wall. He opened something and took a small object in his hand. "Viagra. Very interesting."

He opened it and looked inside. The other humans were watching him. He closed it and put it back.

"What does that mean?" E.D. asked.

"I'm not sure. It's funny how people always forget to empty their bathroom medicine cabinets when they move out of their houses."

We walked to the end of the hallway and stopped at a closed door. My human tried to open it. "Birk, you're up. It's locked," my human said.

Birk nodded. "I got this. Let's check out this last room and get the hell out of here." He walked up to the door and took something from his pocket. I felt the cold thing from the stairs behind us. I didn't hear it walking or smell it, but I knew it was there.

I turned and looked at it. I said something, and the hair raised on my back. The humans didn't see it. It made a loud noise, and all of the humans turned around. They pointed the lights at it, but it was gone.

"I'm sure we're the only ones here. It was probably just the house settling," my human said.

"We told you, Careless," Sarge said. The thing was behind us. I could feel it. Then it was gone. The humans turned back around.

Birk asked, "Careless, wasn't this door just locked?"

My human narrowed his eyes. "Of course it was. You saw it."

"Well, not only is it not locked—the door is open. And I didn't touch it."

E.D. tightened her lips. "That's not funny, Birk."

Birk thrust up his hands. "It wasn't me. Let's get out of here."

"No," my human said, "let's go in, look around real quick, and leave. We need to find a copy of the will."

They stepped into the room. Things were scattered all over the floor. My human whistled. "You weren't kidding, Birk. Somebody really made a mess in here. It looks like a tornado hit it."

"I bet they were looking for something. I wonder what it was," E.D. said.

My human nodded. "Someone was looking for something. The question is—did they find it? I bet not. Otherwise, everything in this room would be gone, just like in the rest of the house. I smelled something strange on the floor and nosed it. When it moved, the humans pointed their lights at me.

"It's just Dudley. You gave us a fright, boy," my human said.

I said something.

"Hold on. What's that next to you?" my human asked. He picked up some things from the floor. "Look what was under all these papers and books. A Holy Bible and a wooden box. The box has *FOR GALLANTRY IN ACTION* inscribed on it. This is a Silver Star medal display box."

"Let me see the medal," Birk said.

"Sorry, Birk, the medal's missing. Who would take the medal out of the display box and discard it this way?"

"A dumbass, that's who," E.D. said.

My human handed the Bible and the box to E.D. "Hold on to these. We're taking them with us for my clients."

The thing on the stairs was back, standing next to a desk. It got cold. My human sat in a chair next to it.

My hair went up, and I said something. It was right next to him, but he didn't see it. I was ready to attack.

My human pulled a paper from the desk drawer and looked at it. "Yes," he said. He folded it and put it in his pocket. The thing was gone. I never hear or smell it coming or leaving. *It confuses me. I don't like it.*

My human got up. "Let's have a look in the closet." He walked over and pointed his light in the closet. "Just as I thought. Empty. The gun collection's missing. Okay, I think we've seen enough. Let's get out of here."

The humans headed toward the door. The thing on the stairs was back and pushed the closet door closed. It made a loud noise. They all turned around and pointed their lights at the closet. The thing was gone.

"Wasn't that closet door open, Careless?" Sarge asked.

"I believe it was. Time for us to leave," my human said.

CHAPTER 56

Birk drove the truck to our home, and E.D., Sarge, and my human got out. I followed them and did my business on the way to the door. We walked up the stairs, and E.D. said, "Well, I have to admit, that was pretty strange."

"That's right, man." Sarge shook his head and walked away.

"Here's the Bible and box you gave me," said E.D. "Do you think we'll be able to solve the case?"

"With Dudley, anything is possible," my human said.

I said something.

E.D. bent down and rubbed my ears.

"You were a good boy tonight, Dudley. Thank you for protecting us," she said.

I said something. My tail spun around in circles.

"I think there really is a ghost in that house, Careless," she said.

"Perhaps," he said.

He walked into our home, and I followed him. He put the Bible and box on his desk and took a paper from his pocket. He looked at it and set it on his desk.

When he decided to go into the little room and do his business, the thing from the stairs at that house appeared next to his desk. My hair went up, and I growled. My human didn't hear me. The thing now hovered next to our bed. I watched it. My human was still in the little room. The thing left.

My human emerged from the little room and said, "You know, Dudley, I want to have a closer look at that Bible and box. Maybe I can find some clues."

I said something.

He walked to his desk and stopped. "Dudley, where's the box? I put it right here next to the Bible. Did you take the box?"

I said something.

He looked at me, picked up the Bible, and opened it. "Linda Swift. Her name's in the Bible. This must have belonged to Suzie's aunt. Why would someone throw it on the ground? I'll call Suzie and tell her I have it. I bet she'll want it."

He picked up the telephone. "Suzie, hi. We found out some interesting things tonight. I found your aunt's Bible. Yes, I'll bring it to you. I also found a wooden Silver Star medal display box. It's empty. It was right here . . ." My human stopped talking. He was looking at our bed.

"Careless? Careless? Is everything okay?" I heard Suzie say.

My human put the telephone down and walked to the bed, where he picked up the box on the table. He looked at me and frowned.

"Careless?" Suzie said.

He took the box and walked back to his desk.

He picked up the telephone. "Suzie, everything's fine. It's just since we went to your uncle's house, weird things have been happening."

"It's strange that you say that. Since the funeral, I've felt like Uncle Ike is still with us. I can't explain it. It started at the funeral. When we drove to it, there wasn't a cloud in the sky. My sister, Burtha, decided to speak during the service. She read off of a yellow tablet she'd written some things on. Just as she started reading, clouds filled the sky, and it rained so hard, no one could hear a word she said. We were standing underneath a tarp, and the rain hit it so hard, it sounded like a stampede of cattle.

"I overheard several people say they couldn't hear a thing she'd said. And the strange thing was, as soon as she stopped reading and sat down, the rain stopped, and the clouds disappeared. And unexplained things in my house have been happening. Things moving around by themselves. I've even found some of our framed art crooked on the walls. Sometimes I think these are signs if you take the time to see them. Don't you think all this is bizarre?"

"Something like that just happened to me. I think someone's trying to tell us something. And Dudley and I will find out what that is. I'll bring the Bible to you when we meet again," he said.

"I have to go put the children to bed. Let's talk later. I want to hear all about what happened."

My human put the telephone on his desk.

"Let's have a closer look at that box, Dudley. It seems like someone wants us to examine it," my human said.

He opened a drawer and picked up something round. "This magnifying glass should do the trick. It seems like a pretty sturdy box. But there looks like a small crack in the back of it. I wonder . . ."

He went to the room where he makes his drinks and picked something up. He walked back and sat down. "Let's see if this knife does anything." He pressed it up against the box, and it moved. "I knew it! There's a secret compartment. And it looks like someone added it after it was originally made. Look at this, Dudley."

I said something.

He pulled something out and held it in front of his face. "It's a key, Dudley. An old-fashioned key. I think I know who put it there, but what does it unlock? What do you think, boy?"

He looked at it and then at me. I wasn't sure what he wanted, but he was happy.

I said something.

"Oh, Dudley, I think we're well on the way to solving this case. I'd have never found this without you. You're a good boy," he said.

I said something again.

"Let's hit the sack, Dudley. Tomorrow's Saturday. Let's get up early and solve the case. What do you say?"

CHAPTER 57

The next morning, my human picked up the telephone. "Good morning, Suzie. Yes, I'll tell you everything. But first, I need you to do something for me. Send an email to Burtha. Oh, she'll answer this one. Yes, I'm certain. I want you to tell her you don't know why she's avoiding you, but you have it on good authority that Ike's gun collection has been removed from the house and that one of the weapons is a fully automatic machine gun that's registered with the federal government. Tell her if it's not put back, you'll be forced to report her to the ATF. Also, explain that she may be sentenced to ten years in prison for moving the rifle. Can you do that for me? Great. Let me know when you get a response."

My human looked at me and said, "The plan is in motion, Dudley. Now all we have to do is wait for the dirty rat to expose herself."

I said something.

My human ate some food. When the telephone rang, he looked at it. I looked at it, too. He gave me the rest of his food and picked up the telephone.

"Hi, Suzie. She already responded? Splendid. She said you don't know what you're talking about and the gun collection is still there? Interesting. You've done well, Suzie. We're about to solve the case."

He pushed the telephone again. "Birk, I need you to case the Swift house. No, you don't have to go in. Just tell me when Big Nasty gets there. How quickly can you be there? Five minutes? Great. Call me."

My human sat on the sofa. I sat with him. He looked up in the air. I looked up to see what he was looking at. I didn't see anything. He smiled and put his arm around me.

"This is going to work out fine. You'll see, boy."

I said something.

The telephone rang. My human stood up, picked it up, and held it to his head. "Is that right? She went into the house with something and left it there? Interesting. Can you stay there for a little bit? Great. I need to bait the trap. I'll see you shortly."

He pushed the telephone again and said, "Detective Present, please. It's a personal call. Thank you. I'm on hold, Dudley," he said, pointing to the telephone.

I said something.

"Detective, how are you, sir? Yes, I'm doing fine. How would you like to solve a murder? No, it's not one of your cases. In fact, you'll be able to solve it before anyone even files charges. What do you think about that? Perfect. I'll text you the address. Can you meet me there in twenty minutes? Terrific. See you then," he said.

He pushed the telephone again. "E.D., I'm about to bust the case wide open. Want to help out? Great. Meet me downstairs in ten minutes."

He pushed the telephone again. "Sarge, are you awake? Well, wake up. We're going to solve the case today, and I need the gang there. Okay, meet me downstairs in ten minutes."

He put the telephone down. "Okay, boy, are you ready to catch a bad person?"

I responded.

He went to the door, and I followed. We trotted down the stairs and found Sarge and E.D.

"Well, let's go catch a killer," my human said.

"What? A killer? What are you talking about? I thought we were looking for a will," E.D. said.

My human grinned. "Well, where there's a will there's a way."

"I'll drive. Where are we going?" E.D. asked.

"To the Swift house. And be swift about it," he said. They all got into the car, and I jumped in. I sat between my human and E.D.

The car stopped in front of the house where the thing on the stairs lives. Birk and Detective Present were already there. Birk walked over to my human.

"Birk," my human said, "I'll go talk to Detective Present. While I do that, I want you and Sarge to open the door and disable the alarm. We don't need him to see that."

"You got it." Birk walked away.

My human and E.D. strode up to Detective Present. "Good morning, Detective. I think you're going to find this interesting. Let's go inside, shall we?" my human said.

Detective Present raised his eyebrows. "Okay, but this better be good."

"Oh, I think you'll be pleasantly surprised," my human said. We walked in the house, climbed the stairs, and entered the room where I'd seen the thing. It wasn't there this time.

My human walked to a smaller room and opened a door. "Dammit, the guns aren't here. Birk, I thought you said Big Nasty brought them in the house."

Birk crossed his arms. "She did. You can't miss a person of that size. I saw her bring them in, and she didn't bring anything out when she left."

"Well, my plan's not going to work now. I'm sorry, Detective. I believe I've wasted your time," my human said.

"No problem. You've done me enough favors in the past. But I'll want a full report on the alleged murder," he said.

"You got it, sir. Come on, gang. I guess I had this one all wrong. Let's call it quits," my human said.

All of them walked downstairs. I followed. As they reached the front door to leave the house, I saw the thing on the stairs come back. It got cold in the room, and the thing moved down the stairs and to a door underneath the stairs. My hair went up, and I growled.

The door under the stairs began to open. All the humans turned around. They weren't happy. "Did you guys see that?" Sarge asked.

Detective Present frowned. "Maybe it was the wind."

"There aren't any windows or doors open," E.D. said.

"That's what I was afraid of," my human said.

He walked over to the door and opened it further. I walked by his side. The thing was no longer there. I didn't know where it had gone. It had no smell at all.

"Well, well, well . . . look what we have here," my human said. He picked something up. "One World War II Burp Gun," he said. The other humans crowded around to see it.

"That's one nice rifle," Detective Present said.

My human pulled something out of his pocket and pressed it into the back of the Burp Gun. He turned it, and something came off. A paper fluttered to the ground, and he picked it up and put it in his pocket.

"What was that?" E.D. asked.

"That, my dear, is the key to solving the case. And this key, the one I found cleverly hidden in the Silver Star medal box, happened to fit the butt plate of this old rifle. A note was hidden in a compartment in the butt of the Burp Gun. We'll examine it later. Right now, I need to put the rifle back together and get ready to catch a killer. Are you ready?"

All the humans said, "Yes." He did some more things to the rifle, put it back in the small room, closed the door, and walked over to a telephone.

"Hello, Suzie. Would you email your sister and thank her for putting the gun collection back? Yes, she did put the guns back. I'll explain all that to you later. Tell her you really appreciate it. Also, please tell her you found a copy of Ike's will and you'll be waiting to show it to her in your uncle's upstairs office at his house. I know you don't have it, but tell her that anyway. I'll call you in a bit."

He put the telephone down. "Okay, if I'm correct, we're about to have a visitor. Sarge and Birk, you've already met her. We'll all wait upstairs. I'll be in the upstairs office. I need all of you to wait in the small room next to it. Remain out of sight until I need you. But listen to the whole thing. We'll need witnesses to catch this criminal."

Detective Present frowned. "Okay, I'll go along with this for now. But if it gets out of hand, I *will* step in."

My human nodded. "Very well. Let's all get into place. We haven't much time."

CHAPTER 58

All the humans walked upstairs. The thing wasn't there, but I remained on the lookout for it. The others went to a small room next to the room we'd been in earlier. My human walked into the larger room. I followed him. *I must protect my human.*

"Dudley, go wait with the others. I don't want our visitor to see you." He pointed toward the other humans.

I said something and planted my paws.

"Go on, Dudley," he commanded. But this time I wasn't going to obey him. *I must not leave him alone.* If that thing came back, I would be ready. *I am Dudley, and I will not leave my human.*

He bent down and hugged me. "Okay, boy, I love you too. Come on," he said. He closed the door behind us, and I followed him to a desk and chair. He sat down, and I lay on the floor next to him.

I heard the door to the house open and close. I smelled a human I'd never smelled before. It stopped walking, but it was still there. I heard the door open to the little room under the stairs.

My human turned around in the chair and faced the wall. I remained still. I heard the footsteps again. The human was walking up the stairs. Now it was in the hallway moving toward us. It stopped at the door to the room we were in. I didn't like this.

The door opened. I couldn't see the human because I was lying on the floor behind the desk. But it was there—I could smell it. "Do come in, Burtha," my human said. His back was still turned. Mine wasn't.

"You're not Suzie. Who are you?" Burtha asked.

My human turned around in the chair and faced her.

"Well, Burtha, I represent your sister, Suzie. She had some concerns about your involvement in Ike's estate. My name's Careless. I see you brought the Burp Gun up with you. May I ask your intentions?"

She still didn't see me because the desk blocked her view.

"Here's what's going to happen. You're going to give me Ike's will that you somehow uncovered. Then I'm going to shoot you with this godforsaken rifle. Once you're dead, I'll call the police and claim you were an intruder and threatened my life. Then I'll destroy the will. No one will be the wiser. My sister and her wretched family will get nothing. Ike wanted me to have everything. But then he changed his will before he died. I couldn't find it anywhere. He kept everything a secret. It was almost like a game to him. So, thank you for finding it for me."

I could now see the top part of her. She was pointing the Burp Gun at my human.

"Is that why you trashed Ike's office? You were looking for the will."

"That's right. I never found it. Where was it?" she asked.

"To be honest with you, Burtha, I haven't found it yet. It was just a ploy to lure you over here. I was sure it existed. Thank you for corroborating that for me," my human said.

"Too bad no one will ever find out. This conversation is over," she said.

My human grinned. "Just so you know, the rifle's empty. I took all of the bullets out of the magazine."

Burtha was happy and not happy at the same time. I'd never seen that in a human. I didn't like it.

"Well, just so you know, I took the liberty of loading the rifle when I got here. If I were you, I'd start saying your prayers," she said. She walked around the desk.

"Well, if I were you, I'd get acquainted with my friend, Dudley. Okay, boy," my human said.

I sat up. The hair on my back was up, and my jowls were curled up. Water was dripping from them. I growled. I didn't like Burtha. She pointed the Burp Gun at my human. I didn't like this. *I must protect him.*

I jumped on her. The Burp Gun made a noise. It was up against my chest. I landed on her, and she fell to the ground.

"You may have loaded the rifle, but I took the liberty of removing the firing pin. And since you almost shot my friend, Dudley, here, I don't think he'll show you any mercy. Unless you cooperate with us," my human said.

I had Burtha pinned to the ground.

"What do you want? Don't let him hurt me," she said.

"Why did you kill your uncle? Did you work alone? And don't lie to me. Dudley hates it when someone's less than honest," my human said.

"I don't know what you're talking about," Burtha said.

"Let me refresh your memory. Unfortunately, when you were looting the house after Ike died, you neglected to empty out the medicine cabinet in the bathroom. I found his bottle of Viagra that he was probably taking for a heart condition. I counted the remaining pills, and according to the date on the bottle, there was one missing. You slipped him an extra Viagra, and his poor old heart couldn't take it. And I'm guessing your fingerprints are all over that bottle. How am I doing so far?"

Burtha's jaw dropped. "How could you possibly know that? It was Wanda's idea. She said if I did exactly as she said, we'd both be rich. She was worried that Ike would find out her son had a baby out of wedlock and would disown her. She kept the child a secret for two years but was worried he'd find out somehow. We were sure he was going to cut us out of the will. We had to do something. He was a stupid old man and didn't know what he was doing anymore. He would have left us penniless. You would have done the same thing. Besides, you can't prove a damn thing. And no one will believe anything you say. Now, get your damn dog off of me," she said.

My human said, "Come here, Dudley."

I growled at Burtha. Then I slouched toward my human and sat by his side. Detective Present and the other humans walked into the room.

"We've heard enough," Detective Present said. "Ma'am, you have the right to remain silent. Anything you say can and will be held against you in a court of law. You have the right to an attorney. If you can't afford an attorney, one will be provided for you. Do you understand the rights I have just read you?"

He put something on both of her hands.

She walked out in front of him and yelled, "Ike loved me! He only loved me! Where is the will? Where is the will?"

Detective Present said, "Let's go, ma'am. We'll pick up your sister on the way downtown." I heard the door to the home open and close.

Sarge smiled. "Wow, man, that was awesome."

E.D. cocked her head. "Careless, where is the will?"

My human looked at her and said, "It's been right under our noses this whole time. Let's take a ride, shall we?"

They all walked out of the room and down the stairs. I followed them. Everyone left the house except my human. He stopped and looked back. I watched him. The thing on the stairs was back.

"Dudley, do you see that? It looks like an old man smiling at us on the stairs," my human said.

I said something. I did see it. Then the thing disappeared.

"I must be imagining things. There's nothing there. Or was there? Pretty strange, Dudley. Let's go finish up some business."

CHAPTER 59

My human opened the car door, and I jumped in E.D.'s car. Sarge went in Birk's truck, and we drove to Scout's house. Scout was behind the window waiting for me. I watched her stand up and bark. Suzie walked to the window and waved.

She opened the door, and everyone piled in the house. Scout sniffed me, and I licked her snout. The humans sat on a sofa in the front room. Zach walked in. I sat with Scout on the floor.

"You have me so curious. What happened?" Suzie asked.

"Well, to nutshell it, your two sisters plotted to kill your uncle."

Suzie's hand flew to her mouth.

"Unfortunately," my human continued, "they succeeded. My guess is they'll be doing jail time soon. They were trying to empty out his estate, but I think he had other plans. I'll go into that later. All that's left to do now is read the will and see where the chips may fall."

"Well, where is the will?" E.D. asked. My human pulled a paper from his pocket.

"I found this hidden in a compartment of the Burp Gun. I think it'll tell us where the will is. And I think you'll be surprised when you find out where it's hidden," my human said.

Suzie smiled. "That's just like Uncle Ike. He used to hide presents around the house for us every time he came over. It was a little game he enjoyed playing. Sometimes we didn't find them for weeks."

My human looked at the paper and said, "It reads, *In the forest you will find, all you search for, all that's mine.*"

Zach furrowed his brow. "What does that mean? I don't get it."

My human nodded. "Zach, would you mind taking down that nice print Ike gave you and bringing it over here?"

"Sure. But I still don't understand."

My human grinned. "You will soon."

Zach took the print off of the wall and walked over with it.

"You see," my human said, "the print is of a lovely forest. I believe Ike knew he wasn't meant long for this world, and he didn't trust Burtha or Wanda. He wanted to get a copy of his new and improved will in the hands of someone who would respect his wishes. That would be you, Suzie and Zach. He also liked to play games. So, he made a scavenger hunt out of it. You've had a copy of the will since he gave you that print. If you peel the backing off of that frame, I believe you'll find what you're looking for."

Zach pulled something off the print. A piece of paper fell to the ground.

Suzie gasped. "I can't believe the will's been here the whole time. You're amazing, Careless."

"Well, I couldn't have done it without these guys." He pointed at the humans sitting on the sofa. "And I especially couldn't have done it without Dudley. He actually saved my life today," he said.

I said something and reached up and licked his hand.

Zach handed Suzie the paper. She looked at it and said, "Wow, it looks like Ike cut Burtha and Wanda out of his will. Half of his estate is to go into a trust to help charitable organizations and the other half is to be split between me and my brother, Chuck. There's also a note that says those who believe in a clean, decent, honest life and work hard will be rewarded."

E.D. said, "Well, I guess that leaves out your sisters."

All the humans laughed.

"Okay, it's been a long morning. I think it's time for us to leave and let you guys work things out," my human said.

"Thank you," Suzie said. "I promise we'll pay you as soon as we receive money from the estate. We'll never forget what you've done for us."

"All in a day's work, my dear. It was our pleasure. I'm glad everything worked out," my human said.

Suzie walked up to my human and hugged him.

I said something.

She smiled. "I hope we can get Dudley and Scout together regularly. They seem to really like one another."

"I'm sure that can be arranged," my human said. Sarge, Birk, E.D., and my human walked out of the house. I licked Scout's nose, and she licked mine.

Birk nodded. "Later you guys, I have some things to do."

"Birk," E.D. said, "I'm going to prepare a picnic tonight at the loft to celebrate. I'm sure Careless will tell us just how he figured everything out. Won't you, Careless?"

My human grinned. "Yes, dear."

Birk said, "I'll be there." He left in his truck.

E.D. and Sarge got in her car. My human opened the door and got in, and I jumped in. All the humans were quiet on the way home.

"Okay," E.D. said when we got out of the car, "let's all meet at five o'clock in the back, and I'll have a picnic to celebrate another solved case."

My human went to our home and made a good-smelling drink. He sat on the sofa, and I joined him. He fell asleep before he'd finished his drink. I slurped up the rest of his drink to help him out, laid my head in his lap, and drifted off.

When my human woke up, he tried to slip away from me. I pressed my body up against him, but he got away.

"Oh no, Dudley, it's almost five o'clock. We have a picnic to go to. Let's move it, boy," he said.

I said something.

He walked out of our home, and I followed him. We wandered downstairs and out the back door. E.D., Sarge, and Birk were sitting on something next to some good-smelling food. Water dripped from my jowls.

"It's about time," E.D. said. "We were beginning to worry about you. Now, start at the beginning, and tell us everything about the case."

"If you must know, it started with a key I received in Mexico. There was always a key . . ."

I heard a loud noise from far away, and my human fell to the ground. I stood over him to protect him. I smelled the blood like when it comes from my prey when I tear it apart. My human wasn't moving. I licked his face. He wasn't saying anything. He just looked at me.

E.D. yelled, "He's been shot. Call 911. Hurry!"

Water came from her eyes.

"I'm going to meet the ambulance." Birk darted away.

"Move away, boy, let me help him," E.D. said.

I said something. *I will not move away from my human. I will protect him.*

I pushed my head under his hand and licked his face. I could sense his life coming to an end. Dogs know these things. Blood was all over my human and me.

Two humans ran up with Birk. I turned and growled. *I will protect my human.*

"No, Dudley! They're here to help," E.D. said. She pulled me away and held me tightly until they picked up my human and took him away. Sarge and Birk went with them.

I howled. My human was gone.

E.D. released me. I ran to the door to be with him, but it was closed. E.D. walked up behind me. "Oh, Dudley, what are we going to do," she asked.

I sighed.

"Come on, Dudley. Let's go upstairs. I have to go to the hospital to check on Careless."

She opened the door, and I tracked my human to the front door. It was closed. I waited for him to come back through it. He didn't.

E.D. came up behind me and grabbed my collar. I didn't want to go.

"Dudley, let's go! Now!" She pulled me up the stairs and into our home. "Now, stay here. Stay! I'll come back for you. I have to go check on Careless," she said.

I tried to get out to see my human, but she blocked me with her body and closed the door. I ran to the window and saw her get in her car and leave.

I waited by the window. I waited for my human to come home.

CHAPTER 60

I waited for a long time. Finally, E.D. drove up. I didn't see my human.

I heard her walking up the stairs, so I waited by the door for her. She opened it and fell to her knees. "I'm sorry, Dudley. You'll need to stay with me. Come on, boy. I'll get your food and bowls."

She picked up my bowls and food and walked upstairs. I followed her. She gave me food and water, but I wasn't hungry. I didn't eat or drink.

"Come on, let me clean you up," she said. I followed her into a little room. She picked me up and put me in a tub where water came from the wall. She sprayed me with water and put something on me that didn't smell good. Then she sprayed more water on me and rubbed me with a towel.

"There you go, boy, you're nice and clean again," she said. She walked out of the little room, and I followed her. When she sat in a big chair, I squeezed in with her.

She smiled, but water came from her eyes. "Oh, Dudley, I don't think he's going to make it. And I never told him I care about him. Don't you worry, boy, you can stay right here with me. I'll take great care of you," she said.

I said something.

The telephone made a noise. I looked at it. E.D. slipped out of the chair and picked it up.

I could hear Birk's voice coming from the telephone.

"How's he doing?" E.D. asked. "About the same? So he's still in a coma? Dammit, isn't there anything they can do? We can't let him die, Birk. We have to do something. What? They caught the shooter? Wanda's husband? I hope they fry his ass. Really? Because the yellow Corvette he bought with Ike's money got repossessed? Well, maybe if any of them ever got jobs, they wouldn't need Ike's money to buy sports cars. When old men buy sports cars, we call that the Small Weenie Syndrome. I know it's mean, but he shot Careless. I hope he fries. Of course I'll take care of Dudley. He can stay with me till Careless gets better. I'm going to remain hopeful. I'll come to the hospital this evening. Call me if *anything* changes. Okay, thanks, Birk."

E.D. left our home day after day, and I waited for her. She always came back, but she always left again. She fed me and gave me water, and we went on long walks together. But I never forgot about my human. I always stood by the window, waiting for him to come home. But he never did. I stopped going to the office, and I didn't see Pappa smoking his cigars ever again.

I waited a long time.

CHAPTER 61

It had been a long time since I'd seen my human. I liked living with E.D. but I missed him. I was still waiting for him to come home.

One day, E.D. picked up the telephone. "Hi Birk. They're sure? There's no chance of him ever waking up? I can't believe this. Dudley's been sitting by that window for months waiting for him to come back. I want to bring him to the hospital today before they unplug him. I think in some strange way, it'll give Dudley some closure. He deserves that after all he and Careless have been through. Will you ask his doctor if that's okay? Great—I'll bring him over right now. I can't believe we're going to lose him." She wasn't happy. Water came from her eyes again.

"Come on, boy, we're going for a ride," she said.

We walked out of our home, and I jumped into her car. We went somewhere I'd never been. I didn't like it. It smelled bad and reminded of that room Jen took me into a long time ago.

"Come on, Dudley," E.D. said. I walked at her side. She went into a little room. I followed her. She pushed something, and the doors closed. The room moved. I was confused. The door opened, and we got out. Then I smelled something I hadn't smelled in a long time. *My human.*

I held my nose up in the air and followed the scent. *My human is here.* I ran. E.D. darted after me.

I ground to a stop at a door. My human was behind it. My tail spun around in circles. I pawed the door. E.D. ran up and said, "Yes, he's in there. But he can't hear you. You have to say goodbye to him."

I didn't understand what she'd said, but I smelled my human, and I said something. E.D. opened the door, and I saw him. He was sleeping in a bed. Birk and Sarge were in the room.

I ran over to my human and licked his hand. He didn't say anything or look at me. *Something is wrong. Why is he not saying anything to me? I don't like this.*

Another human walked into the room and said, "His family's on the way up. When you're all ready, we'll disconnect him from life support."

I said something. I didn't like this human.

Pappa and Ross walked in. They had water coming from their eyes. So did E.D., Birk, and Sarge. No one was happy.

The human I didn't like said, "Okay, is everybody ready? I can disconnect him from life support at any time. He won't feel any pain."

Pappa said, "Yes."

I said something, too.

I stood between the human and my human. *I will protect my human.*

"I need a few more minutes," E.D. said.

"Yes, ma'am. Take your time. I'll be right outside this door when you're ready," the human said.

"I'm sorry," E.D. said. She put a hand over her mouth.

I put my head under my human's hand and waited for him to wake up. I waited and waited for him to speak. If he would just open his eyes or say my name, I would be the happiest dog in the world. I waited, and it paid off. I finally saw him.

He was sitting next to a river. It was like the river I'd jumped in to save that drowning puppy, a long time ago with Scott and Gayle. There was a horse next to him. It looked just like Red, the horse at Daddy's farm. My tail spun around in circles.

I said something. I wanted him to see me. *I am here!*

I don't know how, but I was now sitting next to him where the horse had been. The horse was gone. I was confused, but I didn't care. I could feel him. I leaned my body into him with all my might and put my head on his shoulder.

He looked at me and said, "I've missed you, boy. I always knew you would find me. I always knew you had the soul of Eagle in you. Did you see him? He was here a minute ago. I had to say goodbye to that fine horse a long time ago. Do you remember, now?"

I did remember. It was as if my human and I had always been together. I remembered everything.

"I have to go away now. I hope you'll understand. Don't be sad. E.D. will take great care of you. She loves you like I love you. I think I'm being called home. I know I'll see you again, boy," he said.

I now knew what he was saying. *I am not letting him go.* If he was going home, it would be to our home. A dog can smell death when it comes for us. And we meet it head on because we know in our heart it's our time. But this was not my human's time. I would have to show him.

"It's okay, boy. You can let me go," he said.

He stood up and walked toward the river. I didn't let him go. I got in front of him and pushed him backwards with my head. He was not crossing that river. Not without me.

He looked down at me and said, "I've never felt love like this. Do you remember the first day I saw you at the shelter? I was thinking about adopting that Red Heeler or the Blue Heeler in the kennel next to you."

I did remember.

"Well, I'm so glad I didn't. Because I didn't need a Red Heeler or a Blue Heeler. I needed a Soul Heeler. You're my Soul Heeler, Dudley."

I was no longer with my human by that river. I was back in that room with my human, Pappa, Ross, E.D., Sarge, and Birk. I was really confused. Some things connected to my human started making loud noises.

Careless opened his eyes.

Thank you for reading another one of Dudley's delightful ditties, dear reader. I know he worked doggone hard on this tail of intrigue and perseverance. Did you notice the dog images at the end of each chapter? It's okay if you find yourself flipping back to find them. It may interest you to know that with some Dudley donations and a lot of help from a lot of people, all of these very deserving dogs—and thousands more—have been saved from destruction. Have no fear, Dudley will return with his human, all his friends, and someone new who will be hard for you to forget.